SAFE

Keren Hughes

ISBN 978-1-936556-27-4

Published 2017

Published by Black Velvet Seductions Publishing

www.blackvelvetseductions.com

I fell in love with him
Not because he silenced
all of my fears
or made me feel so safe;
I fell in love with him
because he awoke a
sleeping lioness within me –
A wild woman who knows
only passion and freedom,
and laughs away her fears.
~ Beth Belleisle ~

This story is dedicated to the real Drew. Thank you for allowing me the pleasure of creating a character based on you. May you one day find your Elise and realise what true love feels like.

Acknowledgements

This is always the hardest part of the book to write. The story itself comes easier than the thank you's do. Only because there are so many of you to thank and such little space to do it in.

As always, I want to thank my nan for being my rock. She is the calm I cling to in the middle of a storm. She's spent 34 years being the one person I can rely on. She picks me up when I am down and celebrates all my successes as though they are the greatest achievement in the world. I can't thank her enough for always inspiring me to follow my dreams. Nan, I love you SO very much, you'll never know just how much.

My son, Calum, is the most important man in my universe. He loves hearing about anything to do with my writing. He may not be old enough to read my books—and by god I hope he never actually does read them—but he always cheers me on. Whenever I am down, all I need is a cwtch and a kiss from my baby boy and I am happy again. Cal, your mom loves you to the moon and back. I will always call you my baby, even when you're 50.

To my BETA reader gals, thank you so much for always supporting me. You've helped me through so many books now and Safe is probably the most important of them all to have got right. I'm happy that you could tell me when I was on-track and how emotional some scenes made you. Or when I was off-track, you steered me back. I am so grateful and I love you all.

Kara Stewart, you are amazing. I love you so much. Trudy Moore, you are one of my greatest friends and I couldn't do this without you. Chele McKenzie at JoB Done Proofreading, thank you for being there for me. You've done everything for me and then some. You have undertaken many a task I have set you without batting an eyelid. Thank you for being my sister, separated at birth. You're amazing.

To all my reader and author friends who continually spur me on, all the thanks in the world couldn't begin to cover it.

There are many authors who—regardless of whether they know it or not—inspire me to be a better writer.

I could sit here all day listing everyone that I love, everyone who has helped me along the way. But that would take me too long. I don't want to give a 'blanket' thank you note here, but I can't list you all because it would be longer than the actual book. So to each and every person I have met on this journey, thank you from the bottom of my heart. You'll never know what it means to have your support.

Thank you to Jessica Greeley for my cover and all the graphics. I am looking forward to having bookmarks to match my book, all thanks to you.

Thank you to Richard Savage at Black Velvet Seductions for taking a chance on my story. You've been a constant support. I like knowing that you are there to help me, no matter how big or small the things I ask of you. I'm glad you liked Elise being a disabled woman, because I felt it was important to the story.

Maybe the biggest well of gratitude of all though is for Andy. You didn't know in the beginning that I was basing Drew on you. But when I told you, you were so supportive. Thank you for allowing me the pleasure of basing a character on you. I'm glad you are a sexy paramedic so that I didn't have to just rely on my imagination. Thank you just for being you. You were and always will be a part of my heart. The fact that I once loved you is something a girl can never forget. Nor would I want to. It's probably one of the reasons I based Drew on you in the first place. I hope one day you can find your Elise and allow yourself to be loved. You deserve to feel the greatest feeling on Earth. Maybe one day you'll let your guard down and see that not everyone is out to hurt you. Maybe one day, the real Elise will do the same. She'll realise that the walls she built to protect her heart are actually suffocating it. Maybe someday.

Thank you to everyone for reading Safe. If you loved it, this author would be so very grateful for a review.

The thank you's may end here in black and white, but won't end here in my heart. I am probably a sappy so and so, but that's just how it is.

Prologue

I've always been a believer that you have to play the hand you're dealt in life and, much like in poker, you have to bluff your way through sometimes. Keep your cards close to your chest; never let anyone see what hand you're playing. I like to think I have a good poker face; that I don't have a 'tell' but those closest to me know I haven't always had things easy. My ex-fiancé left nearly three and a half years ago, leaving me a single, disabled mother. My son, Caleb, is ten years old and is an absolute Godsend. He's my raison d'être. The reason I get up in a morning, the reason I keep going even when the going gets tough. Having Caleb has made me a different person. Becoming a mother is the single most defining thing I have ever done; the very best thing I ever did. It's not been easy, but nothing worthwhile in life is ever easy.

I thought that I wouldn't cope as a single mother. Thank goodness I've managed to prove myself wrong. My son is growing up to be such a wonderful young man. He's not perfect, but then who is? I know I'm not the image of perfection, inside or out. But it's not about him being the model of perfection; it's about him being the very best that he can be, and every day he makes me proud to call myself his mum. He's a clever boy; does well in school. You only have to hold a conversation with him to know how smart he is. The only drawback is that he can have a tendency to be a bit of a loner. At school he has friends, but he'd rather play on his own or in a small group.

The trouble is his tendency to isolate himself is at an all-time high lately. He's becoming more withdrawn, and I wonder whether it has anything to do with my ex leaving. He was the only dad Caleb ever knew. His biological dad has never been in the picture, so Caleb doesn't have a father figure in his life. Is this why his behaviour is changing? Does he need a father figure around? I know I can't just enter into a relationship to give Caleb what he needs. I need to be with someone because I *want* to be. But that's just it. I *don't* want to be.

Caleb doesn't talk about his real dad except to say he's glad he's not in his life. He also doesn't talk about Jensen, my ex. He was Caleb's father for nearly seven years and, when he left, I chose not to talk about him much because I didn't want to hurt my son. I look back now and wonder if I did the wrong thing in doing what's so typical of me; bottling things up. I've come to realize that Caleb doesn't talk about Jensen because he doesn't want to open up old wounds for me, and I do the same; I don't talk about him because I think it will be difficult for Caleb to talk about.

I don't know how to go about it, but I am determined to help Caleb stop closing himself off. I've spoken to his teachers and told them that I won't stand there and make excuses for him, but I think that our family situation is affecting him. They're keeping an eye on him to make sure he doesn't completely shut down.

I blame Jensen for never giving us a reason why he left. It was the typical *'it's not you, it's me'* bullshit. He said we needed to talk and yet he didn't have anything to say. He just ended up packing his bags and going back to live with his parents. The night he left, I told him to be a man about it and, at the very least, he owed Caleb an explanation. How do you tell a six year old that you're leaving and he'll never see you again? How do you tell him that he'll never see his grandparents or aunts and uncles again? He's not just lost Jensen; he's lost a whole family. We both did. The words he left Caleb with were, "I don't want you to ever think this is your fault. I love you. I always have, but I have to go." That was all he had to say for himself. I told Caleb that it wasn't his fault and that it was because Jensen just didn't love me anymore. Why? I didn't know then and I don't know now.

Did he go because I was told I'd be permanently disabled and he couldn't see past that? That was one of my theories. I've tried piecing things together so many times over the years, but I will never know the real reason. He wasn't someone who talked about his feelings; I knew that before we even got together. But after seven years with me, I thought he was opening up more and learning to talk about things instead of bottling it all up.

There could be so many reasons why he left, but the one that sticks out in my mind is my disability. I don't think he knew how to reconcile the two different versions of me. I was young, carefree and able bodied when we met. Our sex life was better than I've ever experienced with any of the men I've dated. I might have been pregnant with someone else's baby when we first got together, but he knew I was pregnant before we even started dating. We were friends before becoming lovers and he was the second person I told about the baby. It never put Jensen off being with me though, and he was with me as Caleb was brought into the world. He was the best father I could have wanted for my son. But then came the other version of me; disabled, left with irreparable nerve damage in my right leg and foot. That meant our sex life suffered as I had to have operations on my spine and, when I was left with nerve damage after the second operation, it affected our sex life to the point where we weren't exactly intimate for the last year of our relationship. Sex wasn't possible for me without being in too much pain or my leg cramping up at the most inconvenient times.

Maybe our lack of intimacy is the reason, or at least one of the reasons, why he ended our relationship. I can go round in circles for hours asking myself why Jensen did what he did. Like a dog chasing its tail, I could chase the reason but never actually get it. We tried staying in contact after he left, as I wanted us to stay friends because we'd been such a big part of each other's lives that I couldn't possibly conceive us not being friends. But we stopped talking two and a half months after he left when he told me that he couldn't talk to me anymore because his new girlfriend didn't like it. They'd been seeing each other for a week and already it mattered most what was fair to *her*, not what was fair to me and Caleb.

Since then, I've become more cynical and guarded. I feel like there's a piece of my heart missing, so what's left of it is under lock and key, not to be shown to anyone else. Jensen owns that missing piece and it's one I can never get back. He can't even give it back to me. It's just not possible. When someone has been in your life for so long, they carve out a place in your heart and when they leave, it's the emotional wounds that are the deepest. They say you can judge how deep a cut is by how long it takes to heal. But sometimes, words leave permanent scars. It's the scars to your soul that hurt the most.

So now I am a fiercely independent woman who won't allow any man close to her. I don't want to put my heart on the line only to have it wounded again. It's already been through the wood chipper and come out broken and completely useless. I can't enter another relationship only to have it all fall apart around my ears. Not only would it hurt me, but Caleb too. He's my priority now, the only man I'll ever allow entrance to my heart.

Chapter One
Elise

"It's been three and a half years, Elise. Isn't it time you braved your fears and got back out there?" Sam asks.

"I'm not sure I know how, Sammie. I mean, it's harder now. I haven't been on a date in over ten years. I was with Jensen for so long and he shattered my heart. I didn't just lose him, I lost a family too."

I sit back in my armchair and sip at the glass of prosecco I've allowed myself, even though I shouldn't drink much, if at all, because of the tablets I have to take. Sam looks like a goldfish, sitting there opening and shutting her mouth, no sound coming out. We've had this conversation so many times; too many to count.

"All I'm saying is that I think you should go on this date and, even if it comes to nothing, at least you're dipping your toes back in the water."

Sam's spent the best part of the last hour trying to convince me to go on a blind date with a guy she knows from work. She's a nurse at the local hospital and this guy she wants to set me up with is a paramedic.

Apparently he's so hot he'd 'melt my panties'. That's one thing I love about Sam; her sense of humour.

"My toes are pretty happy being on dry land, thank you," I say as I take a larger gulp of my drink than intended.

I choke a little and Sam's face brightens as she laughs.

"See, you're choking. You need a good paramedic on hand."

I laugh and swat her away with my hand.

"You're hilarious. Fine! If it will shut you up, I'll go on this date. But you're on baby-sitting duty."

"Sure thing, babe, you know I'll always look after Caleb for you. He and Josh get on like a house on fire, just like their mums, so he'll be fine stopping over at ours."

"I didn't say anything about stopping over. Do you think I'm going to take this guy to bed on a first date? Or let him go all cave man and drag me back to his for a night of passion?"

Sam looks at me and bursts out laughing, spraying the prosecco that was in her mouth all over my coffee table.

"What's so funny?" I huff out, trying my hardest not to laugh along with her.

"You! You never know, you might want exactly that. A good fuck to get rid of the cobwebs up there. Plus, like I said, Andrew is pantie-melting hot. I'd totally go there if I wasn't a happily married woman."

"Cobwebs? You cheeky bitch!"

We both laugh so hard we have to catch our breath before being able to talk again.

"Look, seriously, Elise, you never know what might happen. Andrew is a genuinely nice guy, well, what I know of him anyway. He hasn't been at our hospital long; he transferred about two months ago. Go on one date and just see for yourself. Not all men are like Jensen. They don't all leave. Look at me and Karl."

"I've already agreed to one date, so you don't have to sell this guy to me anymore. Just tell me when and where to meet him, and I'll give him one chance."

"I'll text him now if you like?" she asks as she whips her phone from her pocket.

"Go on then," I reply with a forced enthusiasm.

I'm doing this to shut her up. I'm happily single, just me and Caleb. Or at least that's what I tell myself. If I were to admit the whole truth, I do miss the companionship. The sex too, but mostly I miss having someone there to come home to at the end of the day; someone to cuddle up to, to talk to, to share my life with. But I've been so guarded for so long that I don't know how to let anyone in.

I hear Sam's phone beep with a reply and she looks up at me with a smile.

"How does Saturday at Olive Grove sound?"

"This Saturday…I didn't expect it to be *that* soon…" I sputter.

"He's keen. You might as well do it sooner than later. There's less chance of you chickening out."

"Okay, but he knows about me, right?! About my disability and that I walk with a stick?"

"Yes, he knows. It doesn't put him off. He's not that shallow, babe, honestly."

I'm relieved to hear those words. I've tried dating since Jensen left but they've ended in disaster, mainly because of my disability. They only see the label, the stigma of it, not the woman behind the stick. So it will be a nice change to meet a guy that can see the real me past the issues I have. Will it be this Andrew guy? I haven't a clue. But Sam's words give me something I haven't felt for some time. Hope.

***

Saturday came quicker than I thought. Now I'm finishing getting ready for my date with Andrew. I have gone through my wardrobe several times and ended up getting Sam to help me choose the right outfit.

I haven't always had such little confidence in my appearance. I used to be way more comfortable in my own skin. My grandmother used to tell me I was vain because I never left the house without makeup and I never had a hair out of place; it was always styled perfectly. I also had good taste in clothes and loved shoe shopping. Nowadays, I'm more of a jeans a t-shirt kind of girl. I don't wear dresses or skirts anymore because they show my legs; something I'm more conscious of lately. As for makeup, I don't really bother with it much anymore unless I'm going out somewhere special, which isn't often. I can certainly leave the house now without wearing any.

"Seriously, babe, you look great," Sam says as she finishes applying my makeup.

"Thanks. It's just nerves, I guess."

"You have nothing to be nervous of; you'll knock Andrew's socks off."

She steps back to take a look at me and a smile lights up her face.

I turn to look at myself in the full-length mirror on my wardrobe door. A smile graces my own lips as I look at how Sam has styled my hair and applied minimal makeup. She said she was going to *'enhance what's already naturally beautiful'*. I think she's done a great job, even if I don't really agree that I am naturally beautiful.

"What time is it? Do I have time to have a mini freak-out?" I ask as I turn back to face my best friend.

"No, you don't. Your taxi will be here in about five minutes."

Andrew had wanted to come and pick me up, but I didn't like the idea of a stranger knowing where I live. So I had agreed to meet him at Olive Grove.

Caleb walks into my room and gives me the biggest grin before wrapping his arms around me.

"Have a great time, mum," he says as he pulls away to look up at me.

"I'll try. You be good for Auntie Sam and Karl."

"I will, mum, I promise. Josh and I will play Minecraft and probably kill some chickens."

I chuckle at my boy as I ruffle his gorgeous sandy blond hair. He has a fascination with that game and when he and Josh play it together, they find it funny to kill chickens and then put them in the furnace to cook.

A car horn beeps, indicating the arrival of my taxi. Nerves pool in my stomach as I look at my reflection one last time.

The restaurant is busy but not full to capacity as I arrive. I look around, unsure what Andrew looks like. I look at each guy I see from my place at the bar. I'm slightly earlier than we planned to meet. I'm always early or on time; I can't stand being late. I order my drink as the barman walks to serve me. I need something stronger to calm my nerves, but I'm being good and only drinking wine.

I know that Andrew has told Sam he'll be wearing a grey shirt and black trousers and I know he has brown hair with a slight salt and pepper look by his temples. I keep my eyes fixed on the door as I slowly drink my white wine spritzer.

A face I never imagined seeing again makes me nearly spill my drink all down myself. I thought he was off travelling the world and didn't put two and two together when Sam told me his name was Andrew and he was a paramedic. Sam couldn't possibly have known we knew each other. She never got to meet him back then, because we were only a 'no-strings' arrangement. I'm finding it hard to take a breath. Surely it's a coincidence and he isn't really my date?

Looking at what he's wearing, I find that it *has* to be him. He hasn't changed much, really. Sure, he's older, but then so am I. He's just as handsome as I remember. Seeing him looking around for someone, I know the instant his eyes land on me. Like a magnet, our eyes are drawn to each other's and he holds my gaze as a bright smile graces those soft, full lips. In that moment, I am pulled back to the memory of the night we met.

"I have to get going, Nat. Thanks for a great night."
"Don't go yet, the party isn't over."

"We've seen all the gorgeous underwear that Bella brought with her, we've drunk far too much wine. How is the party not over?"

Nat had invited me to an Ann Summers party being held in her flat; the flat above the one I once shared with my ex, Dave. We'd become good friends when Dave and I had moved in and I was damned if the two of us splitting up would get in the way of me staying friends with Nat and her husband, Rich.

"Well, I've text the boys and they're on their way round."

"Oh."

Rich had gone round to a friend's flat in the block next to ours. His friend was having a poker night for the boys to get them out from under our feet while we played party games, checked out sexy lingerie and got drunk whilst investigating the sex toys Bella had brought along.

It's been a good laugh, despite me being out of my comfort zone. Underwear parties really aren't my thing, but that didn't stop me from buying some of the things Bella had on offer. For whom, I don't know, considering I'm newly single.

Dave recently decided to go back to his wife and kids, even though we've been together for two years, and I thought he was happy with me.

"Stay a little longer, please?" she asks as the front door opens and the boys come in laughing.

One of the guys catches my eye, so I find myself agreeing to stay. My god, he's breathtakingly handsome. Dark hair, slim build, his eyes twinkle as he laughs at something Rich said.

I look at his ass as he passes me by. Wow. If there's one thing I like about a man, it's a great ass and this guy sure has one of the nicest I've laid eyes on in a while.

We drink and laugh some more, but I start to feel a little sick, so Nat takes me to her bedroom. The guy I was checking out follows us and asks if I'm okay.

"I'm fine. I should just head back downstairs. I'm a tad tipsy," I respond as I look at his beautiful hazel eyes. They have flecks of gold in them and I find that I can't look away.

"Stay here and I'll grab you a glass of water," Nat says as she leaves the room, leaving me alone with Mr Tall Dark and Definitely Handsome. Oh, so handsome.

I drink the water Nat brings and we stay in her room chatting, just the three of us.

"I'm Drew, by the way," Mr Handsome says.

"I'm Elise, pleased to meet you."

I smile down at him as he crouches at the foot of the bed. He smiles back *and I see beauty in his slightly crooked smile. His eyes seem to shine; maybe it's the light in the room or maybe it's because of the alcohol I've consumed. Either way, I can't look away from his steady gaze.*

We chat a while longer before I tell them I really must go.

"Don't I get a kiss goodbye?" I ask Drew cheekily as I sway slightly on my feet.

I feel those soft, full lips press down over mine and I melt into his arms. In the movies they talk about 'foot-popping kisses' and I've always thought it was a made up thing until now. His tongue probes my mouth and I get lost in his kiss. Our tongues dance together and I suddenly feel less drunk than I did before. There's a clarity that comes with this kiss.

"Do you know what time it is?" Dave asks as I enter our flat. I say' ours', but really it's just a place he's staying until he moves back in with his family in a couple of months' time.

"Does it look like I care? Who are you, my dad?" I reply, my tone dripping with its usual sarcasm.

"You're drunk," he states, his voice laced with spite.

"Again, are you my dad? No! So get off my back. You know where I've been. I was at Nat and Rich's, you know, the flat above us. It's not like I was far away."

I'm really tired and all I want to do is go to bed. I don't even know why I let Dave talk me into staying the night. I live with my grandmother now after us splitting up. But as I was coming to a party at Nat's, he asked me if I wanted to stay and the part of me that still loved him made me agree. But now I'm regretting my decision.

"I'm going to bed," I say as I open the bedroom door and begin to take off my shoes.

My phone beeps, indicating an incoming message. I open it and see it's from Drew.

Drew: Goodnight Gorgeous. Thanks for the kiss. I really hope we get to do that again soon.

I smile to myself as I close my stupid flip phone and continue undressing.

"What the hell is this?" Dave demands as I slide into bed.

I look over at him and see my phone in his hand.

"What the hell? You're going through my phone now?"

I'm suddenly angry and I feel my blood boiling as I look at his face, his features marred with anger.

"I asked what the hell this is?" he spits at me.

I sit bolt upright in bed and try to rein in my own anger.

"It's my phone. Are you stupid?"

"I mean the message on it. Who is Drew?"

"That's absolutely none of your business. You and I are no longer together. You're going back to Tracey, so why shouldn't I be moving on?" I seethe, my fists clenching the sheets.

"Because you're still sleeping with me."

His face is blood red and I have a feeling mine is the same.

"You and I have had sex a couple of times since we split up, but the fact remains that I am single. I'm not discussing this with you. Goodnight."

I lie back on the bed seconds before I hear something clatter against the wall. I look over and see it's my phone. I reach over for it and plug it in to charge on the bedside table next to me. I'll be surprised if it's still working in the morning with how hard he threw it, but I'll deal with that tomorrow. Right now, I'm too tired to care.

As I'm drifting off, I feel Dave lie on the bed next to me. I feel my anger begin to dissipate as sleep takes me away.

***

Shaking myself out of the memory, I look at Drew and see him move in my direction. How the hell is he here? How is it possible that he's my date?

"Elise," my name is a mere whisper from his lips.

"Drew…long time no see…how are you?"

I feel myself getting more anxious by the second. I've suffered with anxiety since 2012 but I'll be damned if I'm going to let it get in my way tonight.

"I'm good. How are you? You're looking well."

"I am well, thank you. It's been so long since I last saw you. Last I knew, you were renting out your flat and going travelling. Did you do that? Did you finally go travelling like you always wanted?"

I'm beginning to ramble, something I typically do when I'm nervous, but also when I'm getting anxious. But I also find myself wanting to know what he's been up to since 2005 when we last saw each other. Twelve years have passed and I realize I know only the Drew of old, not the man sitting next to me at the bar. This version of him still oozes confidence and sex appeal, just like he always did. But there's something different about him and I can't put my finger on what.

"I did. Shall we find a table and I'll tell you anything you want to know?" he asks as he steps down from his stool and offers me his hand.

I place my hand in his and instantly feel a crackling like electricity in my veins. We always had great chemistry, but I had to go and ruin it all. Now he's here and I don't know what will happen after tonight, so I'm going to make the most of it while I can.

Chapter Two
Drew

When I started working at the local hospital, I made friends with a few of the doctors and nurses as well as other paramedics. I've spent a long time travelling and now I want to settle down at home again, for now, at least. I still have the travel bug, but money being what it is, I have to settle somewhere for a few months or so to be able to afford to travel. Plus I enjoy my job and I like meeting new people.

Sam was one of the first people to befriend me. She's a sweet natured woman and has a real sunny disposition. She wanted to set me up on a date with a friend of hers and I kept saying 'no'. My lifestyle doesn't allow for lasting relationships. A woman would have to cope with me being away for large chunks of the year or she'd have to come with me, and I'm not sure I want a travel companion. I guess if I met the right woman, I might settle down and travel less. But the right woman is beginning to sound like a myth rather than a reality, or at least that was the case until Sam showed me a photo of this 'best friend' of hers. To say I was taken aback is an understatement. I couldn't believe my eyes. The years have changed her, but I couldn't forget those beautiful blue eyes even if I wanted to. I met her twelve years ago and we had a brief 'no-strings' thing going on. But one day she just disappeared and all contact ceased.

I got the feeling that Sam didn't know I knew the woman in the photo. She certainly didn't sound like it when she was telling me all about Elise. I didn't know whether to tell her I already knew her friend or not. But if she wanted to set us up on a date, I thought it might spook Elise if she knew it was me she'd be meeting. Sam told me that she was going to tell Elise when and where to meet me, but she wouldn't divulge anything about me other than my name, age and occupation. I gave her my mobile number and told her to text me if Elise was up for our 'blind date'.

***

As I walk into the restaurant and see Elise, I'm taken back to the time when we first met. I sit next to her at the bar and she seems genuinely shocked that it's me that she's here to meet. I'm guessing Sam really can't have known we knew each other in a previous life. If she knew, then Elise wouldn't have nearly spilled her drink when she noticed me.

I notice she still has gorgeous red hair that flows long and straight, just like it always did. Her blue eyes shine brightly and her lips are painted a soft pink. She looks gorgeous in black leggings and a purple tunic style top. As beautiful as she ever was, just the sight of her has my heart beating a little faster.

I sit down next to her and order myself a drink. I whisper her name, finding it hard to believe it's really her sitting next to me, after all these years. She greets me nervously and I observe a slight shake in her hand as she reaches for her drink. Is she feeling as nervous as I am right now?

We move to sit at a table in the large room beyond the bar. As I walk behind her I notice Elise walks with a slight limp and uses a walking stick for balance; but that's not a surprise to me considering the fact that Sam told me she has recently become disabled. Sam didn't tell me much beyond that, saying that it was Elise's decision whether to share information about what happened to her.

Reaching to pull the chair out for her earns me a bright smile. I wait for her to be seated before taking my seat opposite her. I really want to sit next to her and breathe in that intoxicating scent I inhaled at the bar, but I sit facing her so that it's easier to talk and I get to see those breath-taking eyes of hers.

"So, this must be a shock after twelve years," I say as I reach for the wine list.

"It sure is. I didn't know you and Sam knew each other. She wouldn't tell me anything about you, insisting it's called a 'blind date' for a reason."

She giggles and damn if it isn't the most beautiful sound to ever grace my ears.

"I met Sam at the hospital when I first started work. She was the first person to befriend me and, after a few weeks she asked me if she could set me up on a date with her friend. So here I am."

"Did she tell you who she was setting you up with or is it a shock to you too?"

"She told me your name was Elise and I thought it was just coincidental until she showed me a photograph of you."

"Oh."

She fiddles with her glass and looks nervous. I don't want to put her on edge, but I'd never lie to her. I'm not sure why it should bother her that I knew it was her, but her body language suggests it does.

"Are you okay?" I ask after a few moments of silence from her.

"Yes, I just…well I didn't know it was you and I'm a little annoyed at Sam for telling *you* but not me. I mean she said your name was Andrew, that you are thirty four and work as a paramedic. I thought it was coincidental, considering I thought you were off travelling. I really didn't think it was possible that it was you. Of all people to set me up on a date with," she pauses to sip her drink. "Sorry, I don't mean that offensively. That probably came off as quite brusque, but I didn't mean it that way. I just mean… well…" she trails off.

I see her eyes glisten as if they hold unshed tears. I don't know why it bothers her that she's on a date with me, but if she doesn't want to be here, there's nothing I can do, except offer to leave.

"Elise, if you'd rather we… well, what I mean to say is, if you want to go…"

I can't say I won't be offended if she leaves, but I won't hold it against her. It must feel strange to her to be sitting with me after all these years.

"No, I didn't mean that. I'm sorry. Can we start again?" she asks as she reaches for her glass and knocks back the last of its contents.

"Sure thing. I know it's been a long time, Elise. And with the way things ended, well, it has to be a bit weird for you. I mean, I knew it was you, but I was nervous coming here. I take it Sam doesn't know about our past because, I mean, how could she? If she didn't tell you much about whom you were going on a date with…"

I take a sip of my lager and try to think what to say to put her more at ease.

"She knows I once hooked up with a paramedic called Drew, but to be honest, she really can't have known about us. She wouldn't have set this up otherwise. Well, maybe she would have but I'm sure she would have at least warned me that it was you so that I could decide whether to come or not."

"Hooked up?" I scoff.

Shit! We were meant to be starting over.

"I'm sorry, that came out wrong," she replies softly as she fiddles with her empty glass.

I call the waiter over and order a bottle of wine.

After a few moments of awkward silence, Elise looks at me and then excuses herself from the table. I see her walk towards the toilets and let out a breath I didn't realize I'd been holding, thinking she was going to just leave me here.

"Sorry about that," she says as she sits down opposite me once again.

I see her eyes are slightly pink and I am hazarding a guess that she shed at least a few tears while she was gone.

"No problem. I poured you a glass of wine, is that okay?"

She nods in confirmation before taking a sip from her glass.

"Are you ready to order?" the waiter asks as he comes to stand at our table.

I look at Elise and she nods, so I order a sirloin steak with chips, mushrooms and onion rings. Funnily, Elise orders the same and I grin as the waiter leaves. It's refreshing to be on a date with a woman that doesn't just order a salad and sit there pushing it around her plate with her fork.

Our first official date was a night that I cooked for her and she was a little uncomfortable about eating in front of somebody new, but I found that endearing, and she soon devoured the pasta dish I had served up. We laughed and joked like old friends. I wish tonight was like that. I know we seem to have gotten off on the wrong foot, but I hope to put that right.

We make small talk about where I've travelled and the sights I've seen as we eat our meal. She seems less on edge and I feel lighter somehow, as if her earlier reaction was a weight on my shoulders but now it's gone.

It feels more like the old days as we catch each other up on things that have happened over the years. Elise only drinks a glass and a half of wine, telling me about the cocktail of medication she's been prescribed. After that, she swaps to tonic water and I order another lager as we sit and talk for the next hour or so.

I order a taxi as we leave the restaurant and, remembering Elise said something about not living far, I ask her if she wants to share the ride home. She accepts my offer and climbs in the back of the car with me when it arrives.

"Would you like to come back for a coffee?" I blurt as she shuts the door.

"Coffee, or *coffee?*" she asks as she air quotes with her fingers.

I can't help but laugh. I want both, but I don't want to scare her off by saying that quite so soon.

"Just a regular cup of coffee," I reply.

"Okay."

I give the taxi driver my address and we're soon pulling up outside the block of flats where I live. They were newly built flats when I moved in, two blocks of six next to each other. Elise lived on the bottom floor of the block next to mine. It's odd that she'd lived there months and we'd never met until the night of the poker game I held at mine while Nat had the girls round for an Ann Summers party. I'd never even seen her around, as I'd definitely have remembered a strikingly beautiful woman like her. When we met, she was like a breath of fresh air. She was bold and unafraid to speak her mind. She had asked me if she got a kiss goodnight and so help me I couldn't refuse. One look at those eyes and I was weak at the knees. One touch of her lips and my body was on fire. What I wouldn't give to feel that again.

When we enter my flat, she looks around, probably noting that it hasn't changed all that much since she was last here; a new coat of paint here and there, but nothing major.

"It's as if I've entered a time machine," she says as she follows me into the kitchen, where I turn on the coffee machine.

"Yeah, I haven't really made any major changes."

"Do you still have the tank of terrapins?"

"Oh, yes. I still have them. They have a long lifespan, you know."

Elise walks out of the kitchen and I pop my head around the door to see her walking over to the tank. I watch her standing there and it's as if I'm taken back in time.

"What do you feed them?" Elise asks, pointing at my terrapins in the fish tank.

"This," I say as I get up and retrieve a Tupperware tub with their food in.

"I've never known anyone who keeps terrapins before," she marvels as she watches them swimming around.

"They're an unusual choice of pet, granted. But where's the fun in being predictable?"

"They're gorgeous," she whispers as though the volume of her voice will

scare them.

"Not as gorgeous as you," I respond as I slip my arms around her waist and pull her back flush to my chest.

"Such a charmer," she quips as she turns in my embrace.

Her soft, warm lips touch mine and her tongue seeks entrance to my mouth. I grant her access; I don't think I'll ever get enough of her kisses. Our tongues dance and I swallow the moan that escapes her. Her arms go around my neck and she twirls the hair at the nape of my neck around her finger. I lift one of her legs around my waist and she automatically wraps the other around me. I cup her gorgeous ass in the palms of my hands as I carry her to the couch.

Tonight is our first official date. I told her I'd cook up a storm for her and she was pleased to find I am a man who actually knows how to cook. I've been single for a while now, so I pretty much have to cook or starve.

The first kiss we shared was a few days ago and I couldn't wait to ask her on a date. The trouble is, I didn't want to take her anywhere and have to share her with the world. I wanted to be selfish and have her to myself. Now I'm glad I did.

Elise straddles my lap, her arms still around my neck. She deepens the kiss and rocks herself gently over my crotch. Even through the material separating us, I know she'll be able to feel how hard I am.

I don't want to take things too fast with her, but I want her so much. I want to bury myself inside her.

My hands hold her hips and I grind her against me. She moans and grips my hair harder. Shit! If I'm not careful I'm going to come in my boxers.

Her back arches as I reluctantly move my lips from hers. I want to keep kissing her, but I also want to explore more than just her lips. I kiss along her jawline to a spot just beneath her ear before gently nipping the lobe between my teeth. I hear as much as feel her breathing change. Placing a trail of feather-light kisses down the side of her neck, I grasp her hair in one hand while keeping the other firmly on her hip.

Her hand slides down the length of my shaft and it strains impossibly harder against my jeans. I want her something bad. She's incredible. Not only is she beautiful, but she's funny, sarcastic, intelligent, someone you can hold a real conversation with. But conversation is the last thing on my mind as she manoeuvres herself to recapture my lips. Her kisses are urgent and full of desire. This wasn't what I had planned for our first date, but best laid plans go to waste, or so they say.

"Tell me to stop and this doesn't have to go any further…yet," I say as my *hands skim the bottom of her blouse.*

"Don't stop," she whispers in my ear before bringing her mouth back to mine.

I begin to undo the buttons on her blouse and, without breaking our connection she begins to undo the rest.

As she throws the discarded material to the floor, I look at her ample breasts, covered only by a black and pink lace bra. I kiss my way from her lips, down the side of her neck and to the swell of her breasts. Her breathing is laboured and I don't know how much longer I can restrain myself from picking her up caveman style and taking her to my bedroom. I'm beyond turned on at this point and I get the feeling Elise is too.

Elise stands and reaches out for my hand. She must have read my mind because she walks towards my open bedroom door. I willingly follow her, my hand in hers.

We enter my room and Elise pushes me back onto the bed. She unbuckles my belt and then makes quick work of undoing my jeans and pulling them down and off my legs. She moves to pull down my boxer shorts and my hard cock springs free.

Kneeling on the floor, Elise takes the head of my cock in her mouth before pulling back and licking me from the tip to the base and back again. I moan as she uses her tongue bar to further stimulate me. Her left hand wraps around the base of my shaft and I lean up on my elbows to watch as she takes me into her mouth, inch by inch until I feel it hit the back of her throat. My cock throbs as she uses her hand in sync with the movements of her mouth. Her pace quickens and I feel my balls tighten, knowing any moment I am going to come in the back of her throat. I reach out and grasp her hair in one hand, sweeping it aside so I can see her, all of her as she gives me the best head I've had in years. My breathing is laboured, my balls are tingling and with one last stroke, she has me shooting hot streams of come into her mouth. She pulls back slightly and I see her swallow, probably the sexiest thing I've seen her do.

Standing over me once more, she slowly shimmies her trousers down over her hips so that I can see a slight hint of panties that match her bra. I watch as she allows the material to fall from her grip and pool on the floor. She stands before me in just her underwear, a sight that has me growing hard again by the second. Straddling me on the bed, her head dips and she easily captures my lips with hers. My hands roam her body, from her supple ass, up her back and to those sumptuous breasts. I caress them over the material and Elise's back arches. I can feel her heat through her panties and I hear the desire in her breathing.

In one swift motion, I swap places with her. She's now lying underneath me and I watch as her chest rises and falls. I kiss the swell of her gorgeous breasts and pull the material of one cup down with my teeth, to run my tongue in circles around her nipple. It hardens underneath my caress and I nip it gently between my teeth before moving to do the same to the other one.

As Elise writhes beneath me, I want so much to just sink into her, but I want to draw this out as long as possible. I stop what I'm doing and tell her to move to the top of the bed and wrap her hands around the bar of my wrought iron headboard. She does as I ask with no question or hesitance. I smile what I'm sure is a shit-eating-grin her way and am rewarded with a gaze brimming with desire.

I move to discard her bra and allow her to briefly remove her hands from the headboard. Moments later they are back in place and all that remains between us are her panties. I make quick work of removing them and then placing myself above her, my arms either side of her head.

I dip my head and slant my mouth over her full, pink and kiss-bruised lips. She moans as she bucks beneath me, wanting to bring me closer to her but being unable to move her hands to do more.

Moving down her body, I place a trail of kisses as I lower my head to her navel. I stop short of where I want to be, taking a moment to look at this beautiful body in front of me. Her creamy expanse of skin is blemish free and silky smooth. My cock is painfully hard again, so I take an opportunity to stroke myself a couple of times before moving to devour the woman before me. She tastes like the sweetest nectar and I swear I could feast on her for hours. She bucks as I lick along her folds up to her clit. Sucking on it briefly makes her buck harder against me. I can't hold back much longer and I have a feeling that I will be waking Elise in the middle of the night for round two.

I slip a finger inside her and feel how hot and wet she is but at the same time, how tight her sweet little pussy really is. The volume of her moans increases as I slip another finger inside her. Her wetness coats my skin and she writhes beneath me as I pump my fingers in and out of her. Clamping her walls around me, I feel her begin to uncoil. I imagine the pleasure this feeling must bring her. If it's anything like she brought me, then it must be pretty fucking fantastic. Her orgasm rolls over my fingers in waves and I dip my head back down to lap up that wetness.

Removing my fingers, I draw them up to her mouth and she gladly opens her lips to lick her sweet juices from me. She really is stunning. I don't think I've ever met such an incredible woman.

I retrieve a condom from the nightstand beside my bed, tear off the packaging and roll it over myself faster than I think I ever have. Lining myself up with her entrance, I lean down and kiss her. I taste her juices on her own tongue as she eagerly explores my mouth.

Slowly, I ease myself inside her. It takes a lot of restraint not to go faster, but I want to savour the feeling. If I thought she was tight around my fingers, fucking hell, it feels fantastic around my cock. Watching myself ease into her is an incredibly satisfying thing to do. She lifts her head from the pillow to watch it for herself and I can only wonder what it is she sees. What I'd give to see this from her perspective.

"Hell, Elise, you're so fucking tight," I think they are the first words I've spoken since we began making out on the couch.

She mumbles something incoherent as I sink fully into her. Pausing for a moment to allow her to adjust to me inside her, I look up and she locks gazes with me. She smiles at me in such a seductive way and I can't help but want to make this an experience she'll never forget.

I begin to move inside her and feel her legs come up to wrap around my waist. Her arms are still above her head, so she uses the grip of her thighs and the heels of her feet as they dig into my ass to help her match my rhythm.

"Harder, Drew...harder," she manages to pant out.

I momentarily pull out and manoeuvre us so that her legs are over my shoulders. Then I'm back pounding her as hard as I can. This angle has a different feel and allows me deeper access to her.

"Hold on tightly to the bed, baby," I say as I build a punishing rhythm.

Thrusting inside her feels so fucking good; she's tight, wet, hot and needy. Her walls clamp around me and it's all I can do to stop myself from coming too soon. This is about her as much as me.

"So...close...so very close..."

Her words are like music to my ears and it isn't long before we're both falling into the abyss.

I move from the bed only long enough to remove and dispose of the condom. Then I climb under the covers and invite Elise to do the same.

"Come here and let me hold you," I say as she crawls under my duvet and into my heart as much as my bed.

I didn't intend to start a relationship with anyone, but Elise makes me want more than I've wanted before. It isn't just the high from amazing sex talking either. This woman has got beneath my skin and we've only just met. What will she do to me a week from now, a month from now? Lord only knows!

***

Her voice pulls me from my memories and I have to ask her to repeat what she said.

"I was asking how long you've been at the hospital with Sam."

"Oh, umm… about three months."

"I realized I didn't get to ask you that before because we were talking about your adventures. How are you finding being back on home soil?"

"It's…" I'm not actually sure how to answer her question. I wasn't sure how much longer I was going to be around before Sam set me up with the one woman I've never been able to forget, "It's good, yeah; the crew here are good."

"You mentioned getting into search and rescue and water rescue. What made you want to do that?"

"A natural progression of things, I suppose. Plus I get to do two things I love; help people and it's an adrenaline rush."

Elise smiles at me and I want nothing more than to kiss her. I have to stop myself from acting on impulse though. I told her I meant coffee and nothing more.

Chapter Three
Elise

When Drew invited me back for coffee, my pulse started to race. I asked him if he meant actual coffee or if it was '*coffee*', air quoting the word as I said it. A big part of me wanted to hear him say it was the latter and I can honestly say I felt a little disappointment when he didn't.

We're sat in his flat, a place that hasn't changed all that much since I was last here. It makes me feel a little nostalgic.

Looking at him as we sit on the couch, I really want to lean in and kiss him. He smells of the same cologne he used to wear, and I inhale it deeply until I feel my lungs might explode. It's a heady scent and makes me yearn for a time gone by; a time when I wasn't disabled, a time when I was younger and more carefree.

Drew and I have been chatting for a while about the new me, and what happened to put me in the situation I'm in now. I've been telling him about my son, Caleb. If a guy is to come into my life, he has a few things to accept about me first. He has to be able to look beyond the label of disability and also has to get on with my son. That's something that's really important to me. Caleb is ten now and he's my world, so if a guy is interested in me, he has to have a relationship with Caleb, too.

After telling Drew all this, he doesn't seem at all fazed by the facts of it all. He works in the health profession and sees people from different walks of life every day. He's got a very caring disposition; he always did. The fact that he seems able to see the real me beyond my need for a walking stick, that's a definite plus. But even though I allowed Sam to set me up on a date, I'm still not sure if I have room for a man in my life right now. I'm pretty guarded and it'll take a lot to knock down the walls I've built around my heart over the last three years. I was really hurt by Jensen and I guess that's something else that any potential guy has to deal with.

Whether Drew and I end up dating or not, it's been good to see him. Oh, so good. He reminds me of the life I had, but also makes me glad of the life I have today. I've come so far since I was twenty two when we first met. I've gone through a lot and I've had to learn to play the hand that I've been dealt. I've become a mother, which is by far the greatest honour anyone could ever bestow on me.

Drew breaks me from my thoughts as he offers to make another coffee. I look at my watch and see that it's only 10pm. Sam has Caleb for the night, so it's not like I have to get back any time soon and being here with Drew after all these years feels better than I could have imagined, so I agree to stay for a little while longer.

He goes to put the coffee machine back on and I stand to look around the living room. It's pretty much the same room from twelve years ago, with the addition of some photos from his travels. I stand to look out of the blinds and remember the day we had to hide from my jerk of an ex. We sat in this very room for hours, hoping he'd just disappear and leave us alone.

I walk into the living room with the dress from last night in a dress bag and the shoes in my other hand. It was such a great night. Drew finally referred to me as his girlfriend and introduced me to some of his friends from work. At first, when he invited me to his works' Christmas ball at the Thistle Hotel, I wasn't sure I wanted to go. I wouldn't know anyone except Drew, whereas he'd know everyone. I couldn't expect him to stick to me like glue all night and wondered what I'd do with myself while he mingled with his friends. But it hadn't turned out like that.

My grandmother took me to buy a new evening dress as I didn't have anything suitable for such an event. I knew Drew was going in a tuxedo and I didn't want to look underdressed. I settled on an ankle length black dress with a sweetheart neckline, a small train at the back and silver and white bead detailing. I fell in love as soon as I saw it and the guy who owned the shop gave me a discount on it. My grandmother said afterwards that his eyes had popped out of his head when he saw me in the dress and while I was taking it off in the changing rooms, he'd told her I looked stunning. I blushed at her words, but was secretly happy because I hoped Drew would have the same reaction.

The ball hadn't been at all what I thought. Drew didn't leave me on my own; instead he introduced me to his friends and soon we were chatting like we'd known each other for years. We sat around a table, me on Drew's lap with his arms around me, chatting and drinking for hours.

After a great night, Drew and I came back to his flat and spent hours making love before falling asleep in each other's arms.

This morning, Drew is dropping me home where I live with my grandmother. I haven't been able to find anywhere else to live since breaking up with Dave.

I look out of the front window and a chill breaks out over my skin, raising goose-bumps in its wake. Dave's Audi is parked out front in the road directly opposite the flats. It's weird for two reasons. I am pretty sure he should be at work and, whenever he's at the flat, he parks in the private carpark behind the block because he doesn't want anything happening to his precious new car.

I tell Drew and he walks closer to the window to get a better look through the blinds.

"He's in the car," he says as he looks back at me.

"Damn. What do I do? Walk out there with my head held high or wait here a while and see if he leaves?"

I haven't done anything wrong, Dave and I broke up in October and he can't hold it against me for moving on. Can he?

"We could always chill out and watch a film if you don't have to be home yet," Drew suggests.

I agree that would be good. I get to snuggle up to Drew on the couch and by the time the film is over, Dave will have given up waiting and gone back to work. He has to leave at some point. I'm not even sure why he's here and I don't know whether he knew I was here or if it's just a coincidence. But why is he just sitting in the car?

Settling down together, snuggled up under a blanket, Drew and I put a film on. I phoned my grandmother and let her know I wouldn't be home for a while and explained that Dave was outside. I don't have to be home by a certain time—I'm a grown woman after all—but I thought it was only polite to let her know my plans.

The credits roll and Drew gets up to look out of the window to see if the coast is clear.

"Whatever he's doing, he's definitely not giving up waiting out there," he says as he steps back from the window.

I'm pissed off that I feel like he's trapping me here. But there are worse places I can think of being. I get to spend more time with Drew this way, so I'm not complaining.

"I'll make us a coffee and we can put another film on. Just choose one and

I'll be back in a minute."

Drew goes to the kitchen and I look at his DVD collection. I peek out of the slit in the blinds and wonder what on earth Dave is hoping to achieve. It's got to be related to me, the reason he's out there, otherwise he'd surely be at work or back in his own flat, as he's technically still living there and not moving back in with his family until closer to Christmas.

The intercom buzzes and I hear Drew answer it.

"He wants to speak to you," he sighs as he walks into the living room.

"What the fuck? Tell him I'm not here."

The buzzer goes again and I hear Drew tell Dave that I'm not here and he should just go. He replaces the handset and I see the cross look on his face as he returns.

"He wants to come up and check the flat to see if you're here."

The contempt in Drew's voice is evident and I am now wondering who the fuck this psycho really is. I mean, he wasn't jealous, possessive or controlling when we dated.

"I hope you told him where to go."

The buzzer goes again so I get up and walk into the bedroom. I'm sure this is going to put Drew off being anything more than just a 'no strings' thing. He referred to me as his girlfriend for the first time at the ball, but now I'm sure he's reconsidering his options. I wouldn't blame him if he was.

"Just go away man, she isn't here, and if she was, I'm sure she wouldn't want to speak to you. You're acting like a stalker."

I hear Drew replace the handset with a heavier hand than normal. He has every right to be pissed off that my jerk ex is acting like this. I just hope he doesn't blame me.

"Let's just chill and watch another film, babe," he says as he returns.

We snuggle up again and he captures my lips for a sweet kiss. I play with the hair at the nape of his neck and open my mouth when his tongue seeks entrance.

The second film ends and Drew gets up to take the DVD out of the player. He peeks out of the blind while he's there.

"He's gone," he says, relief evident in his voice.

"Thank goodness. It's about time."

We decide to go before he comes back, so I grab my dress bag and shoes. Heading down to the silver Porsche he has parked in the private carpark, we see that Dave's car isn't there, which makes me sag in relief. I feel myself let out a breath I didn't realize I'd been holding.

I put my dress bag and shoes into the boot of Drew's car and then buckle up for the journey home.

We pull down the road to the T junction and before I realize what's happening, Drew swerves the car hard. I look out of the window and see Dave driving his car like a maniac. He's heading for us for what I realize must be the second time. Drew speeds up the road toward the dual carriageway and I look out of the back window to see the jerk trying to catch us up. Why is he trying to run us off the road? I just don't get it.

Unfortunately, we have to stop at traffic lights and, as if it couldn't get any worse, I see Dave get out of his car on the dual carriageway and head around Drew's car to bang on my window.

"What the fuck, Elise? You're wearing different clothes to yesterday, so I know you stayed the night with him."

"It's got nothing to do with you what I do with my life. Just grow up and go back to your wife," I spit before Drew pulls off as the light turns green.

I don't know how he knew what I was wearing yesterday unless he was looking out of the bedroom window as Drew pulled into the carpark. I'm breathing heavily, my heart pounding as I look at Drew and see his face screwed up in concentration. I notice Dave catching up with us and hear car horns honking as he weaves his way through them.

Thankfully, Drew was taught evasive manoeuvres when he learned to drive an ambulance. He manages to pull away from Dave at the next set of lights and there's nowhere Dave can overtake now.

Drew drives me the rest of the way home and I'm shocked to see Dave's car parked outside as we pull up. How he got here before us, I don't know and I don't care. I just wish I didn't have to get out of the car. I've never witnessed this side of him and I'm worried about what he might do to Drew or even to me. I've never had reason to fear him before, but fear is coursing through my veins right now.

I get out of the car and Dave is ranting at me, but I can't make out half of what he's saying because he's so clearly furious. Drew gets in between me and Dave. Taking me by the arm, he guides me away. He walks me to the entrance gate to the house and tells me to just get inside. He gets my stuff from the boot of the car and walks behind me into the house. He closes the door in Dave's face and my grandmother looks at me before asking what the hell is going on.

After we explain the situation to her, Drew says he'd better head home because he's working tonight. I walk him to the door and he draws me close to *kiss me goodbye. I inhale the scent of his cologne and take strength from his hold on me.*

Drew taps me gently on the arm, pulling me from my reverie. He hands me the steaming mug of coffee and we walk back to the couch. We sit close to each other and I smile at him over my cup before taking a sip of the molten liquid.

"You're so beautiful," he says softly.

I feel the blush creep across my face, no doubt turning me the colour of a tomato.

"Thank you," I respond timidly.

"You always were though."

His hand on my arm makes me smile as he traces it up and down. I place my mug on the coffee table as my hands begin to tremble. I don't want to spill the dark liquid on his couch.

I want so much for him to kiss me, but I'm too self-conscious to make the first move.

He places his own mug down and shifts closer to me. Placing an arm along the back of the couch, he twists to face me better, so I do the same. I look into those hazel eyes and I search for the flecks of gold I know are there. His eyes are dark with lust, or at least I hope that's the emotion he feels right now. I know I do.

Gently pulling me closer to him Drew angles us so that it won't hurt my bad leg. *'Ever thoughtful'* I think as I close my eyes involuntarily.

The touch of his lips on mine feels like I remembered and yet somehow different. He carefully wraps both arms around me as he continues to kiss me softly, as if somehow asking if it's okay without speaking.

I open my mouth to grant his tongue access and he brings his hands up to gently frame my face as he deepens the kiss.

My heart races and I feel high from his kiss, like I could soar above the clouds. Wrapping my arms around his neck, I draw him closer. He leans further into me and I twist the hair at the nape of his neck like I used to, though it's definitely a little longer now.

Not wanting to rush this or mess it up, I pull away to take a breath. Looking into his eyes, I don't mistake his lustful gaze this time. He captures my lips once more and desire pools in my abdomen; it feels like a fire igniting inside me, burning me up from the inside out. I let it consume me as I pour all my energy into this one kiss. If here and now is all we have, then I'll make the most of it before I don't get another chance.

I haven't been completely honest with myself. I've missed having a man in my life. Missed the companionship but more so the passion and desire that comes with it. Maybe Drew is the one for me, maybe he isn't, but it feels like he's been put back into my life for a reason.

Call it fate, destiny, kismet, whatever word that describes it best. Drew was placed back in my path for a reason and I intend to discover why.

Chapter Four
Drew

Our lips still fit perfectly and my heart pounds in my chest, as this beautiful woman melts in my arms. Time has changed us both and yet somehow we've found our way back into each other's lives. My thoughts silence as I get swept away in our kiss. Tongues exploring familiar and yet new territory, my hands fall away from her face and wrap around her torso. Her hands are wrapped around my neck and the little hairs rise on the back of my neck as she twirls the ends of my hair. Where do we go from here? I don't want to lead Elise on, I don't want this to end up a one-night stand, but I'm not really looking for a relationship. Or at least I didn't think I was up until now. It's crazy how meeting up with Elise makes me rethink everything. Will she end up changing my mind entirely? I don't want to hurt her and at the same time I want to protect my own heart. I've suffered enough heartbreak of my own to inflict it on Elise.

I stop overthinking things and I really pour my all into this kiss. They way her soft lips feel against mine, the scent of her wrapping around my senses, the way our tongues dance together…I don't want this to end.

Elise is the first to break the kiss. I see as she inhales deeply, trying to catch her breath as if she forgot to breathe the whole time we were kissing.

Her face is glowing and she looks utterly beautiful. I smile at her and she looks up into my eyes, keeping my gaze focused on the blue pools I feel I could fall into and take a swim.

"Drew," she begins but then is silent for a beat before continuing, "What are we doing?"

"Honestly? I don't know. Do we have to think about the future right now or can we just live in the moment?"

"I…I don't know; there isn't only me to consider anymore."

I know she has to think of Caleb in all this, but only if she's thinking beyond the here and now which is something I can't do right now. All I can think of is how much I want her. Can I see a future for us? I don't know. But here, in this one moment in time, I know I want her. I want to make love to her, to feel her in ways I remember all too well and yet not well enough.

"All I know is that happiness is a series of fleeting moments. You have to catch them and keep a hold of them for as long as you can. You never know what's around the corner and, even if we can't promise each other forever, we can promise each other for *now*. I'm not saying we do or don't have a future together, because we need to get to know each other again and work out what we want separately as well as the possibility of what we want from each other. What I do know for sure though is that I've gone through the last few years alone. I've travelled, I've experienced a lot from life, but I haven't had any meaningful relationships. This could make me reassess my life or it could reaffirm that I'm better off alone. I'm just being honest here, Elise. I'm sorry if it's not what you want to hear."

She's quiet for so long that I'm thinking I've definitely upset her. I begin to move away from her but stop when she places her hand over mine.

"I've been hurt, Drew. I told you about Jensen. Before him, I always thought I wanted to get married and have children. I had a child but never got married and it turned out that was for the best. It made me reassess whether I want to get married in the future and honestly, I don't think I do. I am wary about putting my heart on the line only to have it irreparably damaged. I also don't want to flit from one relationship to another because of Caleb; he needs stability. But you're right...we might not be able to promise each other forever, but we can enjoy this moment in time. Right now, we don't have to think about what the future holds, we don't have to push each other away because we're scared. If all we have is here and now..." she pauses and takes a deep breath before blowing it out slowly, "let's make the most of it. What happens tomorrow is a problem for another day."

Drawing me closer to her, Elise looks into my eyes and traces a hand across my cheek. There's a definite attraction between us. Like she says, tomorrow is a problem to be solved another day. As for right here and now, Elise seems to want to explore our connection as much as I do.

Leaning in to claim her lips, she opens her mouth to me and I feel a jolt of electricity run through me. The current has all my synapses firing, driving the lust I feel to dizzying heights. I pull her closer to me and wrap an arm around her waist. With my free hand, I cradle the back of her head. Before I realize what she's doing, Elise moves both of her hands and ties her hair back with a band that I can only assume was around her wrist if it was so easy to access. It exposes her neck to me so I place feather-light kisses across her jawline, to the sweet spot beneath her ear and then continue my journey down her neck. Her breathing changes as I use one hand to pull her ponytail and the other to trace a line along the hem of her top. She doesn't tell me to stop, so I slip my hand underneath and touch her soft skin as I move to recapture her lips.

Elise moves her hands to the hem of my own top and I love the feeling as her warm hands come into contact with my body. She expertly explores the planes and ridges of my abdomen and torso. I feel my breathing hitch as she traces the line along the top of my trousers. She doesn't dip lower, as I expected, and I am momentarily disappointed, until she removes her hands from under my shirt and begins to undo the buttons. I want to help her, to discard my shirt as quickly as possible, but I'm too busy exploring her body and don't want to stop, even briefly.

My hands move to her breasts and I hear her breath catch as I trace the cups of her bra. Pulling one bra cup down a little, I trace circles around her nipple before pinching it between my forefinger and thumb. She gasps and is unable to get the shirt button she was working on out of the hole.

Kissing down her neck, I make my way to the swell of her generous cleavage. I dip my head lower and trace around her taut nipple with my tongue before pulling it in between my teeth. Her breasts are heaving with the breaths she's struggling to take. As I bite down gently, her back arches and I know it still affects her just the way it used to.

With the final button undone—not without difficulty—Elise pulls my shirt down my arms and I have to move them so she can discard it completely. My hands are back on her in a flash and she moans softly as I move to give the same attention to the other nipple. I undo the clasp of her bra with one hand and she slips it off from underneath her top.

Knowing there's only one layer of clothing separating our skin from touching, I move to take her top off. She raises her arms and allows me to quickly divest her of it. I lower her to the couch beneath me as I claim her lips once more. As soon as I lay my skin against hers, I feel like she's set fire to the blood in my veins. I'm careful not to hurt her or put her in an uncomfortable position as I frame her face with my hands and pull away to look into her eyes. I want permission to take this further.

Without words, she implores me not to stop. That look in her eyes tells me she wants more of this; more of me.

Her hand dips under the waistband of my trousers and she strokes the length of me which is hard as rock. I lean slightly sideways so I can undo my belt buckle but she bats my hands away and quickly pulls the belt from the loops holding it in place. She makes quick work of undoing the button and zipper before shoving my trousers down to my knees. I don't want to move from her to remove them, but I stand and allow them to fall to the floor. I kick them to one side and lean down to pick Elise up from the couch.

Carrying her to my bedroom, I lie her down on the bed. She doesn't deserve just a *quickie* on the couch. She deserves to be worshipped, even if only for the night.

I move to pull her leggings down and she raises her sexy ass from the bed so that I can remove them. She lies there in just her panties and I move on top of her in just my boxer shorts. Kissing and touching each other, we continue what we began. Exploring her body, I realize it's changed since we were last intimate. Not in a bad way. She's had a baby since we were last together and he was born by C-section, so she has a scar. I think it's beautiful. This body held another life inside for nine months. Her body gave life to her son ten years ago.

"Drew, I…"

Scared I've gone too far too fast, I look up at her.

"What is it, Elise?" I ask after she's been silent for a moment.

"I haven't…" a blush creeps across her neck and cheeks, "I haven't done this for a while. I'm different now, my body…it's not what it used to be."

As if that makes a difference to me; but then I realize she doesn't know that.

"Elise, you are beautiful. Do you think the changes in your body make me want you less?"

"Well, I…" there are unshed tears in her eyes as she continues, "I find it hard to believe that anyone could find this attractive."

She gestures at her body. I don't see it through her eyes. I see beauty. Sure, she isn't flawless, she doesn't have what models and the media make out to be the 'perfect' body. But her curves make her a real woman. I don't have a particular type when it comes to women, but I know what I don't like. I don't find stick thin women attractive. But that isn't to say Elise is overweight, she's not, and she may not know it, but her beautiful body turns me on.

"Elise, please don't shy away from me," I implore as she moves to try to cover her modesty, "I think you are absolutely gorgeous. Do you honestly think we would be in this position if I wasn't turned on by you?"

I take her hand and stroke it down the length of my cock. A small smile creeps across her face. I lower myself to kiss her, my tongue dancing with hers. I kiss her as deeply as physically possible. When I pull back to breathe, I lock my gaze with hers.

In a flash, gone is the shyness she displayed only moments ago. In its place is a woman who knows what she wants.

"Beautiful," I breathe just that one word out as she reaches to wrap her arms around my neck.

She brings me back to kiss her and if I thought I was turned on before, now I am impossibly harder and finding it hard to regulate my breathing.

I feel Elise move to trace lines with her nails in my back. A rush of desire washes over me and I move to devour every inch of her. The loss of contact with her lips strikes me, but is replaced by a rush of adrenaline as I kiss my way down her neck to her breasts. I reach to squeeze them with my hands and pull each nipple in turn between my teeth. Moving to explore the rest of her with my hands and tongue, I enjoy the way her body moves with my touch.

Lowering myself between her legs, I smile to myself as she opens them further. I kiss my way from her inner thigh towards her pussy. I can see it glisten with her juices; a sign she's as turned on as I am. I lick her gently and it elicits a moan from her, which provokes me to exert more pressure.

I'm consumed by the taste of her. It's a taste I'm familiar with, but something I thought I'd never experience again.

With every moan and buck of her hips, I feel as if I might shoot my load in my boxers. I reach down to stroke myself a couple of times to relieve some pressure.

Inserting a finger, I stroke her as she clamps her walls around me. I'm dying to bury myself inside her but I want to make this last. I insert another finger and her tight pussy stretches to accommodate me. I know that she's on the brink of her orgasm as she writhes on my bed, twisting the sheets in her hands, her moans filling the air around me. I work her faster and it isn't long before my fingers are coated in her juices as she moans my name loudly.

I don't give her time to recover before I remove my boxers and sheath myself with the rubber I wish wasn't going to separate us from touching completely.

As soon as the condom is rolled over my shaft, I lean down to claim her lips, but she brings my hand to her mouth first and sucks her juices from my fingers, and only when she's done does she kiss me. I align myself with her and, inch by inch, my cock sinks into her warmth. I swallow her moans as I ease completely inside her walls.

Her nails dig deeper into my back as she lifts her legs to wrap them round my waist. Whoever said that a little pain is pleasurable was right. She digs deep enough to leave marks, I'm sure.

Digging her feet into my ass, she pulls me ever closer to her. I move slowly at first so as not to explode inside her in seconds. As I up my pace, Elise bucks beneath me to match my every move. She grips my shoulders as I partially pull out of her before pushing back in harder and deeper than before. The tingling sensation begins in my balls and it's such an intoxicating feeling. Elise's moans match my own and I feel her walls clamp tighter around me.

"Drew, I'm going to…"

I silence her last word with a kiss before setting a more punishing rhythm to take us both over the edge.

"Oh Drew," she sighs softly as I get up to discard the condom.

"Will you stay the night?" I ask, hope evident in my voice.

"Yes."

I'm pleased by her answer, and though neither of us knows what tomorrow will bring, I know we'll make the most of tonight before falling asleep tangled in each other's embrace. I'll be damned if this is the only time we make love to each other tonight. I'm determined to make this night count for us both.

Chapter Five
Elise

I wake up under a duvet in a tangle of limbs and am momentarily disorientated. It takes a few seconds to remember where I am. I look over at the pillow next to me and see Drew, his face relaxed in sleep. I study him while I have the chance. He's been working out since we last saw each other; he's also gone and got himself some ink. I can't read what the one phrase on his arm says and can't even begin to fathom what language it's in, but I make a mental note to ask him.

Drew stirs next to me and I get my first glimpse of those beautiful eyes. The way the sun shines through the bedroom window highlights the gold flecks in his irises and I'm blessed with a gorgeous smile.

"Good morning, beautiful," he says as he reaches a hand out to me.

"Morning," I say as I flash him a grin.

He sits up in bed and I get a good look at his gorgeous body; the way the planes and ridges of his torso end with that V shape that I find irresistible. I remember what it used to be like to run my fingers and tongue over that V. It drove me as crazy as it drove him. There's just something about it that I find really sexy, but I can't put my finger on what.

Drew catches my lingering gaze and beams a shit-eating grin my way.

"See something you like?" he asks with a wink.

"Not really," I deadpan with as straight a face as possible.

Feigning shock, he draws his hands to his heart.

"You wound me, Elise Swanson. Don't you know that you've just killed my ego?!"

"Aw, and here was me thinking you were impenetrable."

"Not me. I'm as soft as a marshmallow and your words have cut me so deeply I'm not sure I'll ever recover."

"I could think of a way to make it up to you?" I offer as I smile seductively—or at least I hope that's how it comes off.

"Well, there's bacon and eggs in the fridge..." he trails off before bursting into hysterics at the look on my face that I can only assume comes off as incredulous.

My reaction to his words is to straddle his lap, put my arms around his neck and kiss him deeply. His shock at my reaction is momentary before he kisses me back just as fervently.

***

After working up an appetite, Drew is cooking breakfast for us. I pull my phone out and send Sam a text telling her I'll be by to pick up Caleb after I've had something to eat. What I fail to mention is that I'm not eating at home.

We sit at the dining table, both kinds of appetite sated after our antics this morning. I smile at him before standing to clear the plates away. I'm wearing one of his t-shirts and a pair of boxers and I add a slight sway to my step to make him smile. If I know Drew, his eyes are fixed on my ass.

When things are cleared away, I make my way to get dressed and hear Drew in the shower. He's singing to himself and I realize that I never knew until now that he has got a really nice voice. I can't remember back to him in the shower twelve years ago; suffice to say I've slept since then and I fear I've forgotten more than I've remembered.

I get dressed with a smile on my face as I hear him sing a song I love. Most men don't like my kind of music, but Drew's version of *I See Fire* by Ed Sheeran could give Ed himself a run for his money. I hum along as I finish getting my things together.

Turning at the sound of a door opening, I see him with a towel wrapped around his waist and beads of water dotting his skin. My tongue darts out to wet my lips, an involuntary reaction to the chiselled man I see before me.

"See anything you like?" he quips, echoing his words from earlier.

"I can think of a few things," I reply as I feel the colour rush to my cheeks.

"Shame you have to get back home, I can definitely see something I want."

"To be continued, Mr Wright."

"I'll hold you to that," he says as he removes his towel and begins to dry himself.

He turns his back to me and I can't help but stare at his perfect ass. He has a small patch of hair at the base of his spine and rather than being off-putting—which I imagine it is to some women—I actually like it. He has a muscular back; broad and sexy. He's everything I'd want if I wanted a relationship. However, this can only be a 'no-strings' kind of thing. I don't know how we'll approach that conversation, but I'm sure we will. He wasn't the kind of person to want to settle down before and that doesn't seem to have changed over the years, considering the kind of lifestyle he leads. I don't mean that offensively, it's just an observation that if you spend large chunks of the year away from home soil, then you can't really be expected to be tied down to a woman.

I'm a homebody. I love holidays, but only for a week, maybe two. I certainly couldn't imagine myself being away from home for months on end. Yes, I'd get to experience things I am unable to at home, but when I weigh up the pros and cons, I'd much rather stay here in the UK. I don't know how Drew does it, but I guess that's up to him and not me.

Not wanting to talk about that and break the spell just yet, I don't bring it up on the drive to Sam's. I asked Drew to drop me at the end of her road rather than outside the house. I'm not sure if it offended him, but I reassured him that it was just because I didn't want to have to explain to Sam, but mainly to Caleb. He's old enough to notice things now, obviously, and I'd rather not face questions about 'the man in the car.'

Pulling up at the end of Sam's road, Drew turns the engine off. He turns to look at me as he removes his seatbelt.

"Elise, I…had a wonderful night."

I noticed the pause in the sentence and I saw the bob of his Adams apple as he swallowed before continuing. It makes me wonder what he was going to say, but I don't ask.

"I did too. I still can't quite believe Sam set me up on a date with you. It's surreal. But I loved every minute of last night," I pause and smile at him, "and this morning," I add with a wink.

His hand comes to frame one side of my face and he draws me closer to him. I inhale deeply to imprint his scent on my memory before his lips come crashing down on mine.

The lust in the kiss is unmistakable and I feel a pool of desire beginning to form in my abdomen. I wish we had more time than this. I wish we could have gone back to bed after breakfast. Selfishly, I want a few more hours alone with him to fully satiate my appetite. But even then, I'm not sure mere hours would do.

I pull back, breaking the kiss, to take a breath. Somehow, it feels like I forget to breathe any time Drew's near me.

Flashing me a toothy mega-watt grin, Drew places his hand over mine and gives it a gentle squeeze. Just as my heart feels like it might explode, the ringtone of my phone makes me jump out of my skin. I see Caleb's name flash on the screen. I imagine he tried to call me at home first to see how long I'd be.

"Hey baby," I answer as I press a finger to my lips, signalling Drew not to make any noise.

"Hey, mum. Are you coming to get me yet?"

"Yes honey, I am almost there. You're not fighting with Josh are you? Fed up and wanting to come home?"

"No, Auntie Sam told me you were coming after breakfast and told me not to bother you, but I snuck up to the top of the garden to call you."

"You don't have to sneak around to call me, baby. You can always ring me."

"Okay, well I'll see you in a few minutes then. Got to go, Auntie Sam is standing in the doorway giving me the stink-eye."

"Love you, honey, see you in a few."

I hang up and look at Drew.

"I'm sorry. I didn't really want to play twenty questions with him if he heard your voice."

"Elise, it's fine, honestly. You explained before. And I totally understand. You can't introduce him to just anybody. I get it, don't worry."

I'm not sure that he isn't at least slightly bothered, but it's true. Although I don't date much, I can't be introducing my son to just anyone. I need to know it's going somewhere with someone before I do that, and it's a big step to consider.

"Okay, well I better get going. But before I go, I have something for you."

I lean over and claim his lips in a sweet, tender kiss. His tongue seeks entrance and I allow it as he frames my face in both hands and deepens the kiss. As we pull apart this time, my lips feel bruised and I put a hand to them to check they aren't swollen. I flip down the visor and look in the mirror to double check. Drew laughs at me and, my God, if the sound of his laughter doesn't make me feel all tingly. I have to get out of the car before I straddle his lap right here in full view of any passers-by.

Placing a chaste kiss to his delectable mouth, I bid him goodbye as I get out of the car and begin to walk away from a tiny piece of my heart.

Chapter Six
Drew

Feeling the tiny sliver of my heart follow Elise out of the car was an odd feeling, to say the least. I don't have lasting relationships. I don't allow people into my heart. Women have trampled all over it too many times for me to bare it to another. But sure enough, I feel Elise beginning to knock my walls down. It's subtle; like she's removing them one brick at a time, but it's not something I'm used to allowing to happen. I'm not so sure I'm 'allowing' it to happen now; it feels like she's doing it without even knowing, and there's nothing I can do to stop it.

I arrive back home and, once I'm inside, I notice that the scent of her still permeates the air. I'm not sure even opening the windows or spraying air freshener would rid the flat of the delicious smell. To be honest, I don't even want to try. I find comfort in the way it lingers long after she's gone.

I'm not sure it will help me with trying to block all thoughts of Elise or the past out of my mind, but I can't bring myself to do anything about it.

Sitting on the couch, I lay my head back and close my eyes. The way she straddled me in my bed just a couple of hours ago comes to mind. It plays like a movie behind my eyelids and I feel myself harden at the memories.

After a few minutes, I can't take it any longer and I get in the shower for the second time today. The only difference this time is, it's a cold one. The freezing water doesn't do anything to erase the motion picture in my head, but it does help my raging hard-on go down. I step out and wrap myself in a towel and walk into my bedroom.

The scent of our love-making still lingers in here and I feel my cock twitch, but try to focus my mind on something else so that the shower wasn't pointless. I grab a pair of tracksuit bottoms and pull them on. Picking up the t-shirt from the bed, I put that on too. I'm not sure what to do to stop feeling so bewitched by Elise. I'm also unsure I even want to. That's what scares me.

Grabbing my iPod and a pair of trainers, I decide to go for a run. I slip my house key on a cord around my neck and take my phone in a band strapped to my upper arm. Taking a cold bottle of water out of the fridge, I step out of the flat and shut the door behind me. I walk down the stairs and out of the door at the front of our block. Putting my earbuds in, I turn my iPod up to blast the cobwebs in my head.

Hole In My Soul by Kaiser Chiefs probably isn't the best song to listen to if I want to stop thinking of a certain red haired, blue-eyed beauty, but I find I don't want to skip the track so instead I concentrate on the pounding of my feet on the ground as I begin my two mile journey.

***

Back on shift, I find it easier not to think of the woman I've had in my head since yesterday. Call-outs are at the forefront of my mind tonight. Work has to be a priority. You drop everything personal at the door as you begin your shift, just as you switch off work stuff as you leave.

I am flat out by the end of the shift. It was mainly easy calls but there was one red-haired woman that reminded me of Elise. She wasn't as naturally beautiful, though, and her eyes were green. But the passing resemblance struck me at first. So much for her not being on my mind.

The lads have organised a night out tonight and, as it's my day off tomorrow, I agreed to join them. We're going for a few pints and a curry. Typical blokes.

Running a little late, I catch up with the boys in The Stag's Head. They're in full swing by the time I arrive. I think I have some catching up to do drinks-wise.

By the time we arrive at the curry house, we're all a little bit worse for wear. Seems there couldn't be a better time to line our stomachs. Well, perhaps it would have been wiser to eat *before* drinking, but still, we're here now.

We are seated in a booth at the back of the restaurant and we order a round of drinks before looking at the menus.

***

It's the typical morning after the night before. I get up, take a couple of painkillers with a glass of water, but I also take a multi-vitamin, a tip a friend passed on some time ago. I head to my en-suite for a shower to wake me up and hopefully leave me feeling more refreshed than I do right now.

Last night was fun. The lads I work with are a bunch of characters. When I go travelling, they always see me off in style. That usually means plenty of booze flowing and a choice of curry, kebabs or pizza. We must really feed into the stereotype.

Travelling. Shit! How could I have forgotten? I can't even think of backing out now; the plans have been in place for months. It's all been booked and paid for.

Come to think of it, why am I even thinking about backing out? I'm still me. I'm still single, free to do what I want, when I want. There's no reason for me not to go. Is there? I need to get my head straight and stop second-guessing myself.

If this is how I feel now, how am I supposed to feel in a couple of months' time? I can't push her away in between now and then; I'm too selfish for that. I want her all to myself. But I should consider her feelings above my own, especially as I'm gone for nearly three months. What will come of all this when I leave? Will she turn her back on me for good?

I'm not sure I'm any good for her. I'm not one to commit to a woman, not anymore. But there's a part of me that wants to try. There's a connection between us that was forged long ago. Maybe she's been put back in my path for a reason. Fate? Destiny? Is destiny just a bunch of bullshit people who want to live 'happily ever after' talk about? I'm not sure how to answer that and I don't want to even begin to wrap my head around what might or might not happen in the future. I can't predict what's going to happen and neither can she.

Feeling a headache lurking behind my eyes, I decide to cook a fry-up. Sometimes grease can kill or sometimes it can cure a hangover. Other matters can be dealt with as they arise.

***

Three weeks later…

Elise and I have seen each other on my days off work, but I've always driven her home afterwards so she can be there to do the school run with Caleb.

We've been careful not to be seen by him. Sam knows what's been going on because she's the one who's been looking after Caleb while Elise has been with me.

I get why Elise doesn't want to tell him about me, especially since I've confessed about my upcoming trip to Iceland. We're not a "couple." I don't know what we are because neither of us wants to use labels. All I know is we've been having fun and I've grown very fond of Elise Swanson all over again. She broke my heart once—though I was too prideful at the time to confess it. Will she break it again? Or will I be the one to break hers?

We haven't talked about feelings. We've just enjoyed getting to know each other again. Our time together hasn't always included sex, either, but the times it has have been nothing short of amazing. The fact we haven't talked about feelings hasn't stopped mine from growing. I'm caring more about her each time I see her. I've been trying to put the brakes on it, but my heart won't stay entirely out of it.

It sounds harsh to say, but I'm slightly glad that Elise's job as an events co-ordinator keeps her busy. It means we can see each other, but between my shifts and her appointments, we aren't seeing each other all the time. I don't want us to live in each other's pockets. This way we have a little space between us, something I sorely need at the moment with the way meeting up with her again has put my head in a spin.

I'm seeing her tonight after a few days apart and I'm looking forward to it; possibly more than I should be if we're meant to be *friends with benefits* or *no-strings attached*; whatever you want to call it. But it is what it is and I've decided to cook for her. Sure, eating out at somewhere like Olive Garden is nice, but it lacks the personal touch of a home-cooked meal.

I've been tidying the flat this morning and then I went shopping for fresh ingredients this afternoon. Now I'm starting the preparation for the meal. Having decided to do beef tenderloin with roasted cauliflower and pomegranate salad, it's time I started chopping the shallots, kale and cauliflower.

After tending to various things in the kitchen, it's time to open a bottle of cabernet sauvignon to let it breathe. Elise will be here soon and I need to take a shower, so I open the wine and grab a towel on my way through to my en-suite.

I can't help but close my eyes and picture her beautiful face while

I shower. I wanted to have a quick wash and then get back to lighting the candles and stuff before she got here, but now there's something that either needs my attention or a burst of freezing cold water to help it go away.

I've just lit the last candle when the buzzer to my intercom sounds. Perfect timing.

"Come up, gorgeous," I say as I press the button to release the downstairs door.

I open my front door and am floored. She looks stunning. All the times I've seen her before tonight, she's worn trousers, and whilst she always looked great, tonight is a whole new level. She's wearing a purple dress that accentuates all over her curves. It shows a generous amount of cleavage, but not too much. Cutting off at her knees, it gives me chance to see those beautiful legs. She may not be able to wear heels anymore, but she can certainly still rock a dress, much as she disbelieves that herself.

My jaw must be hanging open because she laughs and then touches a finger to my chin to close my mouth. Placing a chaste kiss on my lips, she then pulls back and looks me in the eye. Her baby blues are twinkling with mirth.

Stepping aside to allow her entrance into the flat, I close the door behind her before turning to see that this time it's her with her jaw on the floor.

"Drew, this is…you did all this for me?" she asks as she takes in the table setting.

There's a vase of calla lilies—her favourite flower—in the middle of the table. Fairy-lights twinkle from where I hung them along the fireplace behind the table. Then there are tea-light candles floating in a round bowl on one of the side tables by the couch.

The flat isn't vast in space, by any means. The living room and dining area aren't separated by walls, but I love the place just how it is. I have the lights on a dimmer switch and tonight they are set so that there's a more romantic feel.

I want to joke with her and say something sarcastic, but it won't pass my lips.

"I did. Do you approve?"

"Definitely. It's beautiful. I can't believe you went to this much trouble."

Turning to face me, I can see the slight shimmer of unshed tears. I decide not to mention it so as not to embarrass her. Instead, I walk and wrap an arm around her.

"You did all this for me?" I echo her words in a low whisper.

"All what?" she asks, perplexed.

"This."

I gesture to her dress and her cheeks glow faintly pink.

"Oh, this. Yes. I thought that you might like it. You comment frequently on liking my legs, so I thought I'd show them off."

"The dress will look better on my bedroom floor," I whisper right next to her ear before gently nipping the lobe.

Elise bats me away with her hand but I can tell that she agrees with my statement. Shy Elise is just as beautiful as bold Elise—who takes what she wants when she wants it—but in a different way. The pink that flushes across her chest and cheeks gives her a rosy complexion and I love that my words did that to her.

I walk to the table and pour her a glass of wine.

"Red wine? Does that have anything to do with the meal you won't tell me about? You're such a foodie, you've probably put a lot of thought into what wine goes best."

"I did."

I pour myself a glass and clink it to hers before taking a sip. I need to start thinking about anything other than that dress on my floor. Anything to take my mind off the pink lipstick she's wearing and how I can't wait to smear it all off. I must think about something off-putting before my twitching cock decides to join the conversation.

"Take a seat, I'll just go and check on things in the kitchen."

Elise sits on the couch rather than at the dinner table and I make my way towards the kitchen.

Rotten eggs, rotten cabbages, rotten tomatoes. What else can I picture to make this go away? Brando's bare ass in the shower at work; that will do the trick. I walked in on him once and although the ladies may think he looks like Marlon Brando, I'm not sure what they make of his hairy ass.

Geez! That's so much better. I can think straight and serve our meal without having to account for a semi hard-on.

"It will be just a few minutes longer," I remark as I retrieve my wine glass and sit next to Elise.

"Then there's time for this," she says before reaching to cradle my face in her palms.

She kisses me softly, nipping gently at my bottom lip. My mouth opens on reflex and her tongue darts inside to dance gently with mine. She tastes like red wine and smoke, not a combination I am averse to. Inhaling her scent, I realise she's wearing my favourite perfume; the same one she wore the night of our first date. I think I'm going to have to keep her in supply of it, I could never get enough.

Cradling her in my arms, I lean in to deepen our kiss. She immediately wraps her arms around my neck and I can feel her chest heaving with her heavy breathing. Fuck! Just when I thought I wasn't going to have to sit through this meal with a hard-on, somebody else had other ideas.

I pull back and take a deep breath.

"Hell Elise, keep that up and the meal will be burned to a crisp because we'll be in bed."

"That's okay, Romeo, we can wait. We have all night, after all."

Her laughter is beautiful and so infectious I can't help but join in.

The timer goes off in the kitchen, so I reluctantly get up to remove the beef from the pan. I cover it with foil while I whisk olive oil, lemon juice and mustard together with salt and pepper to season. I put the kale in with the purple cauliflower and shallots, using the same pan the beef came out of.

While the beef rests, I walk into the living room and stand by the terrapin tank. It's a safe distance from temptation, but I can look at her in all her glory. That purple dress really does hug her figure. I can't help but wonder why she's worn it, considering she's normally so self-conscious of her body. That's not something I'll ask her though, I wouldn't want to make her uncomfortable. The evening would end up going in a completely different direction than I have planned.

We make small talk for a few minutes before I head back to the kitchen to dish up.

Once the food is on the table, Elise looks at me and smiles. I take my seat opposite her after pouring more wine.

"This looks delicious," she remarks as she takes a sip of the water I also brought through to the table.

I knew she couldn't drink too much wine, so I made sure to have some tonic water chilling in the fridge for her arrival. It's something I've done since our first date.

"Thank you."

I nod to her to tuck in and she picks up her knife and fork.

"Did it take long to do?"

"Not really. It's a one-pot kind of recipe."

We talk about our day as we eat and I learn that she's busy planning a wedding reception. She says she's not normally a wedding planner— remarking how she couldn't take that amount of stress—but that she doesn't mind planning the odd reception. This one is for a friend, so she felt she couldn't really say 'no'.

"That was really beautiful," Elise says as I clear the plates.

"Not as beautiful as you."

I walk away with a smile on my face.

I place the slices of chocolate cream pie on the plates before adding whipped cream to the top and lightly dusting with chocolate powder.

Elise's eyes widen when she sees what I put in front of her. What is with women and chocolate?

I play what's on my iPod through my Bose speaker system. It's quiet enough that we can still talk but loud enough that Elise should know I was thinking of her when I selected the music.

"This looks too good to eat," she says as she puts a small bite to lips.

The moan she lets out as it hits her taste-buds is enough to make my pulse spike. I love it when she moans; it's so sinfully sexy, just like she is.

We eat in relative silence, both enjoying our dessert.

"You have Lifehouse on your iPod? Since when?" she asks as *You and Me* begins to play.

"I added an album the other day, just to appease a certain lady."

Her beaming smile is enough to tell me that I did well. I like making her smile; it's almost my favourite pastime. There's only one thing I enjoy her—or should I say 'us'—doing.

"You'll find other songs and artists you like on there now too."

"Really? You're so thoughtful."

"I try to be."

After the dishes are cleared, I turn the speaker system off and walk to the DVD player. Bending down, I insert a film without letting Elise know what it is.

We snuggle up on the couch together under a fleece blanket I had draped over the back. As one of her favourite films begins, she turns and grins at me before snuggling deeper into me and laying her head against me. I have a box of tissues on the table next to my end of the couch. I know full well she'll need them because we've watched this film together before and as she laid her head in my lap, she didn't think I noticed her crying softly, but I did. I know exactly the moment she'll start to cry and she then won't stop until the end credits. I've heard that City of Angels has a tendency to make women all gushy. I may not cry at films, but I can admit to getting choked up a little.

I hand her the box of tissues when Maggie's arms spread as she rides her pushbike, her face turned towards the sun. Elise sniffles and I trace lazy circles on her arm, wondering whether it has any soothing effect.

As predicted, she didn't stop crying until the end of the film. She sits up next to me and gives me a look, but I can't quite figure out what it means.

"You had this planned, didn't you?"

"Umm, well, yeah. Don't you plan if you cook for somebody?"

"I didn't mean that. I meant making me cry."

She digs me gently in the ribs with her elbow.

"I didn't plan to make you cry. Shit! I knew that you cry at this film and I *still* chose to put it on. If ever there was a face-palm moment, this is it!"

"Should've picked a rom-com, huh?"

"I'm sorry. Shall we put on a rom-com now? Or is it too late to salvage?"

I'm such a bloody idiot. It was meant to be romantic, showing her I remember things about her, but that's backfired on me big time.

"Calm down, I was joking."

Her belly laugh shocks me for a second. I really thought she was cross with me or something. Once her laughter subsides, she snuggles close to me again.

"Shall we finish the bottle of wine and then turn in for the night?" she asks with a salacious grin.

My smile must be enough of an answer because she knocks back the rest of her glass in one large gulp before taking me by the hand and leading me to the bedroom.

***

Nights like last night make me start to think about my trip to Iceland. I'm going to be gone for months and I really don't know if I can do it. Elise has somehow made me rethink my feelings about relationships. I've been up and down like a yo-yo, not knowing what to do for the best. However, the group of friends I'm going with reminded me that these plans were laid before Elise and I started whatever *this* is and I'd be letting them down if I pulled out.

Elise knows I'm leaving shortly but we haven't discussed what that means for us. We haven't put a label on what we are to each other, but what I'm beginning to feel goes deeper than just a "friends with benefits" kind of thing. I don't know how to tell her that. I'm not sure if she feels the same. But even if we did have that conversation, the trip is all booked and paid for, meaning I'd lose a lot of money if I pulled out now. Also, if we have 'the talk' before I leave then it might leave her feeling rejected, considering I'm still going.

I'm stuck between a rock and a hard place here. If I don't tell her how I'm starting to feel, there's a chance she'll find someone else while I'm gone. If I do tell her, it could ruin what we have because she may not feel the same. Or it could go the other way; I tell her and she does feel the same, leaving us both feeling torn while I'm gone.

Damn this. This is why I gave up on feeling anything a long time ago. Feeling something for someone only ends in pain. Can I push these feelings to the back of my mind while I'm gone? Possibly, but even if I can, I'm sure that they'll resurface the second I see her when I return.

Chapter Seven
Elise

Last night was so romantic. Drew went to a lot of effort, and I mean a *lot*. The flat was spotless, there was a vase with my favourite flowers in, the table setting was gorgeous and even some twinkling lights on the fireplace. Why did he go to so much effort? It's not as if we're dating. I mean, we're friends who sleep together occasionally and we go out to the movies or for a meal, or Drew cooks for me. Some people might say that's dating, but we haven't talked about labelling what we have. I'm not even sure how I'd feel if we were to label it, especially as he's leaving for Iceland soon. He'll be gone for a few months and it's not like I can up sticks and go with him. I have a son and a business, responsibilities that tie me here. And he wouldn't want me to go anyway. But what do I do when he's gone? How am I supposed to feel? Everything I once felt for him has come creeping slowly back. The problem with that is that neither of us wants a relationship. He's happily single. He can travel when the mood takes him and do whatever it is that normal single guys do. I'm happily single. I'm busy with the business and looking after Caleb. I don't have time for a man; or room in my life for one.

Bloody hell, how contrary can I be? I'm saying I don't have time for a man and he doesn't have time for a woman, but what the hell is it we've been doing up until now if it's not making time for each other? Maybe I'm just running from the possibility of getting hurt again. I've been hurt once too many times in my life and I'm not sure I can handle any more pain. I've survived so far, but anything else might just break me irreparably.

How did I ever think I was impenetrable? I'm obviously not if Drew has come along and started to break the walls down that I kept around my heart. I'm pretty sure it's got something to do with how I felt for him in the past. Feelings I never confessed then and have no plan on confessing this time, either. I'd probably spook him into running a mile. I don't know what I'm going to do. I am starting to feel things I had long since thought were dead, but the moment I tell Drew and fuck up what we have, then he'll disappear.

I find myself in something of a quandary here. If I don't tell him, I get to keep him close but I have to bottle it all up inside. If I tell him, I could lose him completely and it would devastate me to lose him again. How the hell did I get here? I need to do something and fast before I end up head over heels and broken.

Work should take my mind of my problems for a while. I've had a couple approach me about hiring me to organise their wedding reception. I don't do many receptions but they've been let down by the person they were using before me and they are willing to pay good money for my services, so I can't afford to turn them down. The problem is, organising wedding receptions reminds me that I'm always the bridesmaid, never the bride. I don't know if I necessarily want to get married, but to love and be loved in return would be nice. I thought Jensen and I were forever. I was obviously wrong. But I do want 'forever' with someone; maybe even give Caleb a brother or sister. But I've been hurt by so many men in my life; people I thought I could trust, and I ended up becoming this cynical woman who *might* want the 'happily ever after' kind of ending, but I'm not sure they actually exist.

As I'm sitting at my laptop, my thoughts swirl back to a day in the past that I really wish I could forget.

How has it come to this? My body aches from the blows he inflicted. My brain is frazzled because I am emotionally drained. I thought I was out of tears, but they keep flowing. He begged and pleaded, said he'd never do it again, but that's what he said last time. How long am I going to remain his punch bag? Why don't I have the strength to do something about it, to leave him for good? I've tried time and time again, but somehow he always gets me to come back. He's a manipulative son of a bitch that always gets his own way. He lashes out 'supposedly' without thinking and he's always sorry afterwards. He thinks buying me pretty things will make up for the things he does to me. I have a wardrobe full of unused 'gifts' that he's given me by way of an apology. But I don't want 'things', I want a man who treats me better than this. Surely this isn't all I deserve.

"Nobody will ever love you the way I do," he tells me repeatedly.

He loves to take me out and show me off on his arm; the girlfriend that's nearly twenty years younger than he is. He never leaves a bruise where someone might see. When he takes me out, I am told to wear as short a skirt as possible and a top that shows off my cleavage. But when he's not around, he makes me dress like a nun. He says that I'm his and my body is for his eyes only. But if that's the case, why does he insist I wear something revealing when we are out together? I think it's because I'm a trophy. He likes showing me off and it makes him feel good to know that men drool over me but it's him that has me.

I haven't had a job in months. He's scared that if I leave the house, I'll cheat on him. He's so insecure.

So I sit home all day, doing nothing. Well, I say nothing, but actually I am little more than an unpaid servant. I have to make sure the house is spotless, that the floors are so clean he can see his face in the reflection. I have to wash, dry and iron all his clothes for work. He has two jobs, a normal day job and one working on the doors of pubs and clubs as a bouncer. So there's always a lot of clothes to be sorted. His shirt sleeves have to have that crisp crease, his trousers have to be pressed 'just so'. Then there's the cooking. I am meant to have a hot meal ready for him when he gets in from work.

I don't know what I'm meant to do when he leaves my body feeling like this. He still expects me to do all the chores, even when my body is stiff from the beating it took.

I take a deep breath and wipe the tears from my face. My ribs are tender as I take in a lungful of air. I'm not sure if I have a cracked rib, but he'll never let me go to the hospital because I couldn't explain my injuries.

Looking at the packets of tablets on the bedside table, I pick up the bottle of schnapps, the only alcohol in the house. He's tee total, but he 'allows' me to drink, as long as it's in moderation. Well it won't be moderation this time.

Unscrewing the cap, I take a gulp from the bottle. I relish the burn as it goes down my throat. The pills are my only way out. I pop them all out of there packaging and soon have a pile in front of me on the bed.

The phone rings and I know he's out the back with a friend, overhauling part of the garden. I answer the phone before it rings off.

"Hey babe," Sam's breezy tone sends a pang of guilt over what I'm about to do.

"Hey."

"How you doing? What are you up to today?"

"Umm, not much."

I pick up a handful of the tablets and put them in my mouth then I take a swig of the schnapps to swallow them with.

Sam keeps talking to me, but I'm not sure of everything she's saying. The pills are beginning to take effect. I've taken nearly ninety of them, just one more handful to go.

"What are you doing, Elise?" Sam asks.

"Nothing."

My words have begun to slur. I wonder if she's noticed.

"Seriously, what are you doing? You keep going quiet. You haven't answered anything I've asked you. Something's going on and I want to know what."

Her tone is serious and demands I answer. But I can't. I'm too sleepy. I just want to lie here on the floor; goodness knows how I ended up down here.

"Elise? Elise?"

Her voice gets louder, but I feel too far away to speak.

"Elise, you better tell me what the fuck is going on, now!"

"I just want to go to sleep. I'm really tired."

"It's more than that Elise. You're slurring your words. Are you drunk? Has he hit you again?"

"I just took something to numb the pain," I reply.

"What did you take?"

"Paracetamol."

"How many?"

"I don't know."

"Elise, I'm putting the phone down and calling an ambulance. I'll call you straight back."

"I don't need an ambulance, I'm fine."

The line goes dead and I put the phone on the floor. My limbs feel too heavy to place it back in its cradle.

A minute or two later, the phone rings again. I don't want to answer it, but I do anyway.

"Elise, there's an ambulance on its way, can you get downstairs to let them in?"

"I think so. Please don't tell him what I've done."

"Just get downstairs and stay on the phone with me until the paramedics arrive."

I can tell she's stressed. She's worried for me. I probably would be too if I was thinking straight.

Making my way down the stairs is a tricky task. The world feels like it's spinning. Somehow I make it to the bottom of the stairs just as there's a knock on the door. I reach my hand up to the handle and pull it down. I can't get up from my sitting position behind the door.

The paramedics ask me my name and other questions that I can't answer. They ask me if there's anyone else home and I tell them I don't want him anywhere near me.

As if someone had summoned him, he's suddenly looming in the doorway.

"What's going on Elise?" the bastard asks.

"Please don't let him come in the ambulance. I don't want him near me," I plead with one of the paramedics.

"Okay Miss Swanson," he replies before turning to look at the bastard, "I'm sorry sir, but we have to respect the patient's wishes."

They take me out of the house in a wheelchair. I'm strapped to it to stop me falling. They're talking to me, but I'm less and less sure of what they're saying. My head feels foggy. I'm tired and all I want to do is sleep, but they won't let me. One guy drives while the other sits asking me questions.

We arrive at the hospital and they ask what I took. I reluctantly tell them before everything goes black.

***

I'm awake and the hospital lights are hurting my eyes. I keep them closed but the light is bright enough to penetrate my eyelids.

People come in and out of my cubicle but I don't have much to say to them. I didn't want this. I wanted out. I wanted to die. It was my only escape from him. Now I'm here, I don't know what they did, whether they pumped my stomach or what. I was too out of it to know what went on.

Now they're going to release me back to that bastard. Just what I need.

The curtain to my cubicle is pulled back and he looms in front of me.

"What do you want?" I ask.

"Hell Elise, what did you do?"

"I overdosed, you thick twat, what do you think I did?"

He turns on his heel and storms away from my cubicle, leaving the curtain open and people staring at me.

I'm released into the care of my uncle. I didn't want to go straight home so I called my aunt and she sent her husband to fetch me. We're sat in the carpark, talking. He doesn't think I should go straight home. He starts driving and I have no clue where we're going.

We pull up outside a flat. Out walks a monster in disguise. I can't believe I'm expected to get out of the car and spend time with him. But nobody knows what he's done, so I'm given over to the care of the monster and his girlfriend. My uncle says goodbye and drives away. Then the monster turns to me and invites me inside where it's warm.

Once inside, I take a seat. He offers me a cigarette and I take one from him. I don't want anything from him, but he won't do anything to hurt me while his girlfriend is here, so I'm relatively safe, for now.

After a couple of hours, he offers to take me home. He doesn't have a car, so I have to accept the helmet he's offering and ride pillion on his motorbike. I hope he drives me straight home. I don't really want to go back to that house, I'd rather be anywhere but. However, maybe the bastard is the lesser of two evils in this scenario.

A boyfriend that beats me and a stepdad who sexually abused me for years. Talk about being between a rock and a hard place.

I get off the bike, hand him his helmet and head inside the house.

"What the hell did you do that for, Elise?" Peter asks.

"I don't know," I reply as I move to sit on the couch.

"You don't know? That's not a good enough reason. Do you know how I felt, knowing what you'd done?"

How he felt? Why the hell would I care about that?

"I'll tell you, shall I? You obviously don't seem to know why it hurts me so much. Did you forget I overdosed as a teenager? I told you that story once."

He did tell me, during the first year of our relationship, when things were going well.

"I remember, Pete. Can we just not talk about it for now? Please?"

"No, Elise. We need to talk about it. I died that day. It may have only been for two minutes, but I was technically dead. I hadn't wanted to die; it was just a cry for help. I thought someone would find me but they didn't until it was almost too late."

It's a shame anyone found him at all, if you ask me. The world would have been better off without him in it. I'd never have met him. Maybe I would have met a man who cared for me instead of beat me. But it's too late to change the past now.

"I know, Pete. I've heard this story before. Please, I just want to go to bed.

I need to rest."

He looks at me, disdain written all over his ugly features. I don't know how I ever found him attractive. Maybe I'm just a magnet for the sick, perverted freaks in life. I would have been better off if I'd died tonight. Damn Sam for being such a good friend with good intuitions. If she hadn't called the ambulance, I'd be right where I want to be right now. I'd be on a slab in the morgue.

The sound of my phone ringing pulls me from my thoughts. Talk about saved by the bell.

***

Caleb has a part in the school pantomime tonight, so that should take my mind off things for a little while. He's in his costume and ready to get on stage. Sam's here to watch him and she brought Josh and Karl too. It's nice to have other people here for him, considering we don't have much family to speak of. I haven't spoken to my mother in years, so while she has a grandson, she doesn't see him. All my other 'family' stopped speaking to me at the same time. Well, they think they cut me off, but it was really me that cut all ties when I went to the police about the abuse I suffered at the hands of her ex-husband, my stepdad, the monster I grew up with.

We all stand up when the pantomime is over. We cheer and applaud the children for such a fantastic performance. I hated being in plays and stuff at school; forever shy and not wanting speaking roles. Thankfully, Caleb doesn't take after me. He did brilliantly and we're taking him out for a meal to celebrate.

Sam and I catch up over a drink while the boys play on Caleb's X-Box. We had a lovely evening at the pub and now the kids have a couple of hours to play and catch up before Sam and her boys have to go home.

"So, how are things with Drew?" she asks as she reaches for her glass of wine.

"I'm enjoying getting to know him again. It's so weird that you set me up on a date with a guy I already know."

"I know, right?! So weird, but it turned out well. Do you think you'll introduce him to Caleb?"

"I'm not sure. I mean, we're not in a relationship so I don't want to introduce them only for it to come to nothing between us. If Caleb gets attached and then Drew leaves, it would crush him. Look what happened with Jensen."

"That was different, so different. And you might say you're not in a relationship, but you are dating."

"Do people even actually *date* anymore?" I ask as I ponder the question myself.

"Sure they do. You guys are doing it right now."

"How so?"

"Well he takes you out, doesn't he? You go for meals, to the cinema, he cooks for you. Look at the romantic way he cooked for you last time."

"We're just friends with benefits, and friends go out places all the time. You and I do it when you're not working, but we aren't dating."

Sam laughs and takes a swig of her wine.

"No, you and I aren't dating. I'm sorry to say I'm married and I don't swing that way. But if I did, you would *so* be my type."

"I'm not looking for anything deep and meaningful, Sam."

That's a lie, but she doesn't need to know that. I'm looking for someone who could give me the love I yearn for. But I'm not sure that's Drew. I'm not sure I'm fully over Jensen. Well, I'm over *him*, just not the after effects of what he did.

"It doesn't have to be an all-consuming love affair, babe, as long as you're having fun again. It's been too long. You deserve someone who treats you right and so far so good on that front with Drew. Plus have you looked at him? He is hot!"

Karl looks up from where he's sitting with the boys as she says that. She throws a wink his way and he turns back to face the screen.

"Granted, he is very hot. But I'm just not sure it can go anywhere, Sam."

"You deserve someone who can give you the world. It's about time someone put that gorgeous smile back on your face, and you have smiled so much more since reconnecting with him."

She's right, I have been smiling more. He does make me happy. I get butterflies in my tummy when his name flashes on my phone or when I see him and he kisses me so tenderly. He's been good for my self-confidence too. I've started to feel much better about myself recently.

"Well, wherever it ends up, I am just taking it all in my stride. Baby steps, Sam. You know my heart is damaged."

"Wherever it ends up, you need to have fun along the way. So you might not end up marrying him and having lots of mini Drew and

Elise's running around, but you can still enjoy the moment. Happiness is fleeting, hold onto it while it's here."

She's so wise sometimes. Drew and I had a similar conversation about happiness not too long ago.

"I promise to live in the moment and really enjoy my time with him, however long that ends up being."

"That's my girl," she says as she raises her glass and clinks it against mine.

When it's time for them to go, the boys moan, as per usual. They were having fun killing chickens, yet again. Thank goodness it's only a video game.

***

As I'm getting into bed, my phone alerts me that I have a text.

Drew: Miss you. Wish I was off-shift so I could be wrapped in your arms.

I smile to myself. I wish he wasn't working, too. I won't be able to see him until Saturday, which feels like a lifetime away, even though in reality it's only another two days. I message him back;

Elise: I miss you too. Don't worry, you'll be wrapped in my arms soon enough.

It only takes a few moments before he replies.

Drew: I need to feel you in my arms. Naked. Just tangled up together under my duvet.

Elise: Is that all we'd be doing? Just lying there?

Drew: What else would we be doing?

Uh-oh! I should have seen this coming. Now I'm not going to get to sleep for ages and I might have to get my vibrator out to take all my sexual frustrations out on.

Elise: Well, that depends.

Those little dots show he's typing a reply.

Drew: On what exactly?

Elise: Whether you've been a good boy…or very, very naughty ;)

Drew: Oh, I've been a very bad boy!

I laugh as I read the answer I knew was coming.

We text for another hour and I retrieve my vibrator from my drawer. Just as I'm about to use it, my phone rings with a FaceTime call.

"Hello beautiful," he says as his face appears on my screen.

"Hi," I reply breathlessly.

"Are you out of breath? Why would that be?"

He winks at me and the smirk on his face tells me he's just as turned on as I am.

"I'm not out of breath."

"I want to see you as you play with yourself," he states bluntly.

"Pardon?"

"I know you have your vibe in your hand, show it to me."

I hadn't expected this. I thought our conversation was over and now I'm sexually frustrated but I can't play while he's on the phone.

"Show it to me, Elise!"

Reluctantly, I show him my pink vibrator. He's seen it before and used it on me himself.

"Guide the phone slowly down over that sexy body and show me how much you want me right now."

I place the vibrator to one side and take a deep breath before slowly pulling back the duvet and showing him everything he wants to see.

"Imagine I'm caressing your breasts, that I'm tracing circles around your nipples with my tongue."

I involuntarily use my free hand to cup my left breast, caressing myself the way he does. I squeeze my nipple between my forefinger and thumb.

Hearing his breathing deepen makes me bolder, and I trace my hand down my body to cup myself.

"Spread those beautiful pink lips for me, Elise."

I do as I'm told and I hold the phone screen where he can see.

"Now pick up that vibe and tease yourself with it."

Picking up the vibrator, I switch it on and it begins to buzz. I begin to tease myself and I hear Drew's sharp intake of breath when I show him the vibe sinking slowly into my wet pussy. I don't know what's come over me. I never do this. I haven't even thought about where he is for me to be able to do this and nobody from his work see or hear.

"I can almost taste you from here; such sweet nectar. Let me in so I can taste properly,"

"What?" I ask, whipping my phone up so he can see my face.

He turns his phone around and I see my front door. I throw the vibrator to one side, pull on my dressing gown and rush downstairs to let him in.

"What are you doing here?"

"I want you. I finished work and sat outside your house in my car to FaceTime you. Is this an unwanted surprise?"

"Of course not, but Caleb's here."

"Then we'll have to be quiet, won't we?" he asks as he takes me by the hand and leads me to my bedroom.

I just manage to get the door shut before his lips are on mine and his hands are tearing at what I'm wearing.

"I've been imagining this all day," he says as he pulls my t-shirt over my head.

"You sat outside my house so I'd play with myself for your viewing pleasure instead of just knocking on my door and asking me to do it in person?"

"I honestly didn't think you'd do it because you thought I was still at work."

"Well I'm sexually frustrated after all this sexting and FaceTime, so get naked and satisfy me."

I wink at him and his grin breaks out in full force as he drops his trousers. Seems he doesn't have a problem following orders. I should remember that for future reference.

Once he's naked, I place a hand in the centre of his chest and push him backwards until he hits the edge of the bed.

Pulling a pillow from the bed, I place it on the floor. Kneeling down on it, I take his ridged length in my hand. I take the tip of him inside my mouth, using the ball in my tongue bar for added stimulation. Desire swims through my veins as I suck him and stroke him. The moans coming from his mouth are long and maybe not as quiet as he should be with my son in the house, but I can't bring myself to care.

Taking him out of my mouth, I hear him gasp as I lick my way down to his balls. I look up at him and see he's resting on his elbows, watching my every move.

When I trace my tongue bar from base to tip, I see him shiver. He moves a strand of hair back from my face as I take him in my mouth again.

"Fucking beautiful," he whispers.

I work him with my hand at the base and my mouth around the tip. Then I take him in inch by inch until he hits the back of my throat. Drew's hands fist in my hair as I start to up the pace. His breathing becomes ragged and I know he's not far from coming.

Moments after the thought occurs to me, he grunts as he comes in my throat.

"Jesus Christ baby, you drive me crazy when you do that."

He helps me to a standing position before lowering me to the bed.

"Now I think it's time I finished what you started with that vibrator," he says huskily.

If a voice could melt panties—and if I was wearing any in the first place—then it would be Drew's.

Chapter Eight
Drew

I slipped away quietly just after midnight. Elise saw me to the door, kissing me softly once more before letting me go. I fell asleep quickly when I got home. Fully sated and grinning like the Cheshire cat, I must have been out like a light as soon as my head hit the pillow.

When I got up this morning, there was a spring in my step. Until I saw the calendar and noticed the big red circle indicating the day I'm due to leave. I can't believe I'll be gone for so long. The day seems to be looming and I want to spend as much time with Elise as I can before I go. I don't know if she'll be open to spending more time with me or whether she'll distance herself, knowing that I'm going anyway. I have to try though.

The day shift seemed to drag. I had hoped I'd be so busy that there'd be no time for thoughts of Elise to consume my mind. But no such luck. We didn't receive many call outs; all in all a quiet day. My thoughts were at odds with each other. There were some thoughts saying I should back off now while I still can, whilst others were more encouraging that I should spend as much time as possible with her before leaving. In a way, it seemed like my mind went onto autopilot and made a list of pros and cons for each stream of thought.

If I back off now, the big thing is I won't end up falling head over heels for her and being broken-hearted when I leave. But on the flipside of that, there are already feelings there.

If I spend as much time with her as possible, then I know I'll end up feeling something more than I already do, and I don't know if I can afford to do that; firstly because I'm not used to opening my heart and letting people in. I'm used to being on my own thanks to heartbreak from previous relationships, including Elise herself and secondly, because I'll be gone for three months. That may not seem long in the grand scheme of things, but it's a lot when you consider that we are in a relatively new relationship, and I'm not sure we can withstand a long-distance relationship until I return.

Hang on; relationship? Did I really just think that? We're meant to be just friends with benefits. But do I really see us like that? I don't know how Elise feels, but the more I think about it, the more I realise that even though we haven't put a label on it, we are actually acting as though it's a relationship. We're going out on dates, I'm cooking for her, she's staying the night, there are definitely feelings there for both of us, I'm just not one hundred percent certain what hers are. How can I be when I'm not exactly positive of my own?

The more I think about this shit, the more my head hurts. I'm going round in circles. I don't want to have this conversation with Elise in case I scare her off, but what else am I meant to do? I've had these thoughts more and more frequently the longer we've been seeing each other. I feel like a broken record. How am I ever meant to make a decision?

***

After a long, hot shower, I grabbed a pair of sweatpants and a bottle of beer from the fridge. There's nothing but crap on the television and I don't feel like doing much at all. I want to distract myself, but I'm not sure I have the energy.

I'm holding back from Elise because of the past we share as well as my own past.

That's really it? We're over, just like that? Okay, sure, we started off as friends with benefits, but I thought we meant more to each other than that. What I don't get is why she won't tell me why she's calling it off.

Elise: I just can't do this anymore. It's not you, it's me. I know that seems like a 'cop out' kind of answer, Drew, but I want you to know that it really isn't you. I really am sorry and I hope you find what you're looking for, I just know it can't be me.

I look at the text again and shake my head. Throwing my phone on my bed, I grab a towel and head for the shower.

The hot water didn't really help to clear my mind. I want to know if I did something wrong and if I did, what it was. But since that text last week, she hasn't replied to a single text or phone call. I thought we were good together. We'd just started referring to each other as girlfriend and boyfriend a mere couple of weeks before that text.

At the hospital Christmas ball, I'd introduced her to my friends and they got on like a house on fire. Elise was in the ladies room with two of the girls from my work and they helped her unpin her hair from the chignon it was styled in. When she came out, flanked on either side by the girls, she'd taken my breath away. I knew she was beautiful but in that moment, she had stolen my heart as well as my breath.

We may not have had a traditional start to this relationship, but I wanted more from it than it seems she did. How does a woman hold the power to totally break a man? They really do hold all the cards here. They can give us so much with one hand and then cruelly steal it away with another.

I decide to ask Nat if she's heard from her; surely they are still friends. Quickly dressing myself in sweatpants and a loose t-shirt, I head round to the block of flats next door.

"So you don't know what's going on?" I ask Nat for what must be the millionth time.

"No, Drew. I'm sorry, I really have no clue. I thought you two were happy. You always seemed it whenever I saw you. I don't know why she'd sabotage her own happiness as well as yours."

"Well, I've tried calling her and texting her but never get an answer. I'm driving myself crazy trying to figure out where I went wrong."

Maybe some people don't think it's very manly to show your emotions, but I think real men do feel, they do cry, they do get upset. Women don't have the monopoly on that. They aren't the only ones who can feel so deeply that they end up getting their heart broken when relationships end. Her text felt like a dagger to my heart. I hadn't seen it coming. The last time we'd seen each other, everything was good. There wasn't even a hint that something was off.

"Then I guess the saying goes 'suck it up, buttercup' doesn't it?! I'm going to have to just let go and get on with my life."

"I'm sorry Drew; I wish I could help you. If she gets in touch, I'll try to tactfully extract the truth from her. But you've got to know, she's my friend and I can't break her trust if she specifically asks me not to tell you. If she doesn't ask, then I don't see the harm in telling you." Nat says as she gives me a hug.

"Thanks, Nat. Tell Rich I'll see him for poker this weekend, yeah?!"

I leave the block of flats and return home. I sit in the lounge with a beer in one hand and the remote control in the other. Let's see if I can lose myself in some mindless television.

***

It's been two weeks since I asked Nat about Elise. Finally she has some news for me, but it's not what I want to hear. It would seem Elise is seeing somebody else. Some guy from her past; Vinnie somebody or other.

That news hit me like a freight train. She ended things with me and then ends up with someone else within such a short space of time? Did I mean nothing to her at all? Damn her! She meant something to me. I had opened up and told her about things from my past. She'd met my nephew when he'd been round my flat for a sleepover. Elise was so good with him. It made me think what she'd be like as a mother. Maybe I shouldn't have thought that way so soon, but I did. It didn't mean I was planning on marriage and babies just yet, but the seed had been planted in my mind. I had envisioned a future with her. That's something I hadn't pictured with anyone.

I'd thought I was content on my own until I met Elise. She opened my eyes to a whole new world that I hadn't known existed. Well, it existed, just not for me, or so I thought. Love. It's a world I don't think I'll be setting foot in again anytime soon. Thanks Elise. Thanks for breaking my heart and taking a piece of it with you.

***

I let go of my thoughts with the more beer I drink. It's probably a bit pathetic to be drinking myself into oblivion alone in my flat, but I have no other solution. The thought of calling Elise to see if she's free enters my mind, but she'd only add to my problems at this point, and she'd see I'm a loser who drinks himself into a stupor.

Heading for bed, I switch off all the lights and slip under the covers. Maybe I'll see things more clearly tomorrow.

Waking with a headache, I take a couple of paracetamol and a multivitamin with a glass of orange juice. I shouldn't have had so much to drink last night. It didn't help in the slightest.

Clearing the empty bottles from the lounge, I take them all out to the recycling bin. I really need to get my head straight. Why am I letting the situation have the power to reduce me to this? This isn't who I am. I'm the type of guy not to get emotionally involved. I keep everyone at arm's length; and for good reason.

My thoughts turn to my trip to Iceland. The lads and I have so many things we want to do when we're there. We intend to visit Reykjavik to do some sightseeing and hopefully some whale watching. Also on the itinerary is glacier hiking in the surreal landscape of Sólheimajökull

Glacier. There's a sheer vertical ice wall that I'm really looking forward to the thrill of climbing. Then we'll be stopping off at Skógafoss, one of Iceland's largest waterfalls. Another day we'll be swimming in the crystal clear waters of Thingvellir Park Silfra. We'll have a tour guide take us across volcanic landscapes, give us lessons in snorkelling and then we'll be able to experience snorkelling between two continental plates. It's a five hour tour in total and will no doubt be exhausting, but also exhilarating. There are so many wonderful sights to see, landmarks to visit and plenty of things to satiate the thrill-seeking side of me.

All this and I still can't help but think of Elise. What will she get up to while I'm gone? Will she meet someone else? If she does, how am I meant to feel about that? We're not exclusive, so I have no right to stop her doing whatever she wants. But just because I'd have to accept it doesn't mean I'd be okay with it. You can't help your feelings, nor am I of the mind that you should ever be sorry for how you feel. But I have a feeling it would be too much to take to have it happen a second time round. She went off with someone else last time because I never told her how I felt. The trouble is, I can't tell her how I feel at the moment when I don't even really know myself.

Deciding I need to clear my head, I gear up and go for a run. I take my usual route and have music blaring from my iPod as my feet pound the pavement. As *You Could Be Happy* by Snow Patrol begins to play, I up my pace. I try to outrun the lyrics. It's a song I listened to on repeat when Elise left. It came out not long after we parted ways and summed up exactly how I felt. It's not the kind of song I normally listen to as I run, it was just the first track on a playlist, but I can't find it in me to turn it off, even though it doesn't help my mental state.

Returning to the flat, I shrug out of my sweaty running gear and grab a towel as I head for the shower. As the water falls over me, I close my eyes and try to block out the images of Elise that assault my mind.

I see her silhouette. She has curves in all the right places. Her more than ample cleavage is imprinted in my memory and I reach to stroke myself as I think of how her silky skin feels on mine. As more images come to the forefront of my mind, I feel myself get harder. It's impossible not to be when this beautiful woman consumes my thoughts. Stroking myself a little faster, I begin to pant and my balls begin to tingle. If she were here, I'd want to make this feeling last, but as she isn't, I finish myself off quickly so I can clean up and get back to distracting myself.

Beer didn't help distract me and I don't intend to drown my sorrows again. I find myself reaching for my phone to send a text.

Drew: Hey! What are you up to?

So much for distraction. It's not long before I receive a reply.

Elise: Not much. You?

Drew: Got the day off and nothing much to do.

Elise: I've got something you could do…

I see the three little dots that means she's typing again.

Elise: Me!

I laugh at her boldness. When we first started seeing each other, she wouldn't be so upfront, but lately she's got better at saying what she wants. However, she finds it easier to sext with me than to say things to my face. That's something I think we need to work on.

Drew: You don't have to fetch Caleb 'til 3pm, do you?

Elise: Correct. There's plenty of time between now and then. But you can always stay home and imagine it instead of experiencing the real thing.

Wow. Way to go Drew. You wanted to distract your mind and instead you've decided to go and text the girl you're meant to be trying not to think of. Now she's offering you herself on a plate and you won't be able to resist.

Giving myself a mental kicking doesn't help, so I shoot her a quick reply before going to get dressed. Sweatpants just will not do.

Drew: Give me fifteen minutes. Open the door wearing something sexy. Something I can remove with my teeth.

Pulling up at her house, I turn off the engine and take a couple of deep breaths. Maybe instead of avoiding thinking about her, I need to see her and get her out of my system, for the time being at least. I know I'm only postponing the inevitable, but I don't know what else to do.

I get out of the car and approach the front door. I lift my hand to knock but am stopped in my tracks when the door opens a crack to reveal a shapely, stocking clad leg. Black stockings always make me horny. I have to hand it to her; she knows how to play me like a violin.

Chapter Nine
Elise

It's been a week since I last saw Drew. He'd mentioned wanting to spend time with me before he went to Iceland, making the most of what little time we have. But though we've talked on the phone and via text, I haven't actually seen him since that afternoon he asked me to answer the door wearing something sexy.

I'd dressed to impress, knowing full well what black stockings do to him. I was wearing matching black lacy underwear and it left little to the imagination. We'd had a lot of fun until he dropped me off at the school to fetch Caleb.

Maybe I'm over-reacting but I think there's more to his absence than he's willing to admit. He says he's not got many days off work seeing as though he's got three months off soon. I guess it's a feasible reason, but when we chat, even via FaceTime, he seems like he's holding something back. I get the impression he wants to say something, but then he clams up or changes the subject quickly.

I know he works hard and doesn't always get chance to respond to my messages but it's been two days since I last heard from him. I get a notification that my messages have been delivered and read, which makes my anxiety kick up a notch when I think he's had time to read them but not reply. Is he avoiding me or is he really *that* busy? Surely it doesn't take thirty seconds to type a text to reassure me it's just because he's swamped at work? But then we're not a real couple, so he doesn't owe me any explanation. That doesn't make it any easier to swallow, though.

Since I've been organising this wedding reception, I've found myself busy during the day, but at a loss at night. When Caleb goes to bed, I sit and chill with some mindless television to distract myself, but it doesn't always work. I shouldn't let it bother me, but it does. Something is off and I want to know what. I just want Drew to level with me and I don't think that's too much to ask.

I grab my phone and type out a text before deleting, retyping and deleting several times.

Deciding to just forget it and go to bed, I turn my phone on silent and change into my pyjamas. After brushing my teeth, I slip under the covers and close my eyes. Trying to keep my mind blank is harder than I thought and I toss and turn before drifting into a light slumber.

Morning comes and I feel more tired than usual thanks to a rubbish night's sleep. I had dreams of Drew, some past and some present memories making their way in during the night.

I get Caleb up and give him breakfast before taking him to school. I'm glad I haven't introduced him to Drew because if I'm on an emotional roller coaster, then Caleb would be too. Not knowing where I stand is one thing; I'm an adult and can deal with it. But Caleb is only ten years old and doesn't deserve to go through the ups and downs of this. This is why I don't date and why I don't introduce my son to anyone I'm not serious about.

This morning there's an activity at school for the parents to get involved. Caleb chatters excitedly in the back of the taxi as we make our way to school. The kid loves school. He's a bright boy and does well when it comes to achieving his targets. This morning is about showing the parents the way the school teaches the children numeracy. The way they teach long multiplication and long division is totally different to how we were taught when I was his age. In fact, I don't think I did either of those things until high school, but schools are upping the ante when it comes to the children's learning these days. They want them to be prepared at a younger age than when I was little.

After an hour of numeracy with thirty kids, I'm ready for some adult company. I know Sam has the day off work, but I don't want to bog her down with my crap. I need to offload but it would be unfair to ruin her one day off with my troubles. She's working six days this week and that's enough stress for her to handle.

I head home and wait for my MacBook to boot up. Social media isn't exactly the kind of company I had in mind, but it'll do. I can talk to my friends and blow off some steam without actually having to say what's bothering me. That's one of the only pluses of having social media; I can spend time reading through my newsfeed and take my mind off myself and more importantly Drew for a while.

I spend an hour online but then have to get some work done. I knuckle down and make sure I have everything sorted. I have to dot the I's and cross the T's. The wedding reception I'm planning has to be executed perfectly. Blowing off steam online helped get my mind off my worries and back in the game for work. If this event goes well, there could be more business put my way because of it.

***

After a pretty hum-drum normal week, I have plans with Sam tonight. Karl is looking after Josh and Caleb while we split a bottle or two of wine and catch up on any gossip. Sam is like a bloodhound and it doesn't take long before she figures out the source of my problems. I haven't heard more from Drew than a quick '*Hey, sorry I've been really busy. I promise to make it up to you soon.*' That was yesterday and now I'm looking at the calendar with the ring around the date he's leaving. Two weeks. Just two more weeks and then I won't see him for three months. If I thought not seeing him this last couple of weeks was bad, how the hell am I going to feel when it's months we have to spend apart? More importantly, why am I even feeling this way? I mean, we're nothing serious, so why do I feel as though he's taking my heart with him when he leaves?

Of course Sam believes it's because we're more serious about each other than we care to admit. She thinks I'm afraid of confronting my feelings for Drew because then I'll have to confess, even if only to myself, that I really do feel something for him.

I swore off men when Jensen left; Sam knows this just as well as I do. But she's still trying to make me see that putting myself out there isn't the worst thing in the world. She thinks Drew must feel similarly, otherwise he wouldn't be blowing hot and cold himself. She says he does that because he can't confront his own feelings either. I don't know whether that's true or not but I do know that putting my heart back out there, only to have it broken again is something I'm not willing to do.

"It's not about what you're *willing* to do, Elise, it's about what is already happening. The heart doesn't wait for the brain's permission. When you fall, you fall. There's no controlling it. You need to accept that before you can really process the rest of the situation."

I hate admitting that she's right and I want to do everything in my power to deny how I feel, because when he leaves, I don't know if I can take the heartache. And what if she's wrong about how he feels? What if I confess how I feel and he says he doesn't feel the same? That means I've put my heart back out there only to have it broken again.

"I'm not doing anything until he gets back from Iceland. If I still feel the same in three months' time, then maybe we do have something worth risking my heart for."

"So you admit you feel something then?" she asks as she reaches to open the second bottle of wine.

"I admit nothing."

I cross my arms over my chest and give her the stink-eye.

"Okay. Don't say it out loud, just admit it to yourself. That's a start."

I huff my annoyance at her and she laughs me off as she puts the DVD in the player.

We're watching Silver Linings Playbook, a film I must have watched half a dozen times already. It never gets old. And who wouldn't watch somebody as gorgeous as Bradley Cooper over and over again?!

As the film finishes, my phone vibrates, alerting me to an incoming text.

Drew: Hey, are you busy?

I think before replying. I don't want to seem too eager, but I equally don't want to seem too dismissive.

Elise: I've just finished watching a film with Sam. Karl is coming to collect her in a few minutes. Why?

Drew: I was wondering if you fancied some company when the little man goes to bed...

Sam peers over my shoulder and I shrug her off as I begin to type.

"Tell him yes," she says as she puts her shoes on ready for Karl to arrive.

"I want to, I just… I don't know, Sam. Is this such a good idea? He's leaving in two weeks. I'll be surprised if my heart can take it as it is. If we see each other more before he goes, it's only going to be so much more painful."

Okay, wow. I didn't mean to admit that much. It must be the wine.

"Some things in life are work the risk. If you want to see the rainbow, you have to feel the rain, because nothing ventured, nothing gained."

"Jeez, someone should hire you to write greetings cards or something."

I nudge her playfully in the ribs and she laughs.

"I read it somewhere and it stuck in my head. Now will you hurry up and answer him."

I type out a reply and wait.

Elise: Depends whose company I'd be getting.

Drew: I was thinking you could call Jeffrey Dean Morgan but if he's busy, I'll gladly substitute.

Elise: Ooh JDM, you know me so well. I've rung him and he's busy, but he's a little jealous that I have you on the subs bench for times such as this.

Sam laughs at my stupid reply and I curse her under my breath.

"I heard that, you bitch."

She digs me in the ribs and then cackles likes some evil clown or something.

Drew: There's a whole subs bench? What number am I?

Elise: I can't tell you that. I made a rule never to tell the others about each other's existence.

Drew: I can see why. We'd all be consumed with jealousy. Now I know that JDM is busy, how 'bout I come and occupy you?

Elise: Can you give me thirty minutes to get Caleb to bed first?

Drew: Sure thing, babe.

I smile like the Joker's infamous 'Why so serious' grin. Sam notices and places a hand on my arm.

"I want you to be happy, Elise. You're such a wonderful woman and you deserve to be happy. When he gets here, don't give him hell about the last couple of weeks, and don't let it get into a row. Just enjoy the time you have together tonight."

"There won't be the time or even need for rowing. I sure hope Karl gets here soon so I can get Caleb to bed and get changed."

"That's my girl."

She throws a wink my way and I hear a car horn sound outside.

***

Drew ended up staying the night for the first time, last night. He waited patiently for me to leave the house with Caleb before moving to the lounge to await my return from the school run. There was coffee waiting for me when I got back and now he's making breakfast.

He looks so at home in my kitchen, wearing only a pair of low slung jeans that I wouldn't find sexy on any other man. I watch as he moves effortlessly from the fridge to the cooker, then cracks a couple of eggs into the frying pan. I don't normally eat a full breakfast, but considering he's gone to so much effort, who am I to say no?!

As he turns around to plate up, I take full advantage of seeing those abs and the top of the V shape that makes me quiver. If this is what he's like every morning, he can cook for me more often. It's definitely not just the food that's making me salivate.

"Breakfast is served," he says with a flourish of his hands.

We sit at the table to eat and make small talk whilst drinking our coffee. Anything to stall the conversation I really want to have. He looks at me, opens his mouth, but then closes it again. I know the feeling because I don't know what to say myself.

"This is silly," he says as he scrubs a hand over the day old stubble on his face.

"I don't know what to say, Drew. It's a hard conversation to start."

"I know, but we know each other, Elise. We've known each other for years, if you count the time we spent apart. We should be able to speak to each other with relative ease considering how much time we've spent together lately."

"Except for the last couple of weeks, when you've been avoiding me for fear of having this conversation."

The look on his face changes to hurt. I really shouldn't have put it so indelicately.

"Shit! I'm sorry Drew. Really, I am. That came out all wrong."

"It's okay Elise, it's the truth. I've been putting this off when I should have come to you all along."

"Can we start this conversation again?" I ask as I move to make another cup of coffee.

"Sure."

Once I've made the coffee, we go through to the lounge and take seats on opposite ends of the couch. I turn to him and take a good look at his chiselled features.

"It might be less of a distraction if you put a top on," I quip in an attempt to make things more comfortable.

"Oh, damn, right. Two seconds."

He takes off up the stairs and retrieves his t-shirt. Moments later he's back and I'm disappointed that the view is now hidden.

"I leave in two weeks."

His words hang heavy in the air.

"I know."

"I'll be gone for three months."

No shit, Sherlock. I think but don't actually say. My sarcasm wouldn't be very helpful right now.

"I want you to know something before I go." He takes my hand and looks me square in the eye, "I am beginning… No, let me rephrase, I *am* in love with you."

I gasp in utter shock. I wasn't expecting that. I pull my hand from his like he burned me and the look on his face says that one movement hurt him more than any words I could have said.

"Drew, I…"

He stands, cutting me off.

"It's okay Elise, I get it. You don't want to get involved because you don't want to get hurt again. I'm the same, or at least I was, until you."

"I already am involved, Drew. I didn't mean to make you think any different. Me pulling my hand back, that was a knee-jerk reaction, just shock. I swear; it's not because I don't feel the same. Drew, I've been in love with you since we first met up again. I didn't mean for it to happen. I didn't want it to happen. That sounds so wrong, but the truth us, I *didn't* want it. I was happily single, happily living my life with just me and my son. I got hurt and I didn't want to put my heart on the line again. Things get messy when emotions are entangled. It was easier to think of us as friends with benefits, I just didn't want to admit to you, to myself, that I had true feelings for you. You'll be gone for three months and..."

He cuts me off as his lips collide with mine. His hands are firmly on my hips and my arms automatically wrap around his neck. He helps me to my feet and takes me by the hand. Leading me up the stairs, he's careful so that I don't stumble. That's one of the things I love about him; he's considerate of my disability and doesn't make me feel any less of a woman.

Once we step inside my room, he picks me up and carries me to my bed. He lays me down gently before slowly undressing me. It's torturous how slow he takes it, but damn if it doesn't ramp up my libido.

Standing at the foot of the bed, he begins to undress. I love the way his muscles move as he takes off his t-shirt. Undoing his belt, he sashays his hips when he sees me watching him. I can't help but giggle.

I begin to sit up to help undo his jeans, but he shakes his head, so I lie back and watch him. His movements are slow and purposeful. A minute ago he was crashing his lips to mine in urgency and now he's all about taking it slow. Damn this fine specimen of a man. If I didn't feel the way I do about him, I wouldn't lie back and take this kind of torture.

When his sinfully sexy body is completely naked, he kneels at the edge of the bed, hooks his hands behind my knees and places my legs on either side of his head. He begins to lick me slowly and with the lightest touch. My whole body shivers in anticipation and he starts to exert more pressure.

Adding a finger, he hits my G-spot and makes my body come alive. Desire burns through my veins and I want him more than ever. He adds another finger, stretching me to accommodate him. He pushes them in and out of me with an increasing pressure and pace. I don't think I can take much more. My back arches and my hands twist the sheets. I know that any moment, he will taste me as I explode. I can't hold it back, my legs quake uncontrollably as he hits that spot once more and I come with a force I hadn't known I possessed.

Drew licks me slowly, tasting me delicately as I ride the aftershocks of my orgasm.

When he kneels up, he catches me watching him and he grins salaciously at me as he draws his fingers to his mouth and sucks my essence from them. A moan escapes my lips; there's just something so sexy about the way he does that.

"Come kiss me, baby," I whisper.

He does as I ask, lowering himself over my body, aligning himself with my entrance as he lowers his lips to mine. I taste myself on his tongue and am unbelievably turned on by how I taste.

Sinking his way slowly into me, inch by inch, Drew stretches me in the most delicious way. He pulls my legs up around his waist and I feel his cock deeper inside me. There are not many feelings on earth better than this.

Drew dips his head and gently nips at my left nipple with his teeth. He knows how much that turns me on, especially on the left side.

I moan as he bites harder before pulling his head back and letting go. The pleasure/pain thing really is more enjoyable than I ever thought.

Pushing myself up from the bed to match his thrusts, I scratch my nails down his back, marking him as mine.

His eyes look straight into mine as if he can see into my soul. If he can, he knows how much I love him. It's in this moment right here, as we make love to each other, that my heart begins to heal. The piece of me I thought was missing is slowly being filled by Drew.

Chapter Ten
Drew

I hadn't meant for it to come out of my mouth like that the first time I told Elise I loved her. I'd meant it to be much more romantic and far better timing. When she pulled her hand away from me, I thought I'd read her feelings for me incorrectly. But she blurted out how much she loved me and my heart began to soar. I took her to bed and we made love for hours before she had to go and fetch Caleb.

We agreed that it would probably be better not to introduce me to him ahead of my time away. I'm going to miss her so much when I'm gone. I didn't want to tell her how I truly felt until I got back because I knew how much more me leaving would hurt us both. But I couldn't help myself. I couldn't love this woman one moment longer without declaring it to her.

We've seen each other as many times as possible over the last couple of weeks, still seeing each other on an evening and whenever Sam could babysit Caleb. I really didn't want to leave her this morning; it was the hardest of all goodbyes. I thought we'd prepared ourselves, but now I'm waiting in Birmingham airport for my flight to Reykjavik Keflavik and all I can do is look at the photos of her on my phone.

The boys had their fun all the way to the airport, making noises like I was whipped—or in their words 'pussy-whipped'—but they've cut it out after I told them to shut the fuck up. I don't generally say anything like that to them, especially not in the tone I used, but they were beginning to wind me up so much that I very nearly turned the car around and went straight back to Elise. I'm normally a laid back kind of guy, but I bollocked them at the top of my voice and I've not heard a peep from them since. Well, not about that anyway.

We're sitting in the airport bar, beer in hand and chatting away about what we'll get up to while we're gone. They're all single, so this trip for them is just another one of our lads' trips. Sometimes I travel alone and other times, when they can afford it and get time off work, we go together. That's what it was meant to be for me too. We've had this trip planned since we got home from the last one, last year. But whilst I'm still looking forward to it, I'm also looking forward to my welcome home from Elise.

I didn't intend to fall in love. I didn't mean to get involved with anyone. I haven't had a relationship for about four years. I've been single slightly longer than Elise. Neither of us was looking for anything serious, and then I met Sam. Why did she have to be best friends with 'the one that got away'?

The first date with Elise made all those feelings come flooding to the surface and I did my utmost to bury them. I've lied to Elise and I've lied to myself. I'm a damn fool sometimes. I feel so much better having told her how I feel. It's like now we can just get on with being together. Well, when I get back in three long months' time, that is.

The sights that await me in Iceland, whether it's the waterfalls, the glaciers, the Aurora Borealis; nothing will be able to captivate me like the baby blue of Elise's eyes. I sound like a lovesick fool; maybe the boys are right. But I would never tell them that. If they hadn't hit a nerve, maybe I would have joined in, made fun of myself. But they said it not long after we said our goodbyes.

Now it's time to board the plane, so I send her a quick text before I have to turn my phone off.

Drew: I feel like everything in my life has led me to you. My choices, my heartbreaks, my regrets. Everything. And when we are together, my whole past feels worthwhile. Had I done just one thing differently, I may never have met you. And that was the best thing I ever did, meeting you, because now I know what love really feels like. I love you, baby xxx

My phone vibrates just as I'm about to turn it off.

Elise: I know you've probably turned your phone off now, but that means you'll get this when you land. I know we have a history,

not all of it good. But we also have a present to make the most of and a future to build, together. You, me and Caleb, we'll be the happiest we've ever been and that's all because we took another chance on loving each other. Have fun while you're away, think of me often, send me some epic selfies, make memories and be happy. I love you too. See you soon. I'm counting the days xxx

I grin like it will split my face open. The boys look at me and I flip them the bird before they start with their mocking. Nothing can bring me down. I feel like I'm floating on air as we board the plane. Elise's words reassure me. This might be three months apart, but we'll have so much catching up to do when I get back. I can finally get to know Caleb and be in a relationship with a woman I love. That's something I never could have predicted. But some of the best things in life are the most unpredictable.

Chapter Eleven
Elise

Drew's been gone for two weeks and so far, I don't feel the loneliness that I was sure would set in. Neither of us had wanted to say goodbye, but he's kept me updated on his adventures by sending me selfies and sweet text messages. The sexting comes late at night when I've put Caleb to bed. It's hard having him so far away when he describes the things he'd do to me if he was here. But it's also exciting because I know we'll more than make up for it when he returns.

I can't put my finger on a specific moment in time when my mind changed about what I wanted from life; from Drew. I really didn't think I'd end up in a relationship after the disasters life threw my way. I was committed to being a good single mum to Caleb; to making the most of our life together. I had to pick up the pieces that Jensen left in his wake, and I was doing a good job of it, keeping it all together and making sure Caleb didn't have too much of a hole in his life where he should have a father figure. But then Sam set me up on the date with Drew, which I only agreed to because she nagged me. Now, I'm in a relationship again and I'm going to have to do the whole 'meet the parents' thing, meet his friends, act like a girlfriend would act rather than a single woman. I'm used to being independent after so long single and I don't want a relationship to take away my independence.

Thankfully, with Drew I don't have to cover things up, I don't need fancy clothes and I never have to put on a show. He loves me for me.

It's refreshing to meet a man who doesn't care about the material things in life. He doesn't care whether I wake up in a morning and don't bother to put my war paint on. Some men prefer their women with a full face of makeup, but Drew says I'm prettier without it. However, I've been invited to attend the wedding of the couple I organised the reception for, so today I am doing my hair and makeup and I'm doing something totally out of the normal for me, I'm wearing a dress.

At the wedding, I don't know anyone, so Sam has agreed to be my 'plus one'. I'm in a sea of unfamiliar faces and I'm beginning to feel clammy. I snap the band around my wrist and take a few deep breaths the way I was taught to try and fend off a full-on panic attack. Sam notices and takes my hand as she says a series of numbers. She wants me to repeat them in the order she said them, so I do. It takes a couple of attempts, but I finally get it right and feel calmer. She says it's because your brain can't freak out and repeat the numbers at the same time, it can't process both. It seems to really work.

We all file out of the church and the vicar thanks us for coming. We wait for the bride and groom, Mr and Mrs Harris, to come out and then throw confetti as the photographer snaps his shots of the happy couple.

The venue for the reception is the Hampton Manor; a truly beautiful place. It sits at the heart of a forty five acre woodland, meadows and a walled kitchen garden. It's a neo-Tudor gothic house in Hampton-in-Arden. Felicity couldn't have chosen a more perfect place to hold her modern vintage reception. It feels like a piece of the countryside, nestled in the city of Birmingham. You wouldn't know that there was a bustling city outside of these walls. I had given Felicity a shortlist of places I thought met her requirements and this was my top choice. I'm so glad she chose it. If I was ever to get married, I'd want it to be somewhere as perfect as this.

Sam and I are seated together at a table with some of Felicity's and Eric's friends. They seem friendly enough, but I'm not exactly a social butterfly. I guess that's one of the reasons I started my own business; to help me conquer some of my fears and take me outside of my comfort zone. I have Sam on hand a lot of the time, which really helps. She thinks I should hire staff and then one of them could come with me, but, as I've told her, my business is still small and I take on events that I can manage to oversee myself. I can't yet afford to employ anyone else, but I hope to get more business if this one goes well and people recommend me. In which case, if it really takes off, I will take on some workers to help with the planning and execution of events.

I'm fixing my makeup in the mirror of the ladies room when a woman walks in and smiles at me.
"Excuse me, would you be Elise?" she asks.

"Umm...Yes. Why?"

Suddenly, I'm nervous. I'm wondering what's gone wrong in the few moments I've been out of the room. Nothing could go that badly wrong in such a short space of time, surely?!

"There's a guy out there; he asked me if I could ask you to wait at the bar for him."

"Pardon?"

I turn to look at her instead of her reflection in the mirror.

"Yeah, it was a bit of an odd request. He saw you come in here and then as I was approaching, he asked me to give you a message."

"Can you describe this guy? I don't even know anyone here except the friend I've come with."

"He's good looking, like panty-melting hot. Brown hair, slim build, wearing a black suit."

"Did he give you his name?"

"No, I'm sorry. I should have asked but I was flustered by how good looking he was and my need to pee."

I laugh, more out of nerves and her forthrightness about her 'need to pee'. I'm curious who this guy is, and how he knows my name, but I am not waiting at the bar for him.

"Okay, thanks. If you see him again, could you tell him I'm here with someone. Hopefully he'll back off."

"Sure thing," she says as she enters a cubicle.

I walk out of the ladies and go straight back to my seat. Sam gives me a puzzled look and I sit next to her, leaning close to whisper in her ear.

Once I've told her, she scans the room discreetly. She knows I don't know anyone here apart from her. She's probably scouting for a hot guy in a black suit, but I don't want to look. The only man I care about is in Iceland.

***

At the end of the couple's first dance as husband and wife, I get tapped on the shoulder. I turn round with a smile on my face, thinking it must be Sam coming back with our drinks.

When I turn, the smile immediately falls. I'm greeted with a sparkling emerald green gaze. Eyes I know all too well. I spent many, many hours looking into them.

"Hello Elise," he says with a smile on his own lips.

"Hello," I respond curtly.

Why is he even here? I didn't realise he knew Felicity and Eric. I didn't need to know the names of the guests in attendance to organise the reception, otherwise I would have at least had some prior warning. I feel sick and I want to run, but he's planted firmly in front of me and I couldn't outrun him anyway, not with my damn leg. Bile rises in the back of my throat and I swallow it down. I don't want to make a scene here. It could kill my business if people found out I was the kind of person to ruin the events she organises, which I most definitely am not.

"May I talk with you?"

"We have nothing to say. We haven't seen each other in years and I would rather it stay that way. If you'll excuse me."

I go to move past him but he blocks my way.

"Please, Elise," he pleads as he puts a hand on my arm.

I shrug him off and see Sam over his shoulder. She approaches and puts a hand on his arm.

"Jensen, how lovely to see you," she says, her voice dripping sarcasm.

"Sam," he responds as he turns slightly.

"However much of a pleasure it may be to see you, you should know Elise is here on business and it would not benefit anyone for you to make a scene."

"I'm not after causing a scene, Sam. I merely want to speak to Elise for a few minutes."

"As I'm sure you are aware of by now, Elise doesn't wish to speak to you. You've had over three years; what warrants the need to talk now instead of before?"

"I don't have to explain myself to you, Sam. I'm sorry if that sounds rude, but you are not the person I came to talk to. If Elise had met me at the bar as I had suggested, then I wouldn't be stood here now."

"Met you at the bar? You're 'Mr Panty-Melting Hot'?"

Sam laughs and Jensen's facial expression turns sour. It mars his handsome features. What a pity he hasn't got the kind of personality to match such a gorgeous face and tantalising body.

"Please, Jensen, just go," I urge quietly, "I am working here and I won't have you ruin this."

"I'll go if you promise me we can talk soon."

I look into his eyes and find my resolve weakening. I loved this man so much and the least he owed me was an explanation when he left, but I don't need that closure now. It's been too long since we split to come and tell me why now. Is that what he even wants to talk about? I don't know and I don't intend to find out. I mentally kick myself for momentarily weakening.

"No, Jensen. We have nothing left to say to each other, now please, move."

I push past him and he moves to give me space.

"Elise," he pleads as I pass.

I'm not going to raise my voice and cause distress but I speak as forcefully as I can.

"I said no!"

I walk away and don't look back. Thankfully, he doesn't move to follow me. Sam hurries to catch me up as I walk away as fast as my bad leg can manage.

"He had no right to do that. I can't believe he's here. What the…" she trails off, noting we're in too public a place to be swearing.

"I'll be fine, Sam. Can we just go to the bar?"

We make our way over to the bar and order two glasses of prosecco. I had been drinking water so as to keep a clear head, but one glass won't hurt.

I stand snapping the band on my wrist. Of course, that doesn't go unnoticed by my best friend.

"Deep breaths, babe," she says as she locks gazes with me.

She breathes deeply along with me and after a few moments, my head begins to clear.

"I'm okay, honestly," I say as I reach for my glass.

The slight shake of my hand is the only outward sign of any distress.

"I don't know what he thinks he's doing. I swear I ought to…"

"Don't, Sammie. Seriously, I'd rather forget him. I am not going to let him ruin tonight. This has to go off without a hitch."

"Sorry, I'm just angry. Let's forget. We drink, we dance, and we don't let him see that he's got to you."

The rest of the evening goes by without any further distress. Jensen stays a good distance away from me, although he tries to catch my eye several times.

Once I'm home, I get undressed and slip into my pyjamas. A mug of hot chocolate is what I need right now. Sam has gone home to her boys.

Karl dropped Caleb back with me when he picked Sam up. Caleb is tucked up in bed, so I have an hour or so of peace before I intend to go to bed.

My phone rings and I realise it's a FaceTime call from Drew. My face lights up as I answer. Suddenly, I feel calmer.

"Hey baby," he says.

I can see a headboard in the background, so I know he's in his room. Presumably none of the boys are around, he doesn't normally call unless he's alone.

"Hey gorgeous!"

"How did the wedding reception go?"

My face must drop because his expression changes.

"What happened?"

"The reception went off without a hitch, at least for the bride and groom."

"Then what's the problem? Baby, you can tell me anything."

I see him settle back on the bed and I wish I was there with him. No, I wish he was here with me. It's too cold in Iceland for me.

"Nothing, really. It's just…" I sigh before continuing, "Jensen was there."

"Jensen? Your ex? What would he be doing there?"

"I don't know. I didn't ask and I don't care. He approached me, wanting to talk. I'm not sure of his reasons for that either because I didn't hang around long enough to find out."

"Wow. I'm sorry I'm not there, baby."

"It's okay. Your call came at the perfect time."

"Shall we change the subject?"

"I'd happily talk about the weather, as long as it's with you."

My heart feels lighter as Drew doesn't probe further. Even though nothing happened to warrant discussion, he knows just how to make me feel at ease with just a smile.

We talk for a while and he tells me about his day. He says he'll email me some photos of the sights. I'm happy that he's having so much fun, but I can't help wishing he was here with his arms around me. Apparently the boys have been making fun of him for staring at my photo when he should be having fun with them. That makes me smile, knowing he's missing me too.

After we say our goodbyes, I put my mug in the sink and head to bed. Today has been a long day and I can't wait for it to be over.

Two Weeks Later...

My phone rings and the display shows a number I don't recognise. I wouldn't normally answer the phone unless I have the contact stored in my phone, but as it's my business phone, not my personal one, I pick it up on the third ring.

"Good afternoon, Memories Made, Elise speaking. May I help you?"
"Good afternoon Elise."

My stomach plummets as I hear the dulcet tones of Jensen's voice.

"What do you want? How did you get this number?"
"I just want to talk, Elise. I found your number on your website."
"Well I'm sorry, Jensen, but this is my business line and you are tying it up when potential customers could be calling."
"Then meet me and hear me out. Please Elise. I don't beg for anything, but I would for this."

I don't want to meet up with him. I don't have anything to say to him and I don't owe it to him to listen to anything he has to say. He's the one that left, not me, so I'm not obliged to give him the time of day.

"I can't Jensen. I'm sorry."
"Can't or won't?"
"Both. Leave me be, Jensen, please. We have nothing further to say to each other. Not after all this time. Some things are better left unsaid."
"I want to apologise, Elise."
"Then apologise and be done with it."
"It's not something that can be done over the phone, Elise. I need to look you in the eyes."
I sigh loudly into the phone so that he can hear my annoyance.
"Please, Jensen. I have a different life now and ours is not something I care to revisit."
I don't know whether he actually wants to apologise because he

knows I deserve an apology or because he needs to get it off his chest
to make himself feel better. After so long, why does it even matter?

"Elise, I implore you, please. The least you deserve from me is an
apology. Call it closure. I need you to know how sorry I am for hurting
you."

I don't know what possesses me, but I finally find myself agreeing
to meet in half an hour at a café. Maybe I do need closure in order to
fully move on. Maybe it's just better to let him say what he needs to and
then he can stop disturbing me at work.

I'm sitting in the café with a cappuccino in hand, watching the door
and waiting with a feeling in my stomach that won't go away. It's like a
lead weight has settled there.
Sitting watching the door, I see the moment he enters. He's dressed
in a simple t-shirt and a pair of black jeans. I can't help but think he
looks good, but then he always did.

As he takes a seat opposite me, I snap the band on my wrist. My
palms are clammy and my head feels slightly fuzzy. I need to snap out
of it. I can't have a panic attack here and now. I clear my mind and focus
on my breathing.

"Thank you for coming, Elise."
"I'd say you're welcome, but…"
There's a brief silence that hangs in the air. Neither of us wants to
say anything to cause a row, I suppose.
"Elise, I'm so very sorry. Truly, I am. I never meant to hurt you."
He looks up as the waitress brings the coffee he ordered.
"I was a coward," he continues once she's gone.
"Too right you were," I snap.
"You're right to be angry, Elise, but please hear me out."
I sigh and take a sip of my cooling drink.
"It was cowardly of me to leave the way I did. I knew it then and
I know it now. The difference is, I couldn't admit it then. Maybe if I'd
opened up about being scared, we would still be together."
"You couldn't handle my disability, could you?"

"No. And you don't know how badly I feel about that. My decision to leave ate me up inside. I lost you and Caleb thanks to my insecurities; my stupidity. I didn't know how to voice my fears and I ran away instead of doing the right thing. I should have stuck by you. I loved you so much. I still do and I always will."

"But that love wasn't enough to make you stay and confront your fears."

"I guess not. I know I hurt you, Elise, and lord only knows how much it killed me to lose you both, but I didn't know what else to do. You know me, I don't do well talking about feelings."

"You made the right decision, Jensen. You couldn't cope and I honestly don't blame you. Not now anyway. I could only guess why you left, but I made the right call, by the sounds of it. I knew it was to do with having a disabled girlfriend. You couldn't reconcile the young, carefree Elise who was non-disabled with the woman I became. But I didn't change on the inside. I still had a heart, feelings…both of which you tore to shreds. But your decision to leave made me stronger. I had to learn to survive for me and for Caleb. And I did it, Jensen. I became wiser, tougher, and I focused on being the best mum I could be."

A lump lodges in my throat and I know I'm going to cry if I have to say anything else.

"You're right, Elise. You were still the same person on the inside, the person I fell in love with. But I was blind to her, only seeing the physical aspect of things."

"If only you'd waited it out… If only you had been on the same journey I was, you would have seen… I…"

Tears begin to stream down my face and I'm glad I didn't bother with makeup today.

"I know," he says as he reaches a hand across the table to grip mine.

I pull my hand away and wipe my tears away furiously. I promised myself I wouldn't do this but my feelings betrayed me.

"I have to go, Jensen. Thank you for finally telling me the truth. They say the truth will set you free. I hope you're free now."

I get up and grab my coat and bag. Jensen looks at me and his eyes betray the man who doesn't show emotion. They are red and I can see the shine of moisture. He won't cry. He doesn't think it's becoming of a man to shed tears over anything.

I've shed the last of my tears over him now. I have the closure my heart needed to heal. Turning on my heel, I walk towards the door. I make the first steps away from my past and towards my future. Finally free of the weight I carried like a millstone around my neck.

***

Sam was shocked to hear I'd actually met up with Jensen, but she said she immensely proud of me. I told her how I'd nearly broken down and she gently coaxed me into the light instead of allowing my mind to revisit the darkness.

Drew called and I told him the whole truth too. He was understanding and told me I'd made the right decision. I was relieved that he wasn't mad at me for meeting with my ex. But he told me that jealousy isn't a colour he wears well. I happen to think green suits him, just not that particular shade. We talked for a while about his day to distract me. It sounds like the trip is pretty amazing. The sights they've seen, I got to see for myself via email. I didn't think there was much to do in Iceland but he proved me wrong.

Danny, Seb and Luke, his buddies on the trip, made a funny discovery today and it made me laugh out loud to hear of their antics. Having stumbled upon a place called The Icelandic Phallological Museum, they had gone in and discovered over two hundred penises and penile parts from land and sea mammals. The funniest part was when he told me that they'd been shocked to discover the museum had actually obtained a human penis but was on the lookout for another, bigger, better one because their current one had become grey and shrivelled, finally ending up pickled in a jar of formalin. Drew said he'd offered to cut Seb's off and donate it to them, but it probably wouldn't be much better than the one they already had. I couldn't contain my hysterics, especially when he told me Luke actually had to run and find the toilets as he couldn't keep the contents of his stomach down. Lord help me with the dreams, or should that be nightmares I'll be having tonight. All I can see is a dick in a jar, pickled and kept for goodness knows how many years. The thought they are always on the lookout for a bigger, better specimen is, in itself, enough to keep me laughing for weeks. I'm not sure if Luke will be laughing, though, when he sees the souvenir Drew kindly bought him from the gift shop; a wooden, carved dick.

I didn't ask Drew if he took any photos of the museum because I'm not sure if I could sit here scrolling through pictures of different dicks. He said they had one from a whale that was longer than he is tall, but what was weirdest at the time was seeing a box of cocks. There was a display cabinet that housed silver cocks. Apparently they were casts made from the cock of every member of the local handball team. I couldn't help but wonder how they were talked into allowing casts to be made of their genitals. That's a thought I don't want to spend time pondering. The other species, I can sort of understand, if that's the kind of museum you run. But humans? Just…no!!

Chapter Twelve
Drew

Iceland has been amazing so far. There's more to do than people might think. But I also love it when it's night-time and I get to FaceTime with Elise or, at the very least, text her.

Last night, she told me she'd met up with Jensen. Unlike many men, my gut reaction wasn't jealousy. I was a little apprehensive at first, but when she told me about their conversation, I understood why she'd agreed to meet him. Even if she said she didn't, she needed the closure that only he could give her.

He really is the dickhead I thought he was. He never gave Elise a reason for leaving her, but she always had it in her mind it was because of her disability. As it turned out, she was right. In my opinion, if you can't look past the label of disability to the real person beneath, then you aren't a real man. But also, it's one thing if you decide not to date a woman who is disabled, but a completely different ball game if you date a woman for seven years and then, due to no fault of her own, she ends up disabled and you dump her because you can't man up and accept that. He knew Elise, he professed his love for her and stepped up to the plate for Caleb from the moment he was born, even though he wasn't his biological dad. He spent years loving this wonderful woman and ran like a coward as soon as the going got tough. What the actual fuck is wrong with him? What a douche!

I know people see a stigma attached to disabled people; they don't like things they don't understand. I don't get people with that kind of attitude. I know if I had been with Elise and she became disabled, I would have been man enough to care for her until she was able to do more for herself. Actually, thinking about it, I might shake Jensen's hand if I ever meet him. He gave me the best gift I've ever had, albeit unintentionally.

I'm glad I could make Elise laugh last night, regaling her with our trip to 'the penis gallery' as the lads are calling it. We came across the place quite by accident, and boys will be boys, so we found it utterly hilarious. It was great seeing Elise giggle like a schoolgirl when I told her about the human penis they have in the jar. Her whole face lit up and, after telling me about Mr Douche, it was particularly good to see her in such high spirits.

The lads and I intend to go to The Golden Circle today. It's a popular tourist route in southern Iceland, covering about one hundred and ninety miles; not that we intend to walk that far. Apparently, it's the place where most tours happen and there are a lot of travel related activities. Should be fun.

I send Elise a quick text to tell her I'm thinking of her. She replies quickly, saying she misses me too and I can't wait to talk to her tonight. Although I never intended to get into a relationship, you can't help who you fall in love with or when. With this trip, I thought we'd both end up feeling separation anxiety, especially as it's early days for us. But with there not being a time difference between me here and her in the UK, that's made it somewhat easier. It means neither one of us has to do late night nor early morning calls. It's great to spend the day with the lads and then, when we retire to our separate rooms, I can call my girl.

It's a particularly early morning for us today as we have to be at The Golden circle for nine. We're going on an open-top bus tour for eight hours. It's going to be one long ass day, but I have a feeling it will most definitely be worth it. We're starting the day off at Strokkur, a fountain geyser in a geothermal area beside the Hvítá River. It's one of the most famous geysers here and erupts approximately every six to ten minutes. I can't wait to take some photos and email them to Elise. Even on a lads' trip, she's on my mind a lot. I wish she were here to experience it first-hand, but then I couldn't very well ask her to disrupt her life for three months travelling. It would not only affect her, but Caleb too. Plus this is a lads' trip, and that was perfectly fine by me when we arranged it because we were all single. Just because I'm no longer single doesn't mean I could bring my girl along, though. The others wouldn't do that to me, nor I to them.

It's freezing as we stand about to board the bus. I guess that comes with the territory though; it's not exactly Ibiza type weather. We've wrapped up warm and have come prepared with flasks of coffee.

The bus takes us to various different locations throughout the day, but my favourite by far is the Gullfoss waterfall. Danny, Seb and Luke started talking to a group of girls who are also on the tour. They're on holiday from the UK too, apparently. I'm not interested in them; I'm here to see the sights. I thought they were too but, I guess, when they've been travelling with only each other for company for the last few weeks, it's nice to be able to talk to girls. I think the lads introduced them as Katie, Ashleigh, Laurel and Blake. I'm too caught up in sightseeing and taking photos to really care.

By the end of the daytrip, I realise I've missed out on some information regarding the lads and their new friends. It turns out that the girls are staying not too far from us and they have invited us to go for a meal with them tonight. It's five o'clock now and they want to meet at eight. I'm really not feeling it but Danny won't hear a word of it. He seems quite taken with Ashleigh, which doesn't surprise me considering she fits his 'type'. In his own words, he likes a woman with long legs, blonde hair and who looks like she takes pride in her appearance. Well, from what I've seen, she's that alright, but she also looks like she has breast implants and she's as skinny as a pencil; not what I call attractive, but each to their own. Seb and Luke are interested in two of the others, though I'm not sure which. I guess I'll be the odd one out; the only one who isn't single.

"I'd never try to push someone else on you when you're obviously in love with Elise and I'm not asking you to lead Lauren on, but it would be good if you could talk to her. I mean, me and the boys will be talking to the others so it makes her the odd one out," Danny tells me as he comes by my room at seven-thirty.

Laurel. Lauren. Oh well, I was only one letter out. Whatever.

"Well I don't mind talking, but this is meant to be a lads' trip, not overtaken by women, and I have a wonderful girlfriend back home, so don't expect me to chat this Lauren up or anything. I'm not coming tonight if I'm there purely to keep her occupied."

"It isn't like that, dude. Just please, come out with us."

I grab my coat and pull the door closed behind me. I'm not looking forward to this in the least.

***

It turns out I was right. All I've done all evening is babysit Lauren. Okay, so babysitting may be the wrong term, especially if I said it to her face, but I've been lumbered with her since we arrived. I'm so close to just leaving them to it and going back to my room.

All I want is to talk to Elise and get some sleep before our trip out to The Blue Lagoon tomorrow. Instead, it looks like I'm going to have to sit here with Lauren while the boys drool all over the other girls. I'm going to kill Danny tomorrow. I swear, when he's sober, I'm giving it him with both barrels. Thank goodness the girls won't be around for long. I'm not sure how much longer I can babysit, friend-sit; whatever a good word for it might be.

"So, Drew, you're a paramedic. I bet you look good in uniform," Lauren says in a slightly drunken yet flirty tone.

"You'd have to ask my girlfriend about that."

"Ooh, you have a girlfriend? Is she pretty? Prettier than me? You know, we could always disappear back to your room... What happens in Iceland, stays in Iceland..." she trails off as she drags her finger down my arm.

I'm guessing that's meant to be seductive, but it's doing absolutely nothing for me.

"Yes, she's pretty. Do you really want me to tell you if she's prettier than you? I'm supposed to be being on my best behaviour and that wouldn't be a very nice thing to say. But,since you asked and all, yes, she's much more beautiful than you."

"I like a man who's brutally honest. But even if she is prettier, she's not here and she can't give you what you want. I mean, she's not back in your room ready to give you a blowjob tonight, is she?!"

Oh, man. Is there nothing I can say to deter this girl?

"She may not be here physically, but she's in my heart. I'm not tempted by the likes of you or anyone else to cheat on her. We've not been together long and I want to start a relationship as I mean to go on, *faithfully*," I emphasise the last word.

"But she wouldn't need to know, would she? I could keep you company tonight and nobody needs to find out. I mean, I'm not being rude or anything, but she's not here to keep you warm tonight is she?"

"Just the thought of her keeps me warm at night. Thanks for the offer, but it is a definite no."

"But you can't really say no to all *this*," she says as she gestures to her body.

"Can't I? And why is that?"

I'm not even sure why I'm bothering to entertain a conversation with this woman. To her credit, she's not *completely* repulsive. In the old days, when I used to travel, maybe someone like her could have entertained me and kept my attention for one night; based on looks that is. But I'm not looking to hook up. Not tonight or any other night.

"Look at me," she gestures first to her face, then boobs, then her figure.

"I'm looking. What is it I'm meant to be seeing exactly?"

"Wow, you're an ego boost! Way to kick a girl in the teeth."

"I'm sorry, Lauren, I mean no offence, but let me state this for the record; my friends may want to hook up with your friends, but me, I am not looking for any*thing* with any*one*. Not just you, don't take it all to heart. I'm sure you're a great girl, however, I am loyal to the woman I love. Okay?"

Her face drops and she knocks back the last of her wine before pouring herself another glass from the bottle.

"Okay, Drew. I get it. You're fooling yourself that you aren't like every other man."

"How so?"

"Every man has needs; base instincts, desires. Call it what you like buddy, but every man wants to be fulfilled and you aren't right now. You're here and your girl is back in England. She can't give you what you need. I can, but you're choosing to deny yourself. Go figure."

"Look, Lauren, I've tried this the nice way, now let me say it in words you might understand… Go find somebody else to fuck, cos it ain't gonna be me! Now fuck off and leave me alone."

I knock back the rest of my drink and walk away from her before

I say something I'll really regret. Heading towards the boys, I take a couple of deep breaths to calm myself the hell down.

"Hey Danny. Sorry man but I'm outta here."

"What? You can't leave. Who'll occupy Lauren?" he replies, slurring his words a little.

"Bollocks to that, dude, I'm gonna bounce. I can't handle babysitting her all night man. It's taking all my willpower to be polite to her. She can't take a hint that she's not fucking wanted. If she continues to say the things she's saying, then I'll end up ripping into her and she won't handle it well."

"But dude, there's four of them and three of us if you go."

"And that's my problem how? It isn't. So I'll see you tomorrow at nine. Okay?"

I turn on my heel and walk briskly towards the exit. I haven't really had much to drink, knowing I'd need to keep my wits about me to fend Lauren off. She came across as a limpet from the start. I only came out because Danny asked for a favour. A favour I shall never agree to again.

Once I'm back in my room, I slip out of my clothes and head for the shower. It's too late to call Elise; she'll be in bed already. I want to call her. I need to see her face, hear her voice. I need to feel close to her. One thing Lauren pointed out was correct. Elise isn't here to keep me warm tonight and, God, how I wish she was.

The shower beats down, scorchingly hot. I stand there and allow the water to wash over me for a minute before washing myself down and turning the water off. Stepping out, I grab a towel and wrap it around my waist.

Back in my room, I flop down on the bed, phone in hand. I flick to my photos and find one of Elise and me together. Staring at her gorgeous face, I sigh wistfully and throw my phone on the bed. How is it that my heart hurts? Your emotions come from your brain, not your organs, but it feels like a physical ache in my heart that she's not here or I'm not there.

My phone beeps beside me and I reach to swipe the screen and read the message, expecting it to be Danny bollocking me for leaving.

Elise: Hey, baby. I miss you. I hope you're having a good night. Can't wait to talk to you tomorrow. Love you.

That ache in my heart grows. I send her a text back.

Drew: Hey, you're up late. I miss you too. I'm back in my room. The bar was a total bore. Love you too, baby. Can't wait to see your face tomorrow.

Elise: I have a few minutes before I go to bed if you really want to see my face.

My smile could split my face. I dial her number in a heartbeat. Her face lights up my screen and I sigh in relief. I am not pussy-whipped, as the boys would say, but love does funny things to a guy.

"Hey, beautiful. How come you're up so late?"
"It's Friday night, baby. Caleb goes to bed a little later at the weekend and then I have an hour or so to myself before bed."
"Well I'm sure glad to see you. I didn't think I would for another twenty four hours."
"Careful, anyone would think you're love sick."
Her cheeky grin makes me melt.
"Well, if love is a sickness, I never want a cure."
"Oh, cheesy, Drew. Really cheesy!"
"Are you saying you don't like me when I'm cheesy?"

We talk for another ten minutes or so before I see Elise yawn. I tell her to go to bed and blow her a kiss goodnight. My cheesy lines made her laugh and I'm glad I got to see her happy face before bed tonight. After Lauren's shitty chat-up lines, trying to lure me into bed, I'm just pleased I got to see the woman I love and hear her say those magical four words; 'I love you, Drew'.

I slip under the covers and hope that tomorrow comes slowly so that I can dream of my girl and imagine being home in her arms.

How is it that I used to use travel as a coping mechanism? I used it to keep my distance from women, making sure I could never stick around long enough for deep and meaningful relationships. It means I've kept my barriers up and never let a girl close. But why did I do that? Sure, I've had my heart trampled on, but then so have most people at least once in their lives, unless they're incredibly lucky. But I guess if I hadn't been that way for so long, I might not be with Elise right now. I might be with someone else and, whilst I can't miss what I never had, I wouldn't know what it's like to be this happy with a woman. I might be happy, but it wouldn't be the same if it wasn't with her.

I've gone from guarding my heart with walls made of titanium, to opening it up to the possibility of pain, loss, heartbreak, but I've also opened up to the idea of true love. Maybe that sounds kind of sappy, especially as I'm a guy and we aren't renowned for being emotional. But honestly, I think I was meant to wait for Elise Swanson to fall back into my life. I used to want love, marriage, and children; the whole nine yards, until I got hurt so badly that I denied my heart's desires. Now that I have Elise back, I'm starting to see my way to wanting those things again. Lord knows I hope she wants the same. I don't think I could take another woman shredding my heart to pieces.

***

I wake up to a gorgeous day. I open my curtains and see the beauty that surrounds me. Today is going to be a good day. After a quick shower and a light breakfast, the boys and I will be heading for The Blue Lagoon. Until now, I've only seen photos as proof of its beauty. It looks like the epitome of tranquillity. I can't wait to get there and experience it for myself.

It's almost an hour's drive from Reykjavik to The Blue Lagoon. We load into the car and all the boys can talk about is last night.

"I can't believe you blew us out, Drew," Seb says.

"Yeah, man, what was that all about?" Luke adds.

"I couldn't stand another minute of her flirting and draping herself all over me."

"He's pussy-whipped, for sure," Seb says as he makes the sound of a whip cracking.

"Shut up, man. Can we just enjoy today?"

My tone doesn't leave any room for argument.

"Sorry, dude, it's just…" Luke pipes up.

"Knock it off," Danny says in my defence.

He catches my eye and knows I'm about to blow if they say anything else.

The conversation turns to how they all hooked up with the other three girls, whatever their names were.

By the time we arrive at our destination, I am sick to death of hearing about the head Seb received or the wild way Luke's girl fucked him. Danny was decent enough not to chime in except to say he hooked up with the blonde with fake tits and he has plans to see her later.

Later? Oh, hell. I am not putting up with Lauren again. No goddamn way. I'll fake being ill on our return to Reykjavik. But for now, I'm going to enjoy soaking up the atmosphere without any distractions.

This place is a mix of modern buildings against a backdrop of natural beauty. There is volcanic rock all around and you can see the Reykjanes Peninsula. It really is exquisite. The water is the clearest blue. We get changed into swimming trunks before heading for the required pre-swim shower. Being outdoors, it's a shock to feel how warm the water is. I read that it's thirty seven to thirty nine degrees because the water comes from a nearby geothermal power plant which heats the spa and water.

Swimming underwater, I see how clear and divine it really is. The boys are messing around on the surface, but I want to explore. I want to have some fun with them too; of course I do, but exploring is a different kind of fun to goofing off like them. That can come once I have taken in the sights a little.

There are several girls who are serving drinks in the water. Surprisingly, that isn't as odd as it might sound. I had a drink and then found where I was supposed to be. At this moment in time, I'm suspended in the warmth of the lagoon with a woman massaging my feet. I asked for the thirty minute massage treatment and, boy if it isn't soothing more than just my body. I feel weightless in the water and my mind is pleasantly relieved of the stress of last night. I don't know what the others are doing right now, but I bet they aren't as blissed out as I feel.

***

On our return from the lagoon, the boys and I went back to our rooms and I ended up dozing off for a while. Now I'm up and it's time to grab a bite to eat. I knock on their doors and rally the troops, feeling my stomach rumble in protest at running on empty.

We head to a place across the street called Ostabudin. Apparently

they serve the best Icelandic cod, freshly caught every day. I can't wait
to try it.

We walk into the restaurant and are greeted by the sight of the girls
waving their arms crazily in the air to catch our attention. Great, just
what I didn't want. The boys warned me we were meeting them and I
could hardly say no. Danny leads the way over to their table and sits next
to 'fake tits' whose name I just cannot remember. She greets him with a
deep kiss and I have to look away. Seb sits down by Katie but they play
it cooler than Danny; just a chaste kiss on the lips. Luke hooks an arm
around Blake as he sits next to her and I look at the lone empty chair.

"Sorry, guys, but Lauren isn't feeling well so she won't be joining us
tonight. We were going to cancel, stay and look after her, you know?!
But she said we shouldn't have to miss out just because she's not up for
it. She said she's happy to take a couple of painkillers and sleep it off,
whatever it is that's bothering her," fake tits says.

"Sorry to hear that, hope she's feeling better soon. It'll put a real
downer on the rest of the trip if she's unwell," Danny replies before
nibbling on her neck and making her laugh.

"Danny, stop that," she says as she swats him away, albeit not enough
to actually stop him in his tracks.

"Hey, hey, can you two keep the public display of affection to a
minimum. A guy has to eat, and to eat, he needs an appetite," Seb says
with a laugh.

Danny stops what he's doing and has the grace to look sorry.

The waitress hands us menus and we place our drinks order while
we look over the choices. I already know what I'm having, so I wait for
the boys to decide.

After placing our order, we make small talk with the girls about what
they did with their day and how our trip to the lagoon was. Ashleigh—as
I now know her—says that they visited the lagoon the day before we
met. I just find myself glad they didn't come with us. From this short
conversation alone, I am bored of their company. Maybe I'm being
unfair, maybe there's more to them than meets the eye, but I sure can't
wait to escape them after eating.

The conversation takes a sharp turn as I hear Katie say she can't
wait to spend the day with us tomorrow and really hopes Lauren is well

enough to come. What the hell is going on? Nobody asked me how I felt about them joining us. If they had asked, they'd know I'm not a happy bunny. I'd pull a sickie and say I can't make it but why should I miss out thanks to them? No, I'll go and I'll keep my distance from the girls as much as possible.

Since when did our boys' trip turn into a couple's thing? How much more of our trip will be overtaken? When can we shake the girls off?

I may not have the answers right now, but the boys can be damn sure I'll be having words with them when we return to our accommodation. I'll rip each of them a new one if they try to convince me that this way is better. Yeah, they get sex on tap, bully for them. But me? I get my trip ruined. The whole idea of this for me was to spend time seeing the sights and spending quality time with my friends. I didn't sign on to be the third wheel—or in this case the eighth wheel—every day and night.

Chapter Thirteen
Elise

Drew called me last night and something felt off. He told me about some places they'd been, but he lacked enthusiasm about it. He was a little nonchalant about the whole thing, and that bothers me. He's meant to be having fun but his smile seemed forced and there was no twinkle in those gorgeous eyes of his. I can't help but wonder what's bugging him, but when I asked, he brushed it off like I was just imagining things. I can't get to the bottom of it if he won't even tell me what's going on.

I have a ton of work to do for a couple of events I'm setting up, so I don't have the time to figure out Drew's issue and keep my mind focussed on the job at hand. I resign myself to the fact that if something is up, he'll tell me in his own time. For now, I have to keep my head in the game. Right now I have to help find a caterer for one event as the previous one realised he wase double booked and I don't have much time to do it in.

Work takes my mind off my private life and it's good to have a distraction. Finding this new caterer is taking longer than anticipated as I promised the client I would personally taste samples from each candidate and compile a shortlist before selecting 'the one'.

After I get off work, Sam texts me to say she'll be at mine for six o'clock. Karl is looking after Caleb and Josh while we have a little girl-time. She's planned a mani-pedi with face masks and a bottle or two of prosecco. We'll probably watch a rom-com and have popcorn; the whole shebang. Sam knows just how to cheer me up after a long hard week.

When she arrives, she's towing a medium sized suitcase on wheels behind her. Caleb and I say our goodbyes and I help him buckle up in the back of the car before waving the boys off.

"And just what in the world is in that gigantic bag?" I ask as she wheels it into the lounge.

"Don't exaggerate, it's not *that* big. As for what's in it, you'll have to wait and see."

She totters off into the kitchen and comes back brandishing glasses.

"Here, hold these, I'll grab the alcohol," she says as she unzips her bag.

I take a look at the contents of the bag and have to laugh to myself. She's brought two bottles of prosecco, a couple of DVDs, beauty products galore, a big bar of chocolate and some toffee popcorn. Nobody can say she doesn't come prepared.

We've given each other a mani-pedi and are now lying back with face masks on. Neither of us is talking so that we don't crack whatever it is that's spread on our faces. I have two slices of cucumber resting on my eyes and I'm enjoying a few minutes of contemplative silence. It's the quietest we've been since Sam got here. I have to hand it to the girl; she has a knack for making me laugh. I'm never bored in her company.

"So, how's Drew enjoying the cold of Iceland?" Sam asks after we've washed our faces.

"He's having fun, I guess. I mean, he's been to some really cool—no pun intended—places. He visited The Blue Lagoon and sent me some pictures of its beauty. The boys also came across a museum that made them piss themselves laughing and feel sick at the same time."

"Ooh, do tell."

I pour us a glass of prosecco as I talk.

"Well, it's called The Phallological Museum. No prizes for guessing what's inside."

Sam snorts a very un-ladylike giggle and tries to stifle it with her hand.

"Yeah, it's a museum of penises. They have more than two hundred various penises and penile parts from land and sea mammals. I couldn't help but laugh when he told me. Boys being boys, they decided it would be a laugh to visit, but then one of them got sick because they saw a human specimen that was pickled in a jar."

We both burst out laughing and it took a couple of minutes to get it under control.

"That's just...oh my God! I can't wait to rib him about it when he comes back to work."

Sam holds her sides as her laughter begins to subside.

"Yeah, needless to say, I didn't get any selfies with a pickled human dick. Thank fuck for that!"

Sam guffaws and it's a proper, full-on belly laugh. It's really no wonder she's tickled pink.

Once we're over the whole penis thing, we settle down with a drink, a DVD and call for a takeaway.

Sam decided tonight's film should be something totally girlie, so we've got Bridget Jones's Baby on. You're always guaranteed a laugh with Bridget and what with Patrick Dempsey being the hot new addition, I already know I'm going to enjoy it.

We relax on the couch as we watch Colin and Patrick, or at least that's what I'm doing, rather than focussing on what the film's actually about. I think I'm a little buzzed and need sustenance to soak up the alcohol. It's a good job the takeaway turns up before I search the cupboards for anything to snack on.

We plate up our Chinese food and settle back in front of the film. It makes a nice change to have sweet and sour chicken, Cantonese style. I normally watch what I eat and don't eat after a certain time at night. But this is a one-off so I'll make the most of it.

When it comes time for Sam to leave, I get up and pull her into a hug.

"Thank you for tonight. It was just what the doctor ordered. I've been having a stressful week."

"Anytime, babe, you know that. Friends for twenty-two years and counting; what else am I meant to do when you need a little downtime?"

"Seriously, thank you. I think there's something up with Drew, but can't figure out what or if I'm just imagining it. So tonight has been twice as much stress relief."

"Why didn't you say anything?"

I hear Karl knock on the door and step to answer it.

"It doesn't matter. I'll figure it out one way or another. We've both had a busy week and I didn't want to talk about it. I don't even know why I mentioned it. Forget I said anything."

Caleb barrels in as I open the door.

"I missed you, mum," he says as he wraps his arms around me.

"I missed you too, buddy," I reply as I ruffle his hair and lean down to kiss him on the forehead.

"Were you and Josh on your best behaviour?" Sam asks.

"Yes, Auntie Sam. Uncle Karl let us have pizza for tea; he even helped us make our own. We played on Minecraft before Uncle Karl said we'd spent too long on video games and he wanted to show us how to have fun without a controller in our hands."

"Did you enjoy your pizza?"

"It was awesome. We added whatever toppings we wanted. Mine was oozing with extra cheese ,too."

"Well, that's great. I'd better get going back to Josh, but I'm glad you boys had fun."

Sam steps into the doorway but turns before leaving.

"Don't stress about Drew, babe," she says in a hushed tone.

"I won't."

I make that vow to myself as much as to her.

When Sam and the boys leave, I tell Caleb to brush his teeth and put his pyjamas on ready for me to tuck him in. I go upstairs and lie down on the bed next to him. Picking up his copy of *The Prisoner of Azkaban*, I pick up reading where we left off.

***

Two weeks later…

I'm sitting at my laptop, organising a party for a client, when I'm alerted to an inbox message on my social media page.

I click on the notification and bile rises hot and acidic in my mouth. I read and re-read the short message. My head begins to feel fuzzy and I reach to snap the band on my wrist, only to find it isn't there. I took it off when I showered this morning and must have forgotten to put it back on. There's nothing to stop me melting down and a feel myself begin to spiral into a black hole. A couple of sentences on an otherwise blank screen, that's all it took to trigger an attack.

Peter Webber: Hey Elise. You look different. So, you're an event organiser now. That must be fun. What have you been up to lately?

My palms are sweaty and my head is dizzy. I try to take calm, deep breaths but it's hard to control my reaction. Why did he have to get in touch? It's been over a decade since I left him. What could he possibly think he has to gain now? I just don't get it.

Picking up my phone, I see how shaky my hands are as I try to unlock it and pull up Sam's number. Finally managing to do just that, I hit the call button.

"Hey babe," she greets in her ever chirpy tone.

"Hey."

The tone of that one word has her worried.

"Elise? What's happened?"

"Panic…attack," I manage to respond breathlessly as my head swims and my heart rate spikes.

"Repeat after me; one, three, five, seven, nine."

"One…three…"

I can't remember the order she said the numbers in. I try again.

"One…three…five…"

"Elise, calm down babe. One, three, five, seven, nine. Say it with me."

"One, three, five, seven, nine," we say in unison.

She makes me repeat it a couple of times and I feel my heart rate slow back down. My head begins to clear and I take a few deep breaths.

"What's happened?" she asks after a few moments of silence.

I explain how I got a message from Peter and she gasps in utter shock. I forward her the message so I don't have to read the words to her.

"Oh, honey, I'm on my way over. Stay calm and I'll be there soon. Okay?"

"No, it's okay. I'll be fine. I just… I needed to tell someone."

"I'm on my way; no arguments."

We stay on the phone while she makes her way to mine. She doesn't hang up as she drives over, she keeps me on loudspeaker and we talk about anything except Peter.

"I don't know why he did this."

"Neither do I, but what I do know, is you have to block him right now."

"No, I have a few things to say first. He needs to know he can't play his games with me anymore, Sam. I'm not a victim, not this time."

I grab my laptop and click on his message. With shaking hands, I begin to reply;

Elise: How dare you contact me, Peter. I don't know who you think you are or what you want and I don't care. Stay the hell away from me. Forget I exist, the way I have forgotten you. It's been over a decade since I stopped letting you control me. You may have thought you were the master puppeteer, but I stopped being your puppet the day I left and I have never looked back.

Don't contact me again. I mean it Peter. Do. Not. Message. Me. Again. EVER!

My life changed for the better the day I left you. I stopped being a victim and started being a survivor. Turns out that's more my style than being your punch-bag. I don't know what you hoped to achieve by messaging me, but I can tell you all you have achieved is a big fat ZERO. Nada, zilch, nothing. I'm only messaging you back because I am warning you that if you continue to harass me, I won't think twice about contacting the police. I may never have pressed charges against you in the past because you always managed to manipulate me. But they still have it on record, no doubt, that I reported you for GBH. Contact me again and I will get a restraining order. You have no control over me now, you won't get me to change my mind and let you off lightly.

I don't know whether the police have really kept record of all the times I called them and all the times I didn't press charges, but I'm betting he doesn't know either, so I say it because it feels like I have the advantage over him. I am done running from him. I don't know how he found my business page, I don't use my real name, I go by my mother's maiden name so that he can't find me. But he's found me now and I am still reeling in shock.

Sam continues to hold me close and whisper to me.

"It's alright, baby, he can't hurt you now," she repeats over and over again.

I know in my heart I'm not a victim. I'm a survivor of years of abuse. I don't know how I managed to survive some of the beatings, but I did and that's all that matters. His cruelty was both physical and mental. It was Dave that finally helped me see that I was worth so much more than the life I had with Peter. Dave was the one who made me see that I was worthy of love. If it wasn't for him, I would have carried on believing Peter every time he said that nobody would ever love me the way he did. Although Dave and I didn't last, and the last time I saw him he acted like a dick, I'll always be grateful for the fact that he helped me escape that life.

"Sweetie, maybe you should go and lie down for a while. I'll stay with you, I'm not going anywhere. I just think maybe you would feel better if you slept and woke up fresh like it never happened."

"Okay," I agree as she stands and holds her hand out to me.

Sam helps me upstairs and into bed. She covers me with a blanket and I close my eyes. I don't know if I'll sleep, but right now I want to switch off and not have to think.

***

Waking up, I realise I slept better than I thought. As she promised, Sam didn't go anywhere. She lay down next to me and is currently still asleep. My phone vibrates and I'm nervous to look at it, but I pick it up anyway and notice it's Drew.

Drew: Hey baby, how are you? I miss you! Have you got time to talk tonight? I miss your beautiful face lighting up my screen. Love you xxx

My heart feels lighter after reading those two little words at the end.

Elise: I suppose I can be persuaded to make time for you ;)

Drew: Persuaded? Hmm…and what do I have to do to encourage you, huh?

I think about my response and look at Sam, still sleeping, as I feel a blush spread across my chest. I know she can't see the message I'm typing out, but it still makes me a little embarrassed.

Elise: A slow, sensual strip tease. The second the call connects, you remove an item of clothing. Then, knowing my eyes are following your every move, you slowly strip bare.

Drew: Not the answer I was expecting! You continue to surprise me, Elise Swanson. I agree to your terms on one condition…When I'm done, you have to strip for me too…

Knowing Caleb is having a sleepover with Josh, I quickly type out my agreement.

Elise: I'll have my stockings on ready for you. Love you baby. Speak to you later xxx

Drew: I can't wait. My cock is already twitching with excitement. I'll call about 9:30. Love you, always xxx

I can't help the smile that takes over my face. It feels good to smile considering what happened earlier.

Sam begins to stir as I get out of bed, so I go downstairs and make a cup of coffee while I wait for her to clear her sleepy head.

"Hey," she says softly as she enters the kitchen, "How did you sleep?"

"Seems like it did the job. When I have a panic attack, it drains me physically as well as emotionally, so it was good to rest."

"Well don't worry, Karl is fetching Josh from school so I can go and fetch Caleb for you."

I look at the time. Damn! I didn't even set an alarm when I went to sleep and I didn't realise it was so late.

"Thanks babe. Coffee first?"

I hand her a mug and we walk into the lounge.

"You seem happier."

"I am. Drew text me a few minutes ago. He's going to call later tonight. I've really missed seeing him as he hasn't had a chance to FaceTime for the last couple of nights. So that will cheer me up."

"Well when I bring Caleb back from school, he can pack for tonight's sleepover and then I can take him home with me, if you like? That way, you'll have chance to shower and pamper yourself before his call."

"That would be good. Thanks, babe."

***

I have the house to myself and I plan to make the most of it for Drew's sake. He might not be here, but that doesn't mean I can't show him what he's missing.

After showering, I rub in my favourite scented lotion. I dry and straighten my hair, apply light makeup and put on my black lacy bra and panty set with stockings and suspenders. Lastly, I wrap my satin dressing robe around me and lie on the bed. Drew text not long ago to say he'd be calling soon and I can't wait to see his face, especially when he sees how I'm dressed.

I'm still not completely over what happened this afternoon, but I'm trying not to think about it. Talking with Drew will provide a good distraction. Better than good if he keeps to his word of stripping for me.

It's dead on nine-thirty when he calls, just as he promised. I see his handsome face fill my screen. Oh how I ache to reach out and touch him. This next month can't go by fast enough for me. In four weeks, he'll finally be home.

"Hey, baby."

Just the tone of his voice is enough to send goose-bumps across my skin.

"Hey, yourself."

"What you up to?"

"Well, I'm sat here in stockings and lacy underwear. What about you?"

I try for a sultry tone, but I'm not sure I pull it off.

"I've been watching the clock and waiting until I could get out of the bar to come back and call you."

"Wait, what? You were in a bar, having a drink with the lads and it was more important to come back this early to call me?"

"Trust me; I was glad to get out of there. The three of them have these girls hanging off their every word. I wanted to get back and call you like I promised. Plus, I know it's early, but I plan to be on the phone for quite some time."

He winks and blows me a kiss, which sends shivers down my spine.

"Do you now? And what, pray tell, will we be talking about for so long?"

"Oh, it won't all be talking, baby."

"And what else will we be doing?"

"If I had my way, the answer to that would be *each other*. But as it is, we'll have to settle for some virtual entertainment."

He places his phone somewhere at the foot of the bed before coming back into view. I hear music come on in the background and it's the unmistakable first bars of *Pour Some Sugar On Me*.

I wait impatiently for him to take his top off. He wasn't kidding about taking his sweet time. His hands reach for the hem of his top and he pulls it up over his head, exposing that gorgeous torso. I wish I could reach out and feel his warmth. What I wouldn't give to lick every plane of that body, the V that I lust after so much. I'd run my fingers and tongue over every inch of him.

My eyes are transfixed to the screen as he dances to the beat of the song, singing along as he strips until he's standing before me in just his boxer shorts.

My tongue darts out to wet my lips. It's a damn good job I have something holding me up, else I'd be a pile of goo.

"I have one caveat," his voice breaks into my thoughts.

"And what's that?"

Damn, that sultry tone works so much better when he's just reduced you to all but a puddle on the bed. There's no faking the lust in my voice.

"Well, Princess, these here," he indicates to his boxers, "They stay on for now. You can keep your panties and we can remove them together."

"That's something I think I can get on board with."

I blow him a kiss and he pretends to catch it. So cheesy, but so damn swoon-worthy.

***

The way our conversation went last night, I decided against telling Drew about Peter's message. Not because I didn't want to tell him, but with his little strip tease and then mine, there just wasn't a right time to bring it up. There's nothing he can do about it anyway; it's just that I want to be honest with him. The last time we were together, I wasn't as honest as I could have been, so this time, I want us to start as we mean to go on. Even if that means dragging up a past I never want to relive.

I hear the doorbell and get up to let Sam and Caleb in.

"Mum, Auntie Sam said that if we don't have plans today, we could all go to Jump Nation. What do you think?" Caleb asks the second the door is opened.

"I think that's a great idea, buddy. Why don't you go and get buckled up in Uncle Karl's car while I talk to Auntie Sam for a minute?"

Caleb runs back to the car and jumps in next to an excited Josh. The pair of them are so full of energy and it's good to see them not glued to a games console.

"Hey, what's up, chick?" Sam asks as she steps inside the house.

I close the door behind her.

"I've been thinking and I've come to realise I need to tell Drew the truth about why I left the first time round, as well as other things."

"What good will that do you now?"

"I don't know, it's just, well I've been thinking about how he deserves the truth about me. Everybody my age comes with baggage, Drew included, but it's all about whether your baggage is compatible with somebody else's. If we want to be together, then he needs to know about Peter and even about my monster of a stepfather."

Sam gasps in shock. I've barely ever told anyone about the darkest times of my life. Only she knows the complete, unfettered reality of the situation.

"Do you really think dragging up your past will help you move forward?"

Placing a hand on my arm, Sam gives me a look of understanding. She knows better than anyone how much baggage I truly come with and she knows my need to be honest with someone I intend to be in a relationship with.

Jensen knew about my stepdad. Well, he knew about the abuse I suffered at his hands. I never actually told him very much detail. I didn't think it was fair to burden him with such knowledge. I've pretty much kept it all bottled inside for almost thirty years.

"I think it's time I opened up and let someone in. I'm sick to death of keeping people at bay. Especially people I love; and I love Drew. Sam, I've fallen for him again and I don't think it's fair on him if he's fallen for who I am on the outside but doesn't know me on the inside."

"Then I think you should tell him. But only if you think it's the right thing to do."

"I'm just worried that if I tell him, I'll lose him because it's too much for him to handle."

Wrapping me in a hug, Sam whispers in my ear.

"If he loves you, then he'll accept *every* part of you; the good, the bad and the things that are in no way your fault. If he runs a mile, then he's not the man I think he is, and he's not the right man for you. You're a great woman, Elise Swanson; one of the very best. Those things that happened weren't because of you. You didn't make anyone treat you in that way. Drew will say the same thing. I'm sure of it."

I just nod, unable to speak because of the ball of emotion lodged in my throat.

"Let's get going and let the kid's burn off some of that excess energy," she says, taking my hand.

We make our way to the car and she smiles at me. I know she'll be there to help put the pieces back together if Drew isn't strong enough to handle things.

Once we're at Jump Nation, a local trampoline park, the three boys—yes, that includes Karl—run off to play. I swear, Sam married a man who's still a kid at heart. He's so good with the boys. It makes me happy that she's in such a good place. There was a time when she couldn't settle down with anyone. She went from one bloke to the next—not in a bad way—always hoping the next one would be 'the one'. It may have taken her a while, but I'm glad she finally found the man she wants to spend forever with. He knows everything about her; the good, bad and everything in between. Their relationship is yet more proof I need to clue Drew in to what lies beneath the surface. I didn't tell him the first time we were together because, back then, I couldn't talk about it. Plus, we weren't in *that* kind of relationship. Not everybody needs to know your true colours; just someone you want to spend forever with. Although he's been gone for the last couple of months, we've still talked every day and made this relationship work long distance. I have hope in my heart that he is 'the one' for me, so he deserves honesty.

The boys play for a couple of hours while Sam and I drink coffee and chat. I really wish I could do this kind of thing with him, but my leg is unstable on the floor, never mind a trampoline. That's another reason I'm glad to have Sam and Karl in my life. They try to include us in things so that Caleb doesn't miss out. Maybe when he meets Drew, he'll have someone to be a father figure in his life and do this kind of thing with more often.

As they approach us, the boys look shattered. I can't blame them; they've been bouncing around like crazy. Josh and Caleb come to sit at our table while Karl goes to get them a drink.

"Mum, did you see the backflip Caleb did?" Josh asks.

"I sure did, it was amazing."

"It was the first time he's managed to do it without a hitch. Wasn't it brilliant?"

"I know. I couldn't get the hang of it before. It was so good to actually do it!" Caleb says excitedly as Karl passes him a bottle of water.

"He was so good, Elise. Did you see?" Karl asks as he sits next to Sam and takes her hand.

I love how they still show affection, even if it's just the touch of their hands.

"I did. I'm proud of you, buddy."

I ruffle his hair and am rewarded with a slick coat of sweat on my palm.

"What do you say we all go and get something to eat? My treat," I ask.

Sam shoots me daggers.

"You will not pay for us all."

"Oh, really? What exactly do you intend to do about it?"

We continue to playfully argue all the way back to the car. Once we're all buckled in, Karl turns up the volume on the radio and sings along out of tune all the way to dinner.

***

I'm sitting looking at the big red ring on the calendar, marking the last day of the month; the day Drew is due home. It can't come quickly enough. I want to wrap my arms around him, kiss him, amongst other things.

My phone rings and I smile as I see his name on the caller I.D.

"Hey, baby," he purrs sexily as I see his face.

"Hey, how's your day been?"

"Yeah, we've had fun. Seen some sights, it's just a shame we've had those girls in tow."

I couldn't believe it when he'd told me about the four girls that had been hanging around. I found it funny when he told me he'd had to be brutally honest with them one sniffing around him. Apparently she hasn't been able to look him in the eye since.

"Do they have nothing better to do? They've been hanging around for weeks!"

"I had words with Danny; told him this was meant to be a boys only trip. He said that the girls wouldn't be around for long, but then Seb let slip that the girls are on a break between university and getting jobs. They all have quite the cushy life where their parents are rich and they are spoiled little brats."

"Is fake tits—sorry, Ashleigh—still hanging off Danny's arm?"

I try to stifle a laugh but Drew laughs with me, which makes me giggle all the more.

"Yeah. I mean damn, these girls are like what, eight, maybe ten years younger than us. What is he thinking? What are the three of them thinking?"

"Age is just a number, especially when it's casual holiday sex."

"Still…these girls are like limpets. They won't go away. I'm ready to jack it in and come home."

"But you do have days where it's just you and the boys, right?"

If I'm honest, an insecure part of me doesn't like these younger girls hanging around all the time. But I know Drew isn't interested in that Lauren who tried it on with him. Still, she's able bodied and can go out and have fun the way they do. She can do things I can no longer do. That's the problem with the nerve damage I've sustained; it severely limits what I can do. Will he end up seeing that he's better off with someone like her?

"Yeah, we hang, just the three of us. The girls were meant to return home weeks ago, but decided to extend their stay."

"I can see that it wouldn't be easy to get rid of them. It would mean convincing the boys to give up the sex-on-tap they're getting. But you should still stay. You went out there for a reason, right? You wanted to see things like the Northern Lights, the ice wall you hiked up, that sort of thing. You are still there for the same reasons, even if the boys have trophies on their arms for the time-being."

Drew laughs at my way of phrasing how I see the girls.

"I think at this point…" he trails off and takes the phone slightly away from his face.

There's a muffled sound that I can't make out but then there's a knock on my front door which distracts me.

"Hang on Drew, there's someone at the door."

"…I'd rather be here with you," he finishes his sentence as I open the door and come face to face with him.

"What the…? How did you…? When did you…?" I can't seem to finish a single sentence.

"I hopped on an Icelandair plane home. The flight is less than three hours, so it was easy to leave after I text you this morning and get home by now."

"But…"

Drew pulls me in for a hug and I inhale his scent. God, how I have missed his strength and the smell of his cologne. I wrap my arms around his neck and lean in for a kiss. It starts off slow, but soon Drew is kissing me like I'm oxygen and he's a man taking his last breath.

When we pull back, I look at him and he smiles so widely it could split his face in two.

"How did I not see in the background that you were here?"

"I was in a taxi. I made sure all you could see was my face. Easy!"

Leaning into me once more, Drew nips on my bottom lip and I open my mouth to grant him access. I can't believe he's home early, but not all surprises are bad ones. His hands grip my hips and he brushes himself against me, showing how turned on he is. I know Caleb is asleep upstairs and we'll have to be quiet, but all those thoughts flee my mind as Drew crushes his mouth against mine and pushes me inside so he can shut the door.

He turns me round and holds me captive with the door at my back. Pulling my hair gently, he exposes my neck and places a trail of feather-light kisses across my skin. My body comes alive under his touch. The blood in my veins feels like it's on fire and his kisses are adding fuel to the flames.

"What do you say we take this upstairs?" I ask as he continues to kiss down to the swell of my breasts.

"Mm-hmm," he mumbles as his hands move to my ass, "I'd say that's a great idea."

I let him take me by the hand and lead me upstairs. There are butterflies in my tummy like it's our first time all over again. It's been far too long since I've felt his touch; so long that just the touch of his hand has me feeling giddy.

Opening my bedroom door, Drew sweeps me off my feet. He nudges the door closed and carries me over to my bed. He lays me down carefully before stretching himself out above me. Leaning on his forearms, he dips his head to claim my lips. His kiss is slow, languid. He's taking his time to enjoy what we have. Our tongues dance and I can't get enough of the taste of him.

Sliding down my body, Drew kisses me from the sweet spot underneath my left ear, down the side of my neck, to the swell of my breasts. Then he lifts my top, pulls down the cup of my bra and gently traces circles around my nipple with the tip of his tongue. I moan as he gently bites my nipple and caresses my breast with one deft hand.

Lowering himself further, he kisses down my abdomen to the waistband of my jeans. He slowly unbuttons them and then slides the zip down with his teeth. I lift my ass so he can lower the material easier. As he slides them down my legs, I kick to discard them completely.

Drew moves to kneel on the floor and grabs my ass to slide me down the bed towards him. Lifting my knees over his shoulders, he gently caresses my bare skin and places light kisses that start to kindle a flame within me.

I feel Drew lick and nip his way down my thigh, right to where I want, no, need him to be. Grabbing a handful of his hair, I pull him closer to me. It's been too long and I need to feel that expert mouth on me. It doesn't take him more than a few moments to give me what I desire.

With deft fingers and tongue, Drew brings me to my first orgasm of the night. My back arches from the bed, my fists grip the sheets and I feel the tingle from my head to my toes.

Drew stands to remove his jeans while I lie on the bed, basking in the glow of a mind-blowing orgasm. They say absence makes the heart grow fonder. Sure it does, but it also makes the sex so much better when you reunite.

Watching as he undresses, I get excited when I see that V exposed. I want to run my hands over it, followed by my tongue. I lean up on my elbows so that I can watch him better. Once he's naked, he stalks back towards me, eyes hooded and dark.

Lowering himself to the bed, he positions himself above me and leans in to claim my lips. His kiss is urgent and makes the desire I already feel pool in my abdomen. His tongue explores my mouth and I feel him guide himself between my legs. He's in position as he pulls back from our kiss and makes eye contact with me.

With our gazes locked, Drew sinks into me inch by inch. It's excruciatingly slowly for my liking, but I know what he's doing. He's making me feel every inch of him, making up for lost time. He doesn't break eye contact as he pushes himself deeper inside me. I see desire, lust, and love all swirling in those beautiful hazel irises.

Hitching my legs around his waist, I dig my heels into the cheeks of his ass. Dragging my nails slowly down his back, I watch him shiver under my touch. As he bucks into me, Drew's moans reverberate through his chest. I feel it as much as I hear. The sound of his pleasure makes me happy. I enjoy knowing that it's me that does this to him. I whimper as he ups his pace and I lift my hips to match his movements.

My whole body comes alive as I feel my orgasm build. Moving his head to circle my nipple with his tongue again, he bites as he pushes into me. My moans are long and loud as he repeats the motion several times before releasing my nipple and dipping his head to kiss me instead.

Our kisses are frantic; my hands explore the hard planes of his back as I cling to him and match the bucking of his hips. The harder he pushes against me, the more my climax builds. He grips my hips tightly as he begins to move faster.

The warmth I felt in my abdomen has spread to my entire body and now I am on the edge of an abyss. One I could fall into and never want to find my way out of.

Chapter Fourteen
Drew

I couldn't hack it in Iceland any longer. The girls were grating on my very last nerve and the boys were more interested in the sex they were getting rather than anything we'd originally planned. I told them I was going to go home and they didn't even bat an eye. So much for 'bros before hos'.

Thankfully my ticket had been open ended, so all I had to do was to wait for there to be room on a plane, and bingo!

The journey home was uneventful. I ended up glad I'd bought a book at the airport in England before I left in case I had any downtime. Elise had been going on about this book for months and, although I don't normally read romance novels, she'd told me the sex scenes were so hot she very nearly spontaneously combusted as she read it. She was right. I mean, the story was good on its own merits, but the sex scenes; I couldn't wait to try to re-enact some of them with her.

Dropping my cases at home first, I grabbed a quick shower and fresh clothes before going to surprise her. I hadn't let on that I was coming home. I knew she'd try and convince me to stay. It had been a hard decision at first, but the more the girls hung around, the more the boys became wimps. They had the nerve to call me pussy-whipped, but at least I have a real relationship with my girl. They don't. Holiday flings for the three of them. One of them, Ashleigh, even said she'd got a boyfriend back home, so the boys ended up being 'whipped' by girls that only wanted a bit of fun. And that was more important than our boys trip so, in the end, it seemed the decision was easier than expected.

Freshly showered and dressed, I used Elise's favourite of my colognes. I got a taxi over because I couldn't very well FaceTime her while I was driving.

To say she was surprised by my appearance is an understatement. I literally swept her off her feet and made love to her for hours. We fell asleep wrapped around each other, but woke in the middle of the night when Elise chose hard and fast fucking over slow love making. I had no complaints though. She is literally the best lover I've had. It's not just the way she makes love to me; it's the way we seem to have a deeper connection. Not just lust, desire or even love. It's more than that, but harder to explain. It's every little thing she does. She's a very selfless lover. It isn't all about her desire to climax; instead she's all about me. I do my utmost to do exactly the same for her every time we are together. I love the way she moans my name, the way her hands clutch at the sheets and her back arches as she hits her peak. Every time we make love, it's like that connection deepens.

I'm lying here in her bed, waiting for her to return from the school run. She got up early this morning to make sure Caleb didn't see me. She wants us to meet, but not when I'm naked in bed.

I've been thinking about our relationship and where we go from here now I'm home. I'm certainly not going travelling again anytime soon. Not that I don't want to travel anymore; I still have so many things I want to see. But somehow, Elise got under my skin before I left and it hurt like a physical ache in my chest every day that I was away from her.

The more I think about it, the more I know now that I've always used travelling as a way of coping; a way of never having ties or relationships. I kept everyone at arm's length because it was easier that way. If I never got involved, I never got hurt. Putting your heart on the line is difficult, especially when you've had it broken and had to sit and piece it back together. That's a painstakingly long process and I have no intention of going through it again. The only reason I have allowed myself to get attached to Elise is because I've always loved her. From the first time we were together back in 2005, I have never stopped feeling something for her deep down. Recently, she's brought those feelings back to the surface and, even though it hurt to lose her the first time, even though she's the first one to have made me pick up the pieces of my heart, I can't help wanting to try again; for real this time. No more running away. I'm done. I'm hanging up my trainers for good. As long as Elise really wants to make a go of it this time, then I do, too.

The bedroom door opens and Elise stands there with a grin on her face. I don't know what she's smiling at, but it's contagious and I feel my own face light up with a smile.

"You're still here?!" she sighs as she walks over to the bed.

"Of course I am. Where else would I be?" I reply as I sit up.

"I had this horrible feeling last night was just a dream and I'd come home to an empty bed."

She crawls on the bed next to me and I wrap my arms around her, planting a kiss on her forehead.

"It's real, baby. I'm home. I'm not going anywhere anytime soon."

I lean down to kiss her. Her mouth opens to me and I kiss her more deeply. Her hands are in my hair and she kisses me more fervently.

Rolling over so that she is underneath me, I pin her in place. Her red hair is loose and fanned across the pillow while those baby blues have a look in them that says we're not going anywhere for the time being. That's good, because I have plans to make up for being gone so long. Two months without sex has left me frustrated. Normally, it wouldn't bother me; but normally, I don't have a gorgeous red-headed goddess waiting at home for me. I'm definitely going to make the most of having her here in my arms right now.

***

After spending a couple of hours in bed, we showered together and got dressed. Elise surprised me when she asked if I would like to meet Caleb. I'm nervous as hell, but excited too. It's a big step for her; really big. She hasn't let anyone close to her son since Jensen left her. Now she's ready to introduce us and I don't know what he'll make of me. How do I connect with a ten year old kid?

Thankfully, Elise has told me a few key things that I can get Caleb to talk about. Apparently, like any normal kid his age, he is addicted to playing Minecraft. I know nothing about the game, but that's okay, because he can tell me. Elise said when you get him talking about it, he won't shut up. He's also big into superheroes. He loves DC and Marvel, but, like his mother, if pressed, he would say Marvel characters are his favourite. He says Captain America is the best. I have to disagree there, I think Iron Man is the best, but at least that means we have something in common; our love of comic books.

Caleb is also a Harry Potter lover, just like Elise. There's so much memorabilia in her bedroom and his. They took the tour in London and came back with wands and all sorts. So that's another thing we can talk about. He can tell me all about the tour and why he loves the films so much. Elise says they are reading *The Prisoner of Azkaban* each night at bed time, but are nearly finished and ready to start *The Goblet of Fire.*

I can't help but think Elise must be a great mum. The way she talks about Caleb; she does anything and everything she can for him. She's tried her hardest to make up for the loss of Jensen and his family, but she doesn't want to get involved with a man just to give her son a father figure. She told me how hard it's been adjusting to becoming a single mum at the same time as becoming newly disabled. It must be tough with what she's been through and I'm amazed at the strength she has shown. Jensen left her because of her disability, that's his problem. His loss is my gain.

I can only hope Caleb likes me. I'm not going to try to act like a father figure, I just want us to be friends; at first, anyway. I want him to feel comfortable around me and let me into his life. I'll take things as slowly as I need to in order for him to trust me. Trust is a commodity that needs to be earned, not just given freely.

The plan is to go bowling tonight. I'd suggested a movie but Elise said it wouldn't leave room for much talking and getting to know each other. So, after much discussion and searching for a fun activity, we settled on bowling, even though Elise doesn't like it much.

We have the day to ourselves as I'm not working until tomorrow and Elise can work from home. She says she doesn't have too much to do, so she settles at her laptop while I make a cup of coffee.

While she's working, I settle down to watch Avengers Assemble. I have to say, even though you're meant to root for the good guys, I can't help but like Loki. Elise giggles when I tell her this and says she feels the same. She also doesn't think it hurts that Tom Hiddleston is—and I quote—seriously hot. I find Scarlett Johansson pretty damn sexy with her kick-ass skills and lithe body, topped off with a beautiful face and striking red hair. Yeah she's hot and sort of reminds me of Elise.

***

While Elise fetches Caleb from school, I go home to shower and pick up my car. I have a permanent smile on my face as I think of the future and what it might hold for me. I never envisaged a future where

I settled down and had kids. I used to want that when I was younger, but became more cynical of people as I grew up. Now I see a different path laid out for me; one where a woman actually cares about me, loves me and wants me and I feel exactly the same.

Men may not be overly emotional creatures, but that doesn't mean we don't have feelings. It just means we don't wear our hearts on our sleeves. But for Elise, I will learn to open up and share things with her. She brings out that side of me. She assures me that I can trust her with my heart. When she says that she won't break it, this time I trust her implicitly. It's hard giving my heart back to a woman who previously crushed it, but this time she's breathing life back into it.

I shower and change into fresh clothes. I'm wearing dark indigo jeans and a navy blue shirt along with some of Elise's favourite cologne. Not too dressed up, but it doesn't hurt to put a little effort in.

Getting in the car, I turn up the music coming from my iPod. *Panic! At The Disco's* album *A Fever You Can't Sweat Out* is playing and I begin to sing along as I pull out of the car park and head back over to Elise's place.

***

Caleb is beating both Elise and me and I can't help but laugh every time he comes for a high-five from me after he bowls. He seems accepting of me so far and it makes me feel so much better; less nervous than I was earlier.

Elise and I have agreed that I won't stop over tonight because we have to at least look like we're taking things slowly for Caleb's sake. I'll still sneak over from time to time, either during the day if I'm not at work and Elise is home or at night after Caleb has gone to bed or is staying at Sam's. But we won't tell him I'm staying over for at least another few weeks. I can't force my way into his life; it has to be a natural progression of things. I've never dated someone who has a child, so it's all new territory to me. I'll play things however Elise wants me to.

Caleb wins the last game of the night and we go to grab something to eat. There's a Frankie and Benny's right by the bowling alley, so we make our way across the car park. Caleb is a chatterbox and I can't help but smile at Elise as he chatters away. I'm glad he seems to have taken to me and I know it's a relief for Elise, too. Of course the real test will be time, but we seem to have gotten off to a good start.

"Cap could totally beat Iron Man in a fight," Caleb says as he digs in to his pizza.

"Cap only has his shield, whereas Iron Man has his repulsors," I say as I take a sip of my drink.

"Yeah, but Cap's shield is unbreakable, so if Iron Man blasted him, it wouldn't touch him."

"True, but I'm pretty sure Iron Man could find a way to beat his... backside," I hesitate to say ass.

"Whatever, Drew. I reckon Cap would win any day!" he retorts around a mouthful of fries.

"What have I told you about manners? Please eat with your mouth closed and swallow your food before talking," Elise chimes in.

"Sorry mum," Caleb says with an empty mouth as he dips his head.

"That's okay, buddy, just remember that we don't all want to see that mush in your mouth," she replies with a smile.

I try to cover my chuckle with a fake cough.

"Anyway, what about Thor? He could probably beat both Cap and Iron Man," Elise adds.

"Mum," Caleb groans, "Thor is only any good as an Avenger because he has Mjölnir."

"That's not true at all. He's a Norse God. Cap is only good because he has a shield, take that away and he'd be an ordinary man. Same with Iron Man; take away his suit and he's only Tony Stark. Whereas, even if you take away Mjölnir, Thor is anything but ordinary!"

"Oh, my God, you only say that because you think he's hot, mum."

I break out into a loud laugh. These two crack me up.

"Not at all, young man," Elise giggles as she talks, "Do you not remember the fight scene with Thor and Iron Man in Avengers Assemble?"

"Yeah; neither of them wins because they're pretty evenly matched and then it ends with Cap coming along. He tells Thor to put the hammer down, then Thor hits Cap's shield and there's a blast that levels all the trees. So nobody really wins but Cap was awesome," he replies animatedly.

"Oh, I give up."

Elise shrugs her shoulders and picks up her fork, twirling it in her spaghetti.

The rest of the evening goes well and I drive the two of them home.

"It was nice to meet you, Drew," Caleb says as we bump fists at the front door.

"You too, bud, even if you are Team Cap."

He pokes his tongue out at me and I laugh as he runs into the lounge.

"I think somebody likes you," Elise says as she wraps her arms around my neck.

"Good, because I think he's pretty awesome."

I plant a chaste kiss on her lips.

"Just like his mother," I say before leaning in to kiss her more deeply.

She consumes me. I can't get enough of her scent, the feel of her body against mine, her lips on mine.

"Eww, I can hear you two kissing from here," Caleb says.

"Then put your fingers in your ears," Elise replies as she reaches to shut the lounge door.

I press my lips back over hers and seek entry with my tongue. She opens up to me as I slide one hand around her back and the other up into her hair. I pull her ponytail gently and expose her neck to me. As I trace a path of light kisses down her throat, I feel myself begin to harden. Totally not the time for that, but I can't control it. She turns me on with the simplest of touches.

"Shit," I curse quietly as Elise runs a hand over the bulge in my jeans.

"Kiss me, Drew," she says quietly.

I'm only too happy to oblige. I frame her face with both hands and pull her lips to mine. I kiss her tenderly until she takes control of the kiss and leaves me breathless.

Chapter Fifteen
Elise

It's been a wonderful couple of weeks since Drew got home. Since he still had some time booked off work that he didn't use up on the trip, he decided to spend some quality time with Caleb and me. When I haven't been at work, he's been with us, getting to know Caleb and, although they haven't known each other very long, they have a pretty good bond so far. To see them together you'd think they've known each other for years.

When Jensen and I were together, he was good with Caleb. More than good; he was fantastic. Then, when we split up, I worried that any man I had the potential to date may not get on so well with my son. I feared that it would be hard to find someone who couldn't see the real me beyond the label of being 'the disabled woman' and who was okay with the fact that I have a ten year old kid. But it turns out that I needn't have been worried.

Years ago, when Drew and I were seeing each other, I knew he'd make a great dad someday. I'd been there on a couple of occasions when he'd looked after his nephew, Kai, and saw what a loving bond they had. A light shone in Drew's eyes when he was playing hide and seek with him or cooking him tea; the simple things in life. So it's nice to see now that he's at ease with Caleb. Even though he's not his dad or even his stepdad, he's showing he can be that kind of role model and if we are going to last, then that's exactly what I need to see.

Sam has also been kind enough to babysit so that Drew and I can have time alone. We've had 'date nights' where he's taken me out for a meal or to the cinema, or he's cooked for me. We've been using the time to get to know each other all over again. Although we haven't changed fundamentally, we have both grown up a lot in the last twelve years. We know more what we want out of life than we did back then.

I've been trying to pluck up the courage to have a heart to heart with him; to tell him some of what haunts me, but the timing just hasn't been right. After talking to Sam, she helped me realise there won't be a 'right' time, I just have to make the time. I have to face my demons head-on. It's always going to be a hard subject to face, but it has to be done.

There are actually a few things we need to talk about; one of which is my confession as to why I left him the first time around. Though he hasn't asked me why, I get the feeling that he wonders about it but doesn't want to bring it up. I guess I think that way because of my own issues with Jensen never giving me a reason when he left. I don't think the need for closure is only an issue for women, although people may say we're more emotional about it, I think both sexes have an equal desire for it and even though we are together now and it may not seem important to rake over the past, I really need Drew to understand where I was in my life and why it didn't work. Within my heart, I believe he deserves to know why I did what I did. It's a feeling of needing to close that chapter fully in order to move forward. I don't want either one of us to be stuck in the past. I have hopes for our future together and I'm not sure whether they can come to fruition if I'm not one hundred percent honest.

It probably won't be *the* most difficult conversation we have to have, but that doesn't mean it's any less important.

***

Sam is looking after Caleb tonight, so Drew and I are having a quiet night in. I've decided to cook lasagne and open a bottle of wine. I'm going to try and sway the conversation in the right direction for me to say what needs to be said, but at the same time, I don't want to ruin our evening. I can only hope he listens to me and really hears the honesty behind my words.

I tidy up before heading for a shower. Drew said he'd come round at seven so he could spend an hour with Caleb before Karl picks him up for the night. Caleb's sat playing Minecraft mini-games with his buddies online while I finish getting ready.

"You look great mum," he says as I walk into the lounge.
"Thank you buddy," I respond as I ruffle his hair.
"Muuuum," he whines as he drags his fingers through his hair.
This kid is so damn cute. He doesn't like it when I mess up his hair,

but it isn't out of vanity. When he was a toddler, he had this cute habit of twisting his hair around his fingers. I think it was a comfort thing. He still does it on the odd occasion and it reminds me of when he was younger. I look at him sometimes and wonder where the last ten years have gone. How have I been a mum for so long? I was twenty three when I had him and I'm nearly thirty four now. Where has the time gone? It feels like it's gone by in the blink of an eye.

"Are you all packed to go to Auntie Sam's?"

"Yes, mum."

"Do you have your toothbrush?"

"Yes."

"Clean clothes?"

"Yes. I have everything I need, mum."

If he didn't have any clothes or anything packed, he'd still say he had everything he needed as long as he had his 3DS, so I open his bag and double check.

"I don't know why you asked if you were going to check anyway, mum," he says, looking up from his Wii-U.

"Sorry, buddy. I just want to make sure."

I close his bag and put it back on the table.

"Are you taking Mickey? I didn't see him in your bag."

He may be ten years old but he takes his one particular Mickey Mouse plush with him when he goes to stay anywhere. He's had it since he was about five months old. Over the years, I've bought him more Mickey teddies in different sizes and wearing different outfits. Even though he doesn't watch it on the TV, he still loves the character. Some people might think it's immature for a child of his age, but I don't care as long as my boy is happy.

"Oh, I forgot," he says as he puts down the gamepad and dashes off upstairs.

Drew knocks the door dead on seven o'clock. As I open the door, I am greeted with a bouquet of purple and white calla lilies, my favourite flower.

"Aw, thank you, babe, they are beautiful. Let me go and put them in some water."

"Not before you do this," he says as he pulls me in for a kiss.

His lips are soft and full. I love the way they feel against mine. His kisses have the ability to make me weak in the knees. I'm sure if we had a little longer, they'd make me forget my own name.

"Eww, you guuuys…" Caleb says, drawing out the last word.

Drew breaks the kiss and I'm left to catch my breath.

"Sorry, buddy," Drew says as Caleb walks into the lounge carrying the nearly forgotten Mickey.

I walk into the kitchen and grab a vase, fill it with water and unwrap the cellophane around the flowers.

After placing them in the water, I place the beautiful flowers on the windowsill. They go well in my purple and white kitchen. If I had my way, every room in my house would be purple, but I'll just have to settle for my kitchen and bedroom. Different shades, of course.

Drew, Caleb and I spend the next hour playing on the air hockey table that Jensen's parents bought him one Christmas. I'm useless at the game. I'm not really big on games of any kind. To be honest, I'd rather have my nose in a book.

After Caleb won the last round, he took the game back to his room. Karl knocked on the door a few minutes later and, after he spent a few minutes chatting with Drew, he took Caleb home with him.

We're finally alone and I can't wait to snuggle up on the couch together, but first, I have to get the lasagne in the oven. I prepared it earlier today so that I'd only need to put it in to cook when we were ready. I also have a salad to prepare to go with it.

I have my iPod on quietly, playing Snow Patrol in the background.

"Mmm, something smells good," Drew says as he wraps his arms around me from behind.

"I've been told my lasagne is pretty good."

"That it is, but it wasn't the food I was talking about."

He nibbles on my earlobe and a sigh escapes me. If it wasn't for his arms around me, I'd be a puddle of goo right now. He places tender kisses down the side of my neck and I stop what I'm doing. Who needs to cut up salad when there's something far tastier on the menu?

The opening bars of *You Could Be Happy* stop my thoughts from running away with me. I take a deep breath and try not to shed the tears that suddenly threaten to rain down like a waterfall. There are some songs that you can't help but got emotional over, whether that emotion is happiness or melancholy. This song is the latter.

I turn in Drew's arms and nuzzle into his neck. I wrap my arms around his waist and hold him tight.

"Everything okay?" he whispers in my ear.

"Mmm-hmm," I mumble, unable to trust my voice not to break.

He rubs circles on my upper back with one hand while the other holds my hip. It's comforting and I can't help but want to absorb some of his strength.

I steel myself mentally before pulling slightly back from his hold.

"Hey."

His voice is soft and he catches my chin, tilting it up towards him. A couple of tears fall unbidden down my cheek and he wipes them away with the pad of his thumb.

"I'm okay, it's just this song," I say as I reach for my iPod to skip the rest of the track.

Drew doesn't say anything, just dips his head and places a chaste kiss on my lips.

I move back to the salad on the chopping board. His arms come back around me from behind as I grab the ingredients for a light dressing. I'm playing for time, creating a distraction for myself.

When everything is ready, I dish up and take the plates into the lounge. Drew smiles and thanks me, the most he's said in the last half an hour. After I'd finished chopping the salad, we sat in silence for a while, just watching mindless TV. It wasn't an uncomfortable silence, but at the same time, it wasn't exactly what I wanted. It was born of need, not want. I needed a few minutes to gather my thoughts and Drew seemed to sense that I didn't want to talk. He didn't force the issue and I was glad of that. One of the reasons I love him is his ability to sense what I need and give it to me without me having to ask. He's more sensitive than he lets on. He seems to read my mood and gives me space or holds me close without either of us having to utter a word.

We eat and make small talk about our respective days. The mood has become lighter and Drew makes me laugh as he recalls the air hockey game. He had been insistent he was going to beat Caleb but lost two games to one.

Drew clears our plates and I pour us another glass of wine while I watch how his muscles move under his t-shirt as he bends and straightens, loading the dishwasher. His ass is perfection, as though it was sculpted by Rodin himself.

"See something you like, little lady?"

Busted! I must have been so distracted by thoughts of his perfect form that I didn't notice when he turned to face me.

"I'm not really sure; maybe you should turn back around and let me have a little longer to decide."

He whips the dishtowel at me and I step back out of his reach. I see him lunge towards me and know I don't have time to escape. Damn, I don't even want to.

As he wraps one arm around my waist, the other goes up into my hair and he pulls gently to expose my neck. Kissing a light trail from my ear to the swell of my breasts, he makes my skin break out in goose-bumps. My pulse spikes as he retraces his path, making his way toward my lips. I squeeze my thighs together a little to try and tamp down the molten heat running through me.

Claiming my lips in a kiss that's anything but sweet, Drew makes me feel alive. It's like I can feel every nerve ending in my body and they're all on fire. I try to take strength from his hold on me, lest I end up in a sticky puddle at his feet.

***

I didn't intend to end up in bed—at least not before the evening was through—but Drew had other ideas and I couldn't protest even if I wanted to, which I *really* didn't. After amazingly hot sex, we came back downstairs to snuggle on the couch. With one arm draped round me, Drew traces lazy circles on my arm. I'm trying to stop the thoughts racing through my mind, but it's time to tell him what's been bothering me. I'm afraid to start the conversation, but if I don't muster the courage now, I'm afraid I never will. I don't want to burst the bubble we're in; what if he ends up hating me?

"Drew, there's something I want to talk to you about," I start as I reach for the remote and turn off the TV.

Turning to look at me, Drew takes my hand in his.

"What's wrong?" he asks as he strokes circles on the back on my hand with his thumb.

"Nothing is wrong, exactly. There's just something I should tell you about the past, about us. Do you remember when I left? Well, *left* is putting it nicely. I know that in reality, I just stopped messaging or calling you or answering the phone until it seemed you got the message."

"I remember," he says softly.

His gaze locks onto mine and suddenly my throat feels as dry as the Sahara. I reach for my glass of wine with my free hand and take a large gulp.

"Well, I've realised that like when Jensen left me, I gave you no reason or rhyme. I never gave you closure."

"We don't have to talk about this, Elise. Really."

"I want you to know why. I should have told you back then, but I was only looking out for myself. I don't mean that to sound so selfish, but I guess that's what I was. In fact there's no guessing about it, I *was* selfish. Leaving you was an act of self-preservation. I want you to know I am truly sorry for what I did and how I did it but it was only partly a conscious choice."

I reach for my wine and knock back what little remains in the glass, steeling myself for what I'm about to tell him.

"I wasn't in a good place in my life. I mean, a truly *shitty* place. I… This is going to sound contrary but I was falling in love with you and I couldn't allow that to happen. If I had stayed, it would have meant opening up and telling you more about me. The longer you're in a relationship, the more you learn about a person, right?! And I didn't want you to learn more than you already knew. The thing is, because we were 'no strings'," I air quote the words for good measure, "I could control how much you knew about me. About the person I was; what I had endured. But if I fell in love with you, if I laid my soul bare, you would have had to know my inner most demons. There are things you didn't know about me then and don't know about me now. But back then, I couldn't tell you any of those things. It felt as though I would be slitting my own jugular and bleeding out on purpose."

Drew holds my gaze and I see a shadow of sadness flicker across his features. Releasing his hand, I stand and retrieve the cherry brandy I keep in the cupboard for special occasions or when I need to steady my nerves. I pour myself a small amount and knock it straight back. It burns a little, but I like the taste all the same. Pouring two more glasses, one for each of us, I return to the lounge. Drew hasn't moved an inch.

Sitting back down, I hand him a glass. He takes my freehand in his again, showing me strength where my own is failing.

"Elise, are you sure you want this conversation?" he asks quietly.

"I need to get it off my chest, Drew and you need to know more about the woman you are with before you get too involved. If you want to back away after hearing this, then at least it won't hurt as much as if we'd been seeing each other for years or something. I mean…that didn't come out exactly right. Sorry, it's nerves. What I meant to say is…it would hurt like hell if you left me, but what we'd feel if you left now wouldn't leave as deep a scar as if we'd been together longer. You'll be able to move on quicker than if we were more deeply involved. Shit! I'm waffling like an idiot. I should get to the point. I'm sorry."

I sip my brandy and place it on the table beside the couch. I wipe my palm on my trousers, my hands feel clammy and my anxiety level is rising.

Drew traces lazy circles on the back of my hand. I can't tell if it's for his comfort, mine or both. I'll take it though. He may just run a mile when he finds out I have more than skeletons in my closet. The creatures in my closet have flesh, bones and very jagged teeth.

"I was abused, Drew," I blurt.

A look of shock registers in his eyes but he doesn't recoil from me.

"In more ways than one, and by more than one person. I was abused by one man I should have been able to trust more than anyone in this world; my stepdad. He repeatedly sexually abused me for a period of twelve years, even after he and my mum split. She used to send me and my sister to stay with him and he carried on the abuse then. That was until I was seventeen. I had to keep my mouth shut about it because he swore he'd hurt me if I told anyone. I was scared of him, Drew, so very scared. Growing up with him as the father figure in my life, I was conditioned to believe all the crap he spouted. As a naïve child, you believe what your parents say; they'd surely never lie to you?!

But as I got older and I saw less of him, it made me see things more clearly. I was seventeen the day I went to the police and reported him. I sat there with Peter at my side and I told the police every sordid detail. I won't burden you with the intimate details, but you should know it was never penetrative sex. He stopped short of that. To this day, I don't know why and I don't care. What he did was bad enough. I'm merely glad I didn't suffer a worse fate than I did.

My mum didn't believe me. That's why the only family I had were my grandmother, who has since sadly passed away, and an aunt who lives too far away to see regularly. No, instead of taking the word of her daughter, her flesh and blood, she believed that…that *bastard*. So I guess it isn't always true what they say about blood being thicker than water.

What happened never went to court. That was because of my 'mum'," I air quote the term because that's not what she is to me, " told the police she believed him not me and in the end, a police woman came to my house—well, Peter's house—and told me that the CPS didn't have enough to even *try* to prosecute. She told me that if Emily—I hate calling her mum because she isn't one—had been on my side or at least been on the fence about what had taken place, then it would have at least gone to court, but, because she believed him, I had no case. I didn't have a leg to stand on, Drew. I didn't get my day in court to tell them what a sick bastard he really was," my voice breaks and the tears that I've been holding in come rushing forth with as much force as a river breaking a dam.

Drew's arms come around me and he holds me close to him as I shudder and shake with every tear that falls, every breath I take. When I think of what that monster did to me, I mean *really* think about it in detail, I wonder why I wasn't committed to a psychiatric hospital years ago. I suffered from depression and I didn't put it down to being as a result of what he did, but now when I consider it all, I know the two are connected. I don't know how I didn't have a breakdown all those years ago.

Seconds feel like minutes, minutes feel like hours and I don't know how long ago the tears dried. I'm lying with my head on Drew's chest, his arms wrapped around me and we're snuggled into one corner of the couch. His slender legs stretch out next to mine and his warmth gives me comfort.

"That wasn't all, Drew," I say quietly into the silence that was, until this moment, a sort of comfortable one.

"Elise, baby, that's enough for tonight."

A hand strokes my hair, soothing me gently, but I muster the courage to sit up and spit the rest out.

"No, Drew. I need to tell you all of it now and then never speak of it again."

"If you're sure?"

I'm not sure. I don't think I ever could be. But I know I need to do this. I need to finish what I started.

"The rest isn't as bad as that. I mean, it was bad enough, but it's nothing compared to what *he* did to me. No, Peter left scars like the one I have on my calf. The one I told you I got riding a bike. His torture was another kind."

"Elise…"

I cut him off because I can't afford for him to dissuade me.

"Peter spent three and a half years beating the shit out of me. His abuse was both physical and mental. He was a master manipulator. Actually, I take that back because he'd probably like that title. He was a cunt. I hate that word, but it describes the man I despise.

I was seventeen when we met. Peter was a bouncer at a pub where I was a regular. He thought I was eighteen, obviously, otherwise I wouldn't have been able to get into the pub. Anyway, we went back to his the night we met and I didn't really leave the house until four and a half years later. I fell in love with him, or what I thought was love. He simply asked me to stay for a couple of weeks and it ended up being years. For the first year, he was a real gentleman. Little did I know, he was the devil in disguise.

I don't remember how long we'd been together exactly when he hit me the first time, but I do remember what happened. He held me up against the wall by my throat. I don't know what I did to deserve it, but he held my neck in both hands and squeezed until I couldn't breathe. Suddenly, he let me go and I gasped for air. I tried to walk out of the room, but as I got level with the bed, he grabbed me again and this time he squeezed my throat as he forced me onto the mattress. He loomed above me and I just floundered. I had no strength, barely any air…But somehow, I managed to pull my knees up to my chest, planted my feet on his chest and kicked him backwards with just enough force to make him crash into the computer table at the foot of the bed. As he struggled to stand, I reached for my phone and dialled 999.

When the woman on the phone asked me which service I required, I managed to recover enough breath to speak in broken sentences. I told her I needed the police and then told someone else what had happened.

I'd been strangled by my boyfriend and I was petrified of him."

Drew's hand reaches out and wraps around mine. He squeezes gently as I take a breath before continuing.

"Peter sat at the top of the stairs, sobbing, begging me to forgive him. I was stupid enough to give in when he said he was sorry and it would never happen again. But the first time wasn't the last.

I was too scared to stay with him, but too scared to go. Many times I left him and every single time he managed to convince me to come home. Sam was there for me throughout it all. I went to stay with her sometimes for a night, sometimes for a week. And once, I even managed a whole month. But eventually, he coerced me back. Don't ask how because I truly don't know. I was weak and he exploited that fact. I even overdosed one day in the hope of getting away from him. But Sam was too intuitive and called an ambulance that got to me in time. I don't remember whether they pumped my stomach or gave me charcoal or what. I was too out of it. I just remember my uncle collecting me from the hospital and delivering me to the door of my other abuser, my step-monster, Clive.

Anyway, yeah, I really shouldn't have taken an overdose, I know that now. But at the time, I thought it was my only escape. I still went back to him afterwards though. I still put up with another couple of years of being a fucking doormat. A sponge for his abuse. He was trained in ju-jitsu; a black belt, and he was clever enough never to leave a mark where it could be seen.

I never told anyone what he did until I met Dave. See, Peter wouldn't let me work because he thought I'd cheat. I was his trophy girlfriend for him to show off, but I wasn't to leave the house on my own. Then one day, when he said he could trust me, I started working for Dave. Long story short, I cheated on Peter with Dave for just over a year. I woke up one morning in bed next to Peter and began to cry. He asked what was wrong and I told him I was having an affair. The blows I expected never came, instead, he told me to pack and leave, so I did. I moved in with Dave in the block next door to you.

Looking back, I can't regret having an affair because I was sick of being his punch bag and Dave showed me love where Peter showed me nothing but pain. I'm not a cheat, I swear I'd never do it again. I've done a lot of growing up since that time in my life and I promise you that's not the woman I am anymore.

When I met you, Dave and I had split, he was going back to his wife and kids, even after two years with me. I was hurting inexplicably. I felt like I'd gone from one crappy situation to another and I built walls around my heart. I told myself if I started to think that I was feeling something for you, I would leave. So when you began to burrow through those walls, when your kindness, openness and caring nature began to wear down my defences, I knew I had to leave."

"Oh Elise, baby, come here."

Drew wraps me in his warm embrace and I sink into him.

"You were scared of falling in love with me because of what love had done to you before. I get that, and you don't need to say any more. I'm sorry, I am so very fucking sorry that you suffered at the hands of those bastards, that you felt an overdose was your only way out of a crappy situation. I'm sorry that I didn't know all this at the time because if I had, I would have shown you what the love of a real man was like. I fell in love with you back then and I wish like crazy that I could go back in time and absorb all of your pain, to take it all away from you."

"That was something I needed to do for myself, Drew. I needed to figure out how to love myself and how to become the woman I am now."

"Well, I loved the woman you were then and I love the woman you are now. I'm not letting you get away again."

He kisses me softly. It's not a passionate kiss, but it sets my heart alight all the same. It's soft, tender and all too brief for my liking.

Pulling me to my feet, he walks towards the stairs. He guides me up them, opens the door to my room and pulls the duvet covers back. Undressing to his boxers, he sits on the bed and pats the space next to him.

I sit down next to him and he moves us so that we're lying side by side. He pulls the duvet back up, covering us both, then turns to hold me in his arms.

My eyes feel heavy and it isn't long before Drew's deep, steady breathing lulls me into a slumber.

Chapter Sixteen
Drew

Elise is tucked safely in my arms, sound asleep. But me? I'm lying here with a tumultuous roller coaster twisting and turning in my mind. I don't know how I managed to stay so calm when she told me what happened to her. I could feel my blood boiling in my veins. I wanted to lash out, to get in my car and hunt down the bastards that hurt her. Making them pay would have been small retribution after what she's been through. But beating them to a bloody pulp wouldn't help Elise and would only land me in trouble, arrested for assault. She needed me calm, so that's what I gave her.

My mind is racing with so many thoughts, things I can't begin to put words to. I can't imagine the torture Elise suffered at the hands of two men she thought she could trust.

I had always wondered why she left me, but I never imagined it was anything like this. When she said she had been in a really crappy situation at the time that was the understatement of the century. I remember everything about when we were together—well, friends with benefits—and looking back on it, I think about how she acted and how I simply put it down to being in a bit of a shitty situation because of Dave. I never knew anything about Peter and I certainly never knew anything about Clive. I feel bad for not knowing more back then, but what's done is done and I can't hold it against her that she left me just as I was falling in love with her. At the time, I was heartbroken. She just stopped all contact with me. One of her last messages said she was in a relationship with some guy called Vinnie and I should just move on. Now I'm wondering if Vinnie really existed or if she just said that so that I would move on and not pursue her.

I would have gone to the ends of the earth for her. I was considering not going travelling because I'd finally found a woman I wanted to put down roots with. But Elise put a stop to all that and I had to piece my heart back together after she'd gone.

Now I think back to that heartache and what she told me eases one pain in my chest; the one that was caused by her leaving. However, her words tonight have sliced my heart open in a completely different way. I didn't realise how damaged she was. If I had known, I would have tried my hardest to keep her safe.

Now that I do know, I fully intend to show her what a real man is like. She thought Jensen was meant to be her one true love, but he turned out to be a dick once she became disabled. So now I want to show her what true love feels like. Real love is unconditional. It's pure and feels like the best thing in the world. It sets your soul on fire and you feel free; not caged like a bird, trapped with that person for all the wrong reasons. You don't judge, you don't criticise; you simply love someone regardless of their faults and foibles. You don't love them in *spite* of things they say or do, you love them *because* of those things.

I need Elise to know that she is safe with me, that I'll protect her from harm. I won't stand in the way of her independence, but I'll be there whenever and wherever she needs me to be.

Gently slipping my arm from around Elise, I get out of bed and walk to the kitchen to pour myself a glass of water. My emotions are up and down; everything I thought I knew is upside down and inside out.

Sitting in the kitchen, I leave the light off and just sit looking out of the window, staring at the moon.

I can see why Elise needed to get things off her chest; she felt the need to give me closure on the past, but in the process she has reopened old wounds of her own and poured a whole ocean worth of salt into them. Every gut-wrenching word that came from her mouth is emblazoned on my memory. I had to hold my own feelings in so as not to spook her. If I'd lashed out and smashed something the way I wanted to, it would have been the exact opposite of what she needed from me.

Tonight explains why she hasn't had anything to do with her mum, Emily, or her younger sister, Siobhan, in years. I can't believe her own mother didn't believe her. Elise was her flesh and blood. This woman gave birth to her and yet she cared more about a man who she wasn't even married to anymore. To stick by your ex-husband is one thing, but when you're talking about something like this; when your daughter tells you he sexually abused her for years, you have to be some kind of sicko not to believe her. The woman is obviously self-absorbed, vacuous, spiteful and a complete sociopath. Who doesn't feel some kind of love for her own child? She accused Elise of lying; but what did she have to gain by making things up? She didn't *gain* anything, she lost *everything*. Her grandmother, Lily, and Aunt Becky were the only two people to take her side. When she was alive, Lily and Elise had a really close bond. She was more of a mother to her than Emily ever was, but Lily passed away a while back and Becky lives hundreds of miles away, so Elise pretty much had to deal with things alone after Lily died..

How on earth is Elise the woman she is today? The only person she's been able to rely on one hundred percent since the death of her wonderful grandmother is herself. She has shown an amazing amount of strength to have overcome something so awful. Then add the beatings from Peter on top of all that, she's really been through the wringer.

Yet through all the bad came something good. Caleb. He brought light into her life where before there was darkness. He gave her a reason to keep going, every single day. She suffered post-natal depression after he was born, but it didn't affect the bond between her and Caleb. Instead it affected her relationship with Jensen. She was put on anti-depressants to cope, and she got through it. She told me all that one night a few months back. I thought that was bad enough. Little did I know she was going to tell me all this tonight.

I am in awe of the amazing woman I have come to know and love. She's been down, hit rock bottom and realised the only way from there was up. She's overcome so much shit and I am so proud of her.

Walking back into the bedroom, I see her in the same position as when I left. Quietly, I cross the room and sit gently on the bed. Her luscious red hair fans out around her and she looks so peaceful. I brush a stray strand of hair back from her face and gently stroke the back of my hand across her cheek.

Did she think that what she told me would scare me off? Make me walk away from her? Whatever she thought, she was damn wrong. I plan to be here every single day, showing her with my actions as well as my words that I'm not going anywhere. When I told her I loved her, my love didn't come with conditions, with strings attached. It came from deep within my heart. Whether I expected to fall in love or not, it happened and this beautiful, amazing woman has carved out a place in my soul.

When Sam set me up on a blind date, I was totally blindsided by the fact that it was Elise. I wasn't sure where I wanted things to go. I hadn't gone on the date expecting to fall in love. The two of us have a history and I wasn't sure whether that was a good thing or bad. All I know now is that this strong, intelligent, stunningly attractive, fiercely independent woman came back into my life for a reason. She's like a breath of fresh air. I didn't know then that she would turn my world on its axis.

I didn't believe in fate, destiny, whatever you want to call it. But now I'm changing my mind. If anything was 'destined' to be, it was Elise and me. That much, I'm sure of.

Slipping gently back under the covers, I rest my arm over her stomach. My mind is still racing, but she needs me to be strong, not an emotional mess. I know she doesn't need me to fight her battles for her. And she seems to have put these demons to rest. So unless she brings it up again, I don't want to force her to talk about it. I don't need to know more about what happened, what she told me was bad enough. If she wants to talk some more, I'm here. But I have a feeling she won't want to go into too much detail. She's the kind of person to internalise things and not want to burden others. But Elise could never be a burden to me and, one day, I'll make sure she sees that. I want to show her every day how much she means to me and, though she doesn't need a protector, I will be hers anyway. She doesn't have to like it; she doesn't even need to know that's my plan. But any other kind of crap that comes her way, I'll shield her from it as best as I can. Life won't be easy, but nothing worthwhile ever is.

I used to think I wanted a simple, uncomplicated life. Now more than ever, I realise that life is inexplicably complicated. That's just the way shit is. You do your best for those you love. You risk your heart in the hands of others. Sometimes, they'll take care of it. Other times, they'll eviscerate you, but there will always be someone to help pick up the pieces. Love comes in many forms and it will always come along when you least expect it. That's what happened with me and Elise and I wouldn't change a single second of it.

Easing myself closer to her sleeping form, I close my eyes. They're heavy from lack of sleep and my mind is tired from the roller coaster of an emotional night. I wait for sleep to consume me so that I can switch my mind off for a few hours.

***

Waking with Elise still in my arms, I look at her peaceful face and smile. What makes her so beautiful is that she doesn't even know it. She begins to stir and I wait until her eyes open properly before leaning in to pace a chaste kiss on her lips.

A smile graces her beautiful face as she turns in my arms to face me. She buries her head in the crook of my neck and I inhale her sweet scent. Her arms tighten around me and I pull her flush to my chest.

She lifts her head to look at me and I get lost in the baby blues I've come to learn to just surrender myself to.

"Morning," she whispers.

"Morning, beautiful."

Before I fully think through what I'm doing, my lips claim hers. She opens her mouth to me and our tongues dance together in perfect harmony.

Pulling back slightly, a blush creeps across her skin and there's a hint of bashfulness in her gaze.

"Sorry, morning breath. Let me go and brush my teeth," she says, sounding embarrassed.

"No need," I say before I lean in to kiss her again.

At first she giggles and tries to pull away, but my grasp on her is firm and she quickly realises she's fighting a losing battle. She gives in easily and I place my mouth over hers. I slide my hand underneath the t-shirt she went to bed in. When I notice she isn't pushing me away, I reach up further and unclasp her bra. I don't want to take advantage if she's feeling fragile this morning but she doesn't seem to have any objection to my hands roaming over her.

Sliding her bra down her arms a little to give myself room, I cup her breast in my hand. I begin to kiss a trail downwards but stop at the swell of her sumptuous cleavage. Rolling her nipple between my forefinger and thumb, I squeeze gently, just the way she likes. Her back arches, pushing her breasts closer to me.

Her leg comes up over mine and her hand slides across my bare back. I slept in just my boxer shorts and now I'm glad of that fact. Her nails dig into my skin and I moan as she drags them from the top of my spine to the bottom.

The ringing of her phone breaks the spell she was casting on me and I reach over for it on the bedside table. She smiles as I hand it to her and she sees Caleb's face on the screen. Answering the phone, she sounds a little breathless and I like that I did that to her.

"Morning, handsome."

I hear him giggle on the other end of the phone.

"Morning, mum. I was just wondering something. Auntie Sam and Uncle Karl are taking Josh to Jump Nation and they wanted to know if I could come."

"Of course you can, buddy. Can you just put Sam on the phone for a sec please?"

"Sure."

"Hey, Elise, sorry if we woke you," Sam says as she comes on the line.

"Nah, I'm up. I was about to take a shower. What time are you guys going?"

"Any minute now, babe."

"And what time are you coming back?"

"I was thinking of giving the boys a good couple of hours to play around. Did you need him back sooner?"

"No, that's fine. I was just wondering, that's all."

"Okay, well I'll call you when we're on the way back, if that's alright?"

"Sure thing. Can I say bye to Caleb?"

"Of course, hang on."

Caleb comes back on the line, giggling.

"Thanks mum. I love you."

"Love you too, buddy. Have a good day, and be on your best behaviour."

"You know it, mum. See you later. Love you."

He blows Elise a kiss down the line and she returns the gesture.

Hanging up, she smiles and stretches over to replace her phone. My hopes of picking up where we left off are dashed as she gets out of bed. My eyes roam her body as she strips naked. When she bends to remove her trousers, I can't help that my eyes are drawn to her pert ass. She's absolutely perfect. I know she thinks she's put on weight since her operations and yes, she has a fuller figure than back in 2005, but that doesn't make her any less gorgeous. She isn't overweight as she claims; she's curvy and an absolute delight to look at. And to touch. I love nothing more than grasping her hips as she slides up and down on me. Or reaching up and cupping her full breasts. She's no supermodel, figure-wise, but I'd be disappointed if she was. They are far too skinny for my liking. She's far more enticing the way she is.

Walking around the bed, she grabs fresh clothing and a towel. She goes toward the bathroom and I am left with a semi hard-on to get rid of as she disappears from sight.

Chapter Seventeen
Elise

It's been a couple of weeks since I opened up to Drew. I expected him to walk round on eggshells; treat me differently, like I'm some fragile little thing. I couldn't have been more wrong. He's treated me exactly the same as he always has. He hasn't been scared to touch me or make love to me like I presumed he might be. He's been back at work for a few days, but he's made time to see me and Caleb when he hasn't been on shift.

The bond between Caleb and Drew has grown, as has the bond between the two of us. He's so good to me. I can't believe my luck in love has finally changed for the better. It makes me wonder if what I had with anyone else was even love. If this is what it actually feels like, then I can say with surety that nothing I've ever experienced has come close. What I had with Jensen was as close as I ever got to this before. When we were happy, we really were good together. I thought we were forever, but now I'm glad we weren't.

It feels like some people are only meant to be in your life for a short amount of time; be it weeks, months or years. Then they leave your life and you're free to move on to where you were really meant to be. I think if I'd ever made one decision even slightly differently, it would have affected the outcome of my life, and if being with Drew is the outcome of it all, then all the pain and heartache was worth it. I've been through so much in my life; many highs and way too many lows to count. But now, life is on the up. It can only get better once you've had a taste of rock bottom.

Drew's birthday is coming up and I want to do something to show him how much he means to me. I decide to use my knowledge of event planning to throw him a party, but I need access to his contacts on his phone so as to invite people. How on earth am I going to manage that without him noticing?

This morning he's not at work and wants us to spend some time together, so party planning will have to wait for a little while.

There's a knock at the door and I open it to see the handsome, smiling face of my man. My heart swells in my chest as he beams a mega-watt grin at me. Just the sight of him is enough to make me weak at the knees. He kisses me gently on the cheek as he passes me by. Taking my hand, he pulls me inside and closes the front door behind us. Pushing me up against the back of the door, he places a hand on either side of me, trapping me in place. He doesn't realise that he has no need to do anything to keep me where I am, I'm exactly where I want to be.

As he claims my lips in a tender, loving kiss, Drew wraps his arms around me and holds me close. I wrap my arms around his neck and feel as though I'm completely at his mercy. He could do anything he wants, right here, right now and I wouldn't put up a fight. How did I get lucky enough to find someone that it feels this right with?

"Hi," he says softly as he pulls back from the kiss.

"Hi," I reply a little breathlessly.

"I did have plans for this morning, but they seem to have gone out of the window with that kiss."

"What did you have in mind?"

"It's not a surprise if I tell you."

Pulling me into the lounge, he sits down and pulls me into his lap. Wrapping his arms around me, he nuzzles into the crook of my neck and I sigh in complete contentment. He might have plans for us for the day, but I couldn't think of anything I'd rather do than what we're already doing. I wonder if I can entice him to spend the day in bed with me instead.

***

We get back from the picnic Drew arranged for breakfast, and although that appetite is sated, the one he awoke in me when he arrived this morning is yet to be quelled. We only have a couple of hours before he goes to work, but I intend to make the most of them.

Taking his hand in mine, I lead him upstairs. I turn back to look at him and see a complete shit-eating grin light up his face. His eyes are alight with mirth and my tummy does somersaults at the thought of what comes next.

Walking into my room, I draw the curtains closed. I turn on my iPod where it stands in the dock and quiet music begins to fill the silence in the air. I push Drew to a sitting position at the end of the bed before beginning to slowly strip for him in time to the music. His eyes watch my every movement like a hawk stalking its prey. I move with purpose and the butterflies in my tummy take flight when he reaches out and traces his hands over my curves. I offer him my hand and gently pull him to his feet. Now that I'm naked, I'm at a disadvantage considering how much clothing he's still wearing. I make light work of pulling his t-shirt off over his head and then reach for his belt. As I unbuckle it and begin to undo his jeans, his hands roam purposefully over my body. He traces my hips before reaching up to cup my breasts. Leaning down slightly, he takes my nipple into his warm mouth. My back arches as he bites down lightly.

His jeans pool around his ankles and he steps out of them. Kicking them aside, he stands before me in just his boxer shorts. There's only one item of clothing left between his body and mine now and I reach my hand down to cup his impressive length. He moans as I grip him more firmly, so I stroke him up and down a couple of times, giving him something to look forward to, but stalling for time. I don't want this to all be over before it's even begun. I remove his boxers, leaving him naked and glorious with pre-cum glistening on the head of his hard cock, begging me to lick it off.

Pushing him back down to the bed, I move to straddle him. His hands reach for my hips again and he pulls me closer to where I want to be. Leaning down, I press my mouth over his and lose myself in a lust-filled haze as his tongue dances with mine. Reaching one hand up, he uses it to pull my hair back and expose my neck to him. Tracing feather-light kisses down my throat, Drew ignites a warmth in me. My body feels hypersensitive to his touch. Grabbing my ass with the other hand, he guides me so that his cock is aligned with my already wet entrance. Thrusting himself inside me in one swift movement causes me to moan long and loud. Thank goodness nobody else is home. I don't know whether the neighbours heard, but right now, I don't care.

Moving inside me, Drew hits the spot with every thrust, making me wetter and eliciting moans from within me. His hand shifts from my hair, tracing down the side of my breast, but just when I think he's about to knead my flesh with those deft fingers, he carries on moving down to my hip. My disappointment doesn't last long when I realise where that hand is heading. He rubs my clit with his thumb as he rocks me back and forth on him. My hands are placed flat on his chest, my nails digging into his pecs as I grind myself against him. Tension starts to build within me and I know I won't be able to hold on much longer.

Drew moves his head up so he can suck on my sensitive left nipple. As he sucks and nips at it, I arch my back and dig my nails deep enough to leave marks, branding him as mine just as he brands me as his.

We find a rhythm that sends us both into hyperspace as we both fall apart. I ride the aftershocks as I lean down and kiss him passionately. This man will be the ruin of me. There will never be another like him. Drew is everything I never knew I wanted.

I don't know whether it was his intention from the start, but Drew has made me realise that there will never be anyone else that fits me as perfectly as he does. He's shown me that no other could ever give me what he does. He doesn't just give me love; he gives me safety, protection, a sense of security. Add in the happiness that I feel whenever I'm with him and the sense of peace that washes over me whenever I think of him. Plus there are all the feelings that go along with the love he gives Caleb. It's not just me that's happy; it's not just me he loves. Caleb and Drew are getting closer every day and it warms my heart to know that Drew doesn't see a disabled single mum and her kid. No, he sees Elise, the woman behind her disabilities and Caleb, a wonderful young boy that is starting to look to him like a father figure.

Drew has shown me that home is not a physical place that you live, it's a feeling you get whenever you are with the other half of you. Home is something I have whenever I am with him and Caleb.

I never meant to fall this far, but you can't *plan* love. It's something organic; something that blossoms and thrives in places where you least expect to find it.

***

After a couple of hours in bed, exploring each other's bodies with hands, mouths and other parts of the anatomy, Drew had to go to work. We stayed in bed a little too long, thanks to an insatiable appetite for each other and he ended up running late.

I'm tidying up when I stumble across Drew's phone. He must have forgotten it in the rush to get out of the door. I see it as just the opportunity I need and I sit down with a notepad and pen, a cup of coffee in one hand and the phone in the other. I dial the first number on my list and start making a guest list for the party.

Everyone I call agrees to keep the secret and I sigh happily to myself as I end the last call. Everything is coming together and I hope to give Drew a thirty-fifth birthday party to remember. I dread having to up my own game when it comes to his fortieth.

Chapter Eighteen
Drew

I'm at work but all I can think about is being back with Elise. She's fast becoming the only thing I think about morning, noon and night. When I'm with her, I'm happier than I've been in a very long time. When I'm not with her, she's constantly on my mind. She's brought me out of myself, back to a world filled with love, happiness and a zest for life that was lacking just a few months ago.

I'll be the first to admit that I used to use travelling as a coping mechanism. I didn't want to tie myself down to any one person, only to get attached and then have my heart blown to smithereens. So it was easier to put distance between myself and that type of situation. Going to different countries, experiencing their cultures, seeing the sights I saw, that was a lot of fun. In fact, it was amazing. But I never knew what I was missing. There's more to life than I first thought and sometimes it's worth putting your heart on the line.

Elise and I are so similar in that regard. Neither one of us could withstand the pain that came with putting yourself out there. There are people in this world that will hurt you and others that will heal a broken heart. I don't think either of us knew it at the time, but the more I think about it now, the more apparent it becomes. We were meant to find each other again. We were supposed to help each other heal. And that's exactly what we're doing. The more time we spend together, the more our old wounds heal. The scars of our pasts are something we'll always have to live with, but I know that together, we can overcome anything.

A call comes through from dispatch and that brings me back to reality. Danny is back at work and is back on the ambulance with me. He's still seeing Ashleigh, the girl he met in Iceland. Seems he wants the holiday romance to last; something I didn't think he'd do considering how much of a ladies' man he is.

We're called out to a local address and are greeted by a woman in distress. Her husband is in the lounge and as we walk through, I see classic signs of a heart attack. We get to work quickly. Danny and I are a strong team and we are like a well-oiled machine.

Getting Clive into the back of the ambulance, we allow his wife Jenny to ride with us as we make our way back to the hospital, sirens blasting and lights flashing.

It doesn't take long before we get to hospital and hand Clive over to the doctors for treatment. Danny and I make our way to clean down the rig ready for our next call out.

Sam catches my attention on my way out of the door and Danny goes on ahead to start the cleaning.

"Hey Drew, that guy you just brought in, what's his name? He looks like somebody I know."

"His name is Clive Andrew Swanson. Poor guy suffered a heart attack and we got to him just in time."

Her face falls and I can't help but wonder if she knows him and how. I reach a hand out to her arm and she flinches at my touch. She looks up at me, unshed tears glistening in her eyes.

"Hey, what's up? Who is he? Are you okay?"

She doesn't answer right away and I begin to worry that he's family or a friend. We got to him in time though, and he's being treated right now, so with a bit of luck, he'll recover well in time.

"He's nothing to me," Sam whispers.

"Then what is it? Do you want to go grab a drink and chat? It looks like you've seen a ghost."

If she doesn't know him, then he must have reminded her of someone and it's shaken her up. I start to walk to the coffee shop and Sam follows. I grab two steaming mugs of coffee and sit at the table opposite Sam. I pour extra sugar in hers because it really looks like she's in shock. I know they say sweet tea for shock, but I know she hates tea.

"You really don't know who he is?" I ask as I stir one sugar into my mug.

"Oh, I know who he is. More to the point I know *what* he is and I wish to God you hadn't saved the fucker."

"Woah, Sam, language. Who is he? Or what is he?"

I reach for her hand across the table and she grips it tightly as the next words fall from her lips.

"He's the monster nobody wants to find hiding under their bed, or should I say *in* their bed."

I'm not getting what it is she's saying and I reach for my phone to call Elise.

"Don't!" Sam warns as she sees me reach for my pocket.

"Don't what, Sam?"

"Don't ring her. She won't thank you for it."

I'm completely confounded. What does Elise have to thank or not thank me for?

"Sam, sweetie, you're not making any sense."

I try to move my hand but she still has a firm grip on it.

"Drew, put two and two together. I know she told you about him. She rang me and told me she'd told you everything."

"Holy fuck...no, do not tell me that he is *that* monster," I say as a tear falls down her cheek.

"One and the same. Clive Swanson, step-monster from the seventh circle of hell."

"Fuck!" I exclaim, pushing back from the table and breaking Sam's hold on my hand.

I stand and pace, running my fingers through my hair. It was *him*. I *saved* him. What the hell? I feel like running back in there, grabbing the sharpest implement in the room and driving it into where his heart should be, if he had one.

"I'm sorry, Drew. I shouldn't have told you. I just... I lashed out because of my own anger at the bastard, but I shouldn't have dragged you into it. I'm so sorry."

"It's fine Sam. I'm sorry, but I have to go."

I all but run away from Sam and the monster I saved from certain death. If only we'd been a minute or two later, he would have died. I might not be a killer, I might not wish people dead, but I don't know whether I would have been able to save him if I knew who he was *before* I laid my hands on him.

Danny sees the look of thunder on my face and tries to calm me down, but I can't slow my racing heart. I feel like I can't breathe. My palms are sweaty and my nerves are frayed. I want to lash out but the only thing in reach is Danny and, even though my mind is racing, I know I won't lay hands on my best friend. Instead I walk outside into the cool evening air. I punch the brick wall and expel a long deep breath.

My hand is bleeding from hitting the brickwork so hard. Maybe it didn't do anyone any good for me to lose my cool, but now that I've got that out of my system, I can finally breathe. I can try to restore some order to the chaos.

With a first-aid kit in hand, Danny comes over to where I'm sitting. He looks at my hand and shakes his head. He tuts at me and I see his jaw ticking under his skin. He wants to know what got me so worked up, but I can't tell him the truth. No, that's not my story to tell. I have no business telling anyone, even my best friend who I would trust with my life.

Cleaning my hand and wrapping it, Danny is silent. He's waiting for me to break the silence. I decide to tell him a partial truth. It's the best I can do under the circumstances.

"I ran into someone that I wish I hadn't laid eyes on. He's a vile excuse for a human being who hurt someone I love very dearly. It wound me up, I needed to lash out."

"Okay, buddy, okay. You got it out of your system, right? You don't need to go home early? I mean, I can cover for you if you do. Tell me what you want and I'll do it."

"I just want to work and forget he exists. It's out of my system for now. Let's just finish cleaning the rig and make small talk about anything except him."

"Anything you say, bud. You know you can talk to me though, yeah? I mean, you still look like you want to kick the shit out of someone."

"I do know and you're right, I still want to kick the shit out of the little prick. But it's not my story to tell and so I'd rather just get on with work."

For the rest of the evening, I allow myself to get wrapped up in work and out of my own head for a while.

***

It's been a long day and I'm truly beat. My hand's bloody sore, but punching exposed brickwork will do that to you. Danny didn't ask any more questions. That's one good thing about the guy; he knows when to push me for more information and when to just leave me to work out my own demons.

I unlock the door to my flat, throw my bag in the lounge and head straight for the shower. I grab a towel and some fresh sweatpants on the way through.

The shower is on maximum heat but all it does is scald my skin; it doesn't do anything for what's going on in my head. Having taken just about all I can of the heat, I step out and wrap a towel around myself. I wipe the steam from the mirror over the sink and brush my teeth. With just these mundane tasks, I don't have enough to take my mind off that bastard, especially when I have to re-wrap my hand and take a look at my knuckles, reminding me afresh of who I met and why I'm in such a foul mood.

Pulling on my sweatpants, I walk out to the lounge and feed the terrapins. I am so close to calling Elise, but I know if I do that, it will be really hard not to tell her about today's events. I don't want to hurt her unnecessarily and I know that the mere mention of his name would cause her pain. So instead I pull out my phone—which she'd dropped in at work for me, as I'd left it behind this morning—and send her a text:

Drew: Hey, baby. How's my girl? Miss you xxx

It's not long before I get a reply, almost like she was waiting for my message.

Elise: Hey, yourself, sexy. Miss you too. I'm good. Caleb just went to bed, so I'm watching mindless TV. What you up to?

Drew: Nothing much, just got off shift. We still on for our lunch date tomorrow?

Elise: Of course. Can't wait to see you. I know I saw you earlier today and maybe I'm just being sappy, but I've really missed your company.

Drew: Just my company? ;)

Elise: I'd tell you but then you'd get big-headed and wouldn't fit through the door ;)

Drew: I'd definitely get big-headed if you were here, but not the head you're talking about! :P

Why did I have to go and say that? Now it's got me thinking of the amazing head my girl gives. I've got a semi already, just imagining her hot, inviting mouth wrapped around me.

My phone rings in my hand and I see it's Elise via FaceTime. I answer and am greeted with the sight of her in a sexy black negligee.

"Fancy a midnight snack?" she asks in a tone so seductive that my cock springs to attention.
"Depends what's on the menu."
"Me."
"See you in about fifteen minutes. Love you."
I blow her a kiss and hang the phone up. Scrambling over the back of the couch, I rush to the bedroom to throw on some clean clothes, a little aftershave and my shoes before packing a couple of things in an overnight bag. So much for not seeing her, but I'm hoping that the only thing on our minds will be each other.

Making it to Elise's in record time, I'm not sure I didn't break the law and get myself a speeding ticket or two. I let myself in with the spare key she gave me when I got back from Iceland. The lights are off downstairs and as I get to the foot of the staircase, I see why. The only light on in the house is her bedroom. I take the stairs two at a time and gently push open her bedroom door so as not to make a noise and wake Caleb.

"Hey there, handsome," she says from where she is lying on the bed.
"Evening, beautiful."
Elise gets up and walks over to me. She wraps her arms around my neck and claims my lips with hers. I drop my bag and wrap my arms

around her waist. Her kiss gains fervour and I am only too eager to give her what she wants. Our tongues dance as my left hand glides from her waist to the hemline of her negligee. Sliding my hand gently upwards, I am rewarded with a moan reverberating through her chest. I pull her hair back and expose her neck, but instead of taking my time with her, I go straight for her sumptuous cleavage.

My left thumb finds her clit and she groans as her back arches into me. I move us back towards the bed and sit her on the edge. The stockings and suspenders she has on are such a turn on and I want to see her wearing only them, so I grip the hem of the sexy black satin covering her and remove it in one swift movement.

She is the epitome of beauty as she sits before me, her gorgeous red hair splayed across her full cleavage, her taut nipples, full curves and such elegant long legs covered in black stockings. The look in those stunning blue eyes tells me she's aroused and I can't wait any longer before tearing off my own clothing. Seeing her sitting there without any panties on, knowing I love it when she doesn't wear any, makes me feel like I'm going to spontaneously combust.

I'm naked and my cock is rock hard. Her eyes dart straight from my cock to my face and a blush spreads across her skin. Moving towards her, I kneel at her feet and part her legs. Seeing her soft, wet, pink pussy elicits a noise from me a little like a feral growl. I kneel up high enough to place a soft kiss on her lips before pulling her right nipple into my mouth and nipping it gently before repeating the motion on the left side, knowing it's the most sensitive. Her breathing is becoming more erratic and as I edge my thumb back to her clit, I feel that she's more than a little wet already.

Laying her back gently, I rest back on my haunches. I stroke her stocking clad legs and feel a shiver as it runs through my body. Elise has officially ruined me for life. There's no way I could want anyone else from now until I die. Not only do I love her more than I've ever allowed myself to love anyone, but she is also the best lover a man could ask for and thanks to that, as well as many other reasons, I will never let her go.

As I feast on Elise and push my fingers in and out of her, I feel like I'm high. There's something about sex with this woman that is as addictive as crack cocaine.

My cock is throbbing, aching to be inside her, but she's on the cusp of a huge orgasm and I want her to enjoy the thrill of that first, so I grip my cock in my left hand as my right is busily bringing her ever closer to the edge. I stroke myself a couple of times but it just isn't enough. It will never be enough.

I bring my left thumb to stroke her clit and feel her legs quivering where they lie over my shoulders. I spread her and dart my tongue in and out of her wetness. Inserting another finger, I up the pace and I feel her spiral out of control as her legs shake and she comes all over my fingers. I don't remove my fingers or my tongue until she's over the little aftershocks.

Standing between her legs, I edge her further up the bed and waste no time in thrusting into her. Her fingernails must leave visible marks in my back as she gets her own back on me for not taking my time. I couldn't care less though, even if the lads see my back torn to ribbons at work. Why? A sheer sense of belonging. I'm every bit as much Elise's man as she is my woman. I prove it to her as I make love to her for what feels like an eternity and yet no time at all, before we fall asleep tangled in each other's embrace.

Chapter Nineteen
Elise

It's the night of Drew's surprise party and I'm hoping like hell that he doesn't mind being made centre of attention for the evening. I've never organised a party before for someone I've dated. Jensen hated family get-togethers and Peter wasn't worth the effort, but Drew certainly is. I'm slightly anxious about how it will all turn out, but there's nothing I can do to change it now.

Drew, Caleb and I have been out for the day to celebrate his birthday. He said he fancied spending some quality time together, so that's exactly what we've been doing.

He's downstairs with Caleb, thinking we are going for a meal this evening. It's the only way I can think to get him out of the house without ruining the element of surprise. As I can't be in two places at once, Sam has very kindly offered to be at the venue to oversee things before we arrive. I wrote her a 'to-do' list which made her laugh. She thinks I'm very anal about things, but I have to be. It is a big part of my job and it eases my anxiety.

It was thinking about my anxiety that got me to step outside of my comfort zone and become an event organiser in the first place. Sam is partly to thank for it too. She told me that I needed to learn to cope with all manner of situations and what better to test my ability than this job? I'm just hoping she's done everything I asked her to for tonight. I couldn't think of a way to get rid of Drew, even for half an hour to check, not on his birthday. So it's completely in her hands and it's making my nerves jangle, so I take a few deep breaths as I finish styling my hair and add a touch of colour to my lips.

Tonight, I have opted for a blue dress. Drew says the colour really brings out my eyes, so I'm indulging him on his special night. It has a sweetheart neckline, draped with a kind of chiffon over the top that sweeps up into one strap, diagonally across my shoulder. The strap has small flower detail and is very girly, especially considering my normal tomboy ways. Trailing down the bodice, there are little beads and pearls which accentuate the neckline, down the sides of the bodice and they highlight the way the dress cuts in at my waistline before it flairs out a little more at the bottom. The dress stops at my knee and has a small slit up the one side. Drew hasn't seen it yet, I bought it on a shopping trip with Sam and have kept it in a dress bag so he didn't get to see it until tonight.

I look at my reflection in the mirror and, for a change, I am not repulsed by what I see. Somehow, I have started seeing myself more through Drew's eyes than my own. Before we got together, I felt overweight, ugly, and pathetic. I used to be more confident about my looks when I was younger; my grandmother used to say I was vain, but having had the two operations on my spine and being left with permanent nerve damage in my right leg and foot, I can't really exercise so I have to be careful what I eat in order to maintain a steady weight. Regardless of what I do, I am never actually happy about my appearance. Or I wasn't. Now, I am starting to get more confident because Drew shows me that he not only loves me, but he is very attracted to me. He says that every curve, every freckle, every inch of my skin is beautiful. When his eyes roam over my naked body, I don't cross my arms over my chest in embarrassment anymore. Instead I stand there, unashamed and bold in my confidence. I show him what he desires. Me.

I walk downstairs and head to the lounge where I can hear the boys playing on Caleb's game console. As I walk in, their heads turn and all I hear is "Wow," like it's in Dolby surround sound, because they both say it at the exact same time.

Drew's gaze roams over me from head to toe. The lustful look that takes over shows me just how much he appreciates the fact I am wearing a dress for once.

"You have never looked more beautiful than you do in this moment," he says as he walks around the couch.

Taking both my hands in his, he looks me up and down some more before spinning me around so he can check out my ass. His soft sigh confirms that he does indeed think my ass looks great.

"I love this colour on you. You look…words cannot describe it."

I feel a blush creep across my skin and a warmth settle in my heart at his words.

"You look amazing, mum," Caleb says as he turns off his game console.

He walks over to me and puts his arms around me. It feels so good to have both the people I love with all my heart looking at me as if I am special. To them, I am. I am incredibly lucky to have both of them in my life and it's hard to think what life was like without them in it.

"Thank you, baby. You scrub up well too. So does dad, don't you think," I say without thinking the last part through.

I look at Drew and see the twinkle in his eyes. Then I look at Caleb and see a mini version of the mega-watt grin I associate with Drew.

"Sorry, I…it…it just came out," I rush to explain the slip of my tongue.

"Don't be sorry. It might have bothered me if it was anyone else at this point in my life. But I honestly think of myself as his stepdad anyway. I mean, we're a family, right?! What do you think, Caleb?"

His hazel eyes land on Caleb and shock registers briefly in his gaze as Caleb throws his arms around him. Drew is quick to return the gesture and hugs Caleb tight.

"I think of you as a dad. So it didn't bother me what mum said," my handsome son says as he pulls away from Drew.

"You don't have to call me dad; you can still call me Drew. I understand if it seems too quick. How about we see how things go and you call me whatever you feel comfortable with, yeah?"

"Sounds good."

Caleb holds his hand up for a high-five and Drew slaps his palm against it.

I can't help but beam with pride. If this is what real happiness feels like then I hope to keep feeling it for the rest of my life.

***

We arrive at our destination and I pay the taxi driver, considering I wouldn't tell Drew where we were going and I wanted him to be able to have a drink tonight. I climb out of the car and, although I'd rather be able to walk without it, I grab my cane.

Walking through the double doors, Drew and Caleb are chatting about the game they were playing earlier. I try to stop my smile splitting my face wide open. I whip out my phone and send a quick text to Sam.

Elise: We're here. Everything ready?

The three little dots show she's typing a reply.

Sam: Good to go!

I take Drew's outstretched hand and we walk side by side into the hotel. I don't know whether Drew knows something is up. He doesn't ask why we're at a hotel and, considering they have a fantastic restaurant, I'm hoping he just thinks the three of us are here to eat.

When we walk straight by the restaurant doors, Drew gives me a quizzical side glance.

"There's just something I have to do first and then we can eat."

Walking into the large room that I hired for the party, we are met by darkness until Sam flicks the light switch and everybody shouts "Surprise."

The DJ begins to play music quietly in the background and people come up to say hi to Drew. He introduces Caleb and me to his friends as they wish him a happy birthday.

When everyone seems to drift off to the bar and back to their seats, Drew finally gets a chance to question me.

"So…" he begins, drawing out the word.

"I hope you don't mind," I say, cutting him off.

"Mind? This is fantastic. I was looking forward to an evening with just the three of us, sure. But we can do that any time. You obviously put a lot of thought and effort into tonight, so how could I mind?"

He wraps his arms around me and leans in to give me a soft kiss. It's all too brief, but I'm not giving his friends a show, so it'll have to do for now.

"Sam helped. She's had to be here to oversee some last details today like the caterer and DJ. I couldn't spend the day with you and be here too, so I had to call on the help of my bestie."

I take his hand and lead him to where Sam is sitting with Karl and Josh. She stands and wraps me in a hug. Then she hugs Drew before making way for him to shake hands with Karl.

"Thank you for tonight, Sammie," I say as I look at my best friend of over two decades.

"It's a pleasure. Anything for you. You look stunning, by the way. I told you that you'd totally rock this dress and I am pleased to say I told you so."

"Thanks doll, I feel a tad weird without a pair of jeans on, I must admit."

I laugh nervously and Sam gives me a funny look.

"You rock it, so please do not even go there with the 'I'm a jeans and t-shirt girl' spiel."

"Sorry."

"I'll go and get us some drinks," Drew says from behind me.

I turn round and watch his sexy ass as he walks towards the bar. He looks great in the suit he chose to wear. I told him to wear a blue tie; one I bought when I got my dress as it's the same shade. Caleb looks handsome in a crisp white shirt and black trousers. I might be biased, but my two boys are certainly two of the most handsome men I have ever encountered.

***

It's time for Drew to make a speech. His friends were all chanting "Speech, speech, speech" until he finally caved and took the microphone from the DJ.

"Hi folks," he says as he looks round the room, "I'm so happy you could all be here to spend tonight with me. My wonderful girlfriend Elise says that she's responsible for inviting you all and that you somehow managed to keep it secret. Yes, I'm looking at you, Daniel McMahon," he jokes as he points to his best friend. "I'd like to thank you all for being here. I don't think anyone has ever thrown a party for me except my parents when I was younger. I'd like to say the biggest thank you to Elise for organising such a great night. The cake was probably one of the highlights of the night. As for the baby pictures of me that you've put all round the room… yeah, thanks for that, mum. I know you were only too happy to allow my girl access to photos of me that aren't all the definition of normal. But what are birthdays for if not for embarrassing yourself, hey?! At least I haven't made a fool of myself tonight. So far."

Everybody cheers and I think they are hoping he'll end up drunk and doing something daft.

"I would like to ask my wonderful girlfriend for her hand in this next dance," he continues once the noise has died down.

I look at him and then at my cane. Sam comes up to my side and offers me her arm to lean on instead. She walks me to the centre of the dancefloor as the opening bars of *How Would You Feel* by Ed Sheeran begin to play.

Drew takes me in his arms and we begin to dance slowly in time to the lyrics as Drew sings them quietly in my ear. I feel them as so much more than lyrics of a song. They feel like they are words coming straight from Drew's heart.

As the song comes to an end, he asks me to stay on the dancefloor with him as another Ed Sheeran song begins, this time it's *Thinking Out Loud.* Tears fall from my eyes as he talks about legs not working like they used to and sweeping her off her feet. Drew wipes the tears with the pad of his thumb and wraps me in his arms.

When the last word leaves Ed's lips, Drew steps out of my embrace.

"He's right, we did find love right where we are. Neither of us went looking for it, but fate played her hand and threw us into each other's lives again for a reason. We've both had our fair share of broken hearts, of ups and downs, highs and lows. But together, we have found something that they say you are lucky to experience once in a lifetime. Elise, you are the love of my life. There could never be another. I love you because you are beautiful inside and out, and the best of it is that you don't even know how stunning you truly are. You have a heart as big as the world and a smile that lights up even the darkest of rooms."

Tears begin to fall down my face as he talks and my vision is so blurry I almost believe I imagine it as he gets down on one knee.

"I wanted to do this tonight, wherever we were. It was going to be the three of us, but we have a lifetime to spend together and I only get to ask this question once in my life. Here, in front of all my family and friends, I want to ask you the most important question…Elise Swanson, will you do me the honour of becoming my wife, Mrs Elise Wright?"

I gasp and have to wipe my eyes as I see the ring box he pulls from his pocket. He opens it up to reveal what's nestled inside; a beautiful rose gold Leo diamond ring. Something I always thought I'd want if I got engaged simply because they are gorgeous and I am a Leo.

He pulls it from the box and holds it at the tip of my finger. It's then that I realise I haven't voiced the answer my mind has been screaming on a loop.

"Yes, yes, *yes*!" I exclaim a little too loudly and excitedly.

Sliding the ring on my finger, Drew looks up and his hazel eyes meet my gaze. His eyes glisten with the moisture he's trying to hold back.

Standing from his place at my feet, he wraps his arms around me and kisses me. He deepens the kiss and it steals my breath away. So much for lack of public displays of affection.

Everyone around us bursts into cheers and rounds of applause. We step back from each other and turn to face the room.

"Next time we gather like this, this amazing woman won't be my fiancée anymore, she'll be my wife," Drew says and everyone cheers and hollers at his words.

All of Me by John Legend begins to play and Drew pulls me flush to his chest, taking my left hand in his and looking at the ring he just placed there. He plants a soft kiss on the back of my hand and sways gently to the music.

Chapter Twenty
Drew

I didn't plan to propose to Elise quite like I did, but they do say that the best laid plans go to waste. I had no idea she was throwing a party for my birthday, but when I realised all my family and friends were gathered in the same room, I threw caution to the wind and ended up with the best birthday present money could never buy; a beautiful fiancée.

When she finally said 'yes' after what felt like an eternity of silence, I slipped the rose gold band onto her finger and had to hold back the tears threatening to fall. I'd chosen a Leo diamond because the love of my life is a feisty Leo. The fact that it is made of rose gold is because I know how beautiful she thinks it is and the diamond is princess cut because it looked the best of all the settings I saw.

Cradling her hand in mine as we dance, the lights reflect off the quarter carat diamond and the tears in my eyes are mirrored in Elise's stunning blue gaze. Swallowing a lump in my throat, I lean forward and whisper in her ear.

"I love you Mrs Wright to-be."

All of Me plays like I asked the DJ to if she said yes. We sway in time to the music and I feel my heart swell with all the love I feel. I've never been happier than right this very moment. Elise will be my wife, Caleb will be my stepson and I will be complete.

I asked Caleb earlier tonight as we played Mario Kart if he thought it was okay to ask Elise to marry me. I showed him the ring while she was getting ready and he threw his arms around me.

"There's no way she'll say no, she loves you too much. We both love you," he had said as he held onto me.

"And I love both of you, buddy," I replied as I squeezed him tight.

"I'll have a proper dad in my life, and I can't wait."

His remark had shocked me; I couldn't believe he'd referred to me that way. It made me swell with immense pride.

"How would you feel if I started calling you that, Drew? Calling you 'dad', I mean?"

"I would like that very much."

I had to wipe my eyes with the back of my hand and pretend I had something in my eye.

Then when Elise came downstairs and accidentally called me 'dad', it was what you might call comedic timing. She wasn't aware of our conversation or the fact that Caleb had made me feel like the proudest man alive. He wanted me to be his dad.

If anyone had asked me this time last year if I thought I'd find love and end up putting a ring on her finger, I would have laughed in their face. But now I gladly accept that I was wrong.

Some people may see us as moving too fast and perhaps it would sound a bit clichéd to them if I were to tell them that when you find the one, you just know. I don't think anyone works to a timeline. There are no rules of when you can or can't get engaged. It just happens when it feels right and to me, this feels right. And there are no guidelines that state how long the engagement should be before you marry. I wanted to confess the true depth of my feelings to Elise; it doesn't matter to me if she wants to be engaged for a year or two before actually tying the knot.

I knew I loved Elise back in 2005, and though time has changed us both in some ways, fundamentally we are the same people. We want the same things out of life as we did then, even if we didn't admit it to each other. So although we've only been together a few months, we've actually known each other for over a decade. Okay so we may not have had much to do with each other in the intervening years, but the love we have for each other never fully went away. Whatever some people think, to us, it's what we feel in our hearts that matters most.

I finally found something I never knew I was looking for; the love of my life, and I plan to be by her side for the rest of my days.

***

"Where will we live?" Caleb asks from the back seat of the taxi.

"Do you like our house? Drew doesn't really have room in his flat."

"Yeah, I love our house, mum. I don't want to move, but if you want to then I'm sure I will learn to love somewhere else."

"If you and your mum will have me, after we get married, I'll move in with you guys so you don't have to move. I can either sell my flat or rent it out for an extra income."

"Ooh, I don't know about that. What do you think, Caleb? Should we let him live with us?" Elise asked; mischief evident in her voice.

"What do you mean *after* you get married? Can't you live with us now?" he asks instead of answering her.

"If that's okay with you and your mum, then yeah. Glad someone's on my side dude," I say as I reach to high-five him.

"Seems I'm outvoted two to one," Elise laughs and shrugs her shoulders.

"Then it's decided," Caleb states in a very matter of fact way.

***

"I thought he'd never fall asleep," Elise says as she walks into the bedroom.

As she turns to face me, a lock of shock registers on her face. While she was tucking Caleb in, I spread some rose petals around the room, lit some candles and used the dimmer switch on the overhead light to give the room some ambience.

"Wow."

She walks towards me and I pass her a glass of prosecco.

"A toast to my new fiancée. I just want to tell her how very much she is loved."

I smile at her and she leans down to place a tender kiss on my lips.

"A toast to my husband-to-be for loving me for me. For seeing the real me behind the cane I walk with or the things I cannot do for myself. To both of us for taking a chance on love after our past experiences left us sceptical. I love you, Drew, more than you'll ever know."

I place my hands on her hips and gently lower her to sit in my lap. I claim her lips and seek her tongue. I take her glass and place it on the bedside table without breaking the kiss. Her deft fingers begin to undo the buttons of my shirt and I unbuckle my belt so I can discard my clothing faster. Moments later, my shirt is slipping down my arms and Elise's nails rake trails down my chest, leaving pale marks in their wake.

Elise moves away from me and stands to remove her clothes. She turns and I unzip her dress. As it pools at her feet, I see that she's wearing a new set of matching underwear in the same shade of blue as the dress. She looks incredible and completely takes my breath away.

"See something you like, Mr Wright?" she asks in a sultry tone.

"Definitely, Mrs Wright to-be. You look divine."

I reach out and grab her hips, pulling her to stand between my legs. I want to kiss every inch of her from head to toe.

Leaning down so she's level with me, she places a chaste kiss on my lips as she puts her hands on my shoulders. She pushes me back on the bed and reaches for the waistband of my trousers. I lift my ass from the bed so she can pull them off easier. After discarding them, she straddles me on the bed and leans down to kiss her. I put one hand on her ass and the other in her hair. She settles her body over mine and deepens the kiss, our tongues dancing together. Goosebumps rise on my flesh and my cock twitches in my boxer shorts. If life is a series of fleeting moments, then I want to hold onto this one for as long as I can.

Breaking our kiss, Elise looks into my eyes and her hooded gaze shows lust, love and a whole lot of desire. She slides down my body to a kneeling position on the floor between my legs. I wait while she places a pillow underneath her knees, something we learned helps with her pain.

Elise slides my boxer shorts down and I kick them off. She grips the base of my shaft in her left hand and swirls her tongue around the pre-cum on the tip of my cock. That tongue bar of hers helps heighten the sensation and I feel a shiver run through me. I lean up on my elbows so I can watch my fiancée as she works me over with her hand, all the while she's licking and sucking, drawing me ever closer to my climax. That tingling sensation in my balls is a sure sign I'm about to explode. Knowing exactly how my body works, Elise let's go with her hand and takes my full length into her mouth. I hit the back of her throat and my balls tighten. As she moves her mouth up and down, she cups my balls in her left hand and it is mere moments before I am coming hard right down the back of her throat.

I help her up to the bed and lay her on her back. She's still wearing her sexy blue underwear but I make quick work of discarding the panties and settle myself between her legs. She's already so wet that it makes it easier to slip my finger inside her. She moans out as I do and I look up to see her clutching the sheets in her hands. She's never looked more beautiful than when she cries out as I slip a second finger inside her and hit her sweet spot. Her back arches from the bed and her breathing hitches as I repeat the motion. Using my other hand, I stimulate her clit with my thumb as I trace my tongue from her thigh to her pussy. Her cries of ecstasy make me hard again and I want to make love to her but not until she orgasms from my hands and tongue first.

I work her harder and faster until her legs begin to tremble and her moans come out as a string of muffled expletives. She's on the edge and I'm going to take her over. I up the pace and exert more pressure with my tongue. I read her body as easily as an open book.

Her orgasms hits and crashes over me in waves. She tastes so hot and sweet.

Standing, I lean over her and draw her attention to my fingers as I slip them in her mouth. She greedily sucks her juices off my fingers and moans at the taste. Such a simple thing is so erotic.

I reach beneath her and undo the clasp of her bra. I slide it from her arms, freeing her beautiful breasts. Leaning in to trace circles around her left nipple, I bite down on it gently. Her hand fists in my hair and I know that she wants more. I'm only too willing to give her everything she desires.

Aligning my body with hers, I gently enter her. She's so wet and tight around me that I almost come right away. Taking it slowly at first so it isn't over before it's begun, I set a slow pace. This isn't about sex, there's a difference between that and making love. I intend to show her that difference as I claim her lips in a soft, tender kiss. She steals the breath from my lungs and my heart swells in my chest.

Tonight we make love for the first time as an engaged couple and I can't wait for the first time as a married couple.

So many people say that they don't want to get tied down. Danny, for example, would typically have a different woman on his arm every couple of weeks. He says it would be boring if he had sex with the same woman for the rest of his life.

As for me, I'd rather make love to one woman, *this* woman, every morning, noon and night until the day I die. It could never get boring because it isn't about sex, it's about love. That's the key difference.

Chapter Twenty-One
Elise

I can't stop staring at my engagement ring as I work through some emails for potential events. The way the light catches the facets of the diamond makes it shine like a beacon. I love the fact that he chose rose gold, too. I don't wear yellow gold, only white gold, platinum, silver or rose gold. I love that he knows me enough to know this. How he got the size right, I don't know. But it fits perfectly. I'd bet good money Sam had something to do with it.

An email pops up from a lady at the hospital where Sam works.

To: Elise Swanson
From: Emma Greyling

RE: Help Needed to Arrange a Venue for the Christmas Ball.

Dear Miss Swanson,

I hope this email finds you well. I am in need of urgent help and one of our nurses, Samantha, recommended you. We have an annual Christmas Ball coming up, the invitations have been sent and the staff have replied; however a problem has arisen. The venue where we were holding it at has brought it to our attention that there was an error made and they are double booked for that night. I tried to change the date, but they are fully booked, due to it being the Christmas period. Unfortunately, the other company made their booking before we did, so we need to find somewhere else.

I would hate to have to cancel the event, as our staff work hard and we want to show them how much we appreciate their dedication.

Samantha told me that you are an event organiser and you may have some contacts who might be able to help us out. We would really like to be able to stick to the night of December 20th, but if that doesn't work, we can always work with whatever you can get us. Also, we would need somewhere that can hold around 100 people.

Apologies for the late notice; I know it's less than a month, but I only found out today. Do you think it would be possible to help us? We would be willing to pay extra for the inconvenience of it being such short notice.

You can reach me via email any time or I can call to discuss arrangements.

Thank you for taking the time to read this. I look forward to hearing from you.

Sincerely,
Emma Greyling.

I look through my rolodex. Old fashioned maybe, but I like my contacts on paper because computers can't always be relied on. I start making some calls and cross my fingers that I can help out. I've heard from Sam about the Christmas Ball they hold every year. They charge £15 for a ticket and one hundred percent of the profits goes to the children's cancer ward.

I'm reminded of the time I attended with Drew and a smile tugs at the corners of my lips. That night was one of the most memorable nights of my life. I felt beautiful as Drew held me close on the dancefloor and whispered sweet nothings in my ear. I still have the dress in my wardrobe, even though it no longer fits.

Thankfully, a hotel gets back to me and tells me that they'd be more than happy to accommodate the event, so I email Emma to see if it's okay to book it. She calls me right away and we work out the details. It feels good to help such a good cause and I tell Emma that I don't want paying for my services. After all, the only thing I did was book the hotel and arrange a few minor details. She starts to argue with me, but I tell her that I won't cash the cheque if she tries to pay me. She invites me to attend and I tell her that Drew and I already have tickets. Agreeing to meet her for a drink, I put down the phone and smile. I'm only too happy to help when and where I can and this leaves me with a warm and fuzzy feeling.

I text Sam to let her know that I arranged a new venue, and to thank her for recommending me. She replies asking when we're going dress shopping. Typical Sam; that girl really loves to shop. She's the exact opposite of me because she loves to wear dresses and, as it's a ball, I know she'll help me find the perfect evening gown. I want something that will blow Drew away. I know he's going to look particularly dapper in the DJ he's got hanging in the wardrobe. As he has a simple black cummerbund, I can wear any colour dress I like without having to colour co-ordinate. That works perfectly for me.

***

Drew has been slowly boxing up his belongings in his flat and, as we have no room for his terrapin tank, he's having to let it go. I really didn't want him to have to do that, but there just isn't space in the house.

We go to the flat after work to pick up some of the boxes and Caleb helps feed the terrapins. There's a buyer coming to get them and Caleb will be sad to see them go. He grew to love them the more time we spent at the flat with Drew.

I can't believe he's moving in with us. I said after Jensen and I split that I didn't see myself ever letting a man into my home again. Sam told me I'd feel differently in time and I insisted she was wrong. As it turns out, I'm eating my own words because she was right.

Packing the last of the boxes into Drew's car, we drive home. The guy took the terrapins and I saw the wistful look on Drew's face. He'd had them for so long, but he was insistent that he was fine as long as he could make sure they went to a good home. The guy who bought them was a friend of a friend from work.

We arrive home and Drew unpacks the car while I go to the kitchen to make a start on something to feed our rumbling stomachs. I turn up the music on my iPod and decide to make chilli con carne for tea. Caleb is helping Drew unpack some of the smaller boxes and I can't help but smile. There's a light, happy feeling in my heart and that's because of my two boys.

Perhaps other people would feel we're moving too fast. Perhaps they'd warn me to slow down and take it a day at a time. But I'm following my heart and I know Drew is too. It's not as if we're strangers, even if we hadn't spoken in years until a few months back. We've known each other over a decade and we're taking it a day at a time when it comes to getting to know the things we've missed over the years apart. The thing that matters the most is our happiness. Not just Drew and me, but Caleb, too. We're happier than I can remember being in a long time. That has to be a good thing. If my grandmother was still alive, she'd tell me that I should follow where my heart leads and as long as I'm keeping my eyes open, then that's what matters most. She would have loved Drew. She knew him back in 2005, but it was all too brief. If she really knew him deep down, she'd be so happy for me. All she ever wanted was to see her baby girl fall in love, get married and live happily ever after. She was a hopeless romantic; I guess that's where I get it from. If only she were here to walk me down the aisle when the big day comes.

***

Drew and Caleb have a Sunday ritual; they have breakfast, pop to the shop for a newspaper and a magazine, then back to the house to chill out. This means that I get a lie-in at least once a week, which I'm really grateful for considering how busy Memories Made has become recently. I've been so busy that I've realised I can no longer do it all alone. I have a week of interviews coming up and, because I generally work from home, Drew has offered to help organise my office so that it looks more professional and I can use it to conduct the interviews.

This morning while they went to the shop, I decided to get a head start on the office. I'm starting to wish I hadn't bothered. Why did I decide to redecorate it at the last minute? I'm beginning to regret that decision, but it needs to be done now Drew has stripped the walls and started to put up the new wallpaper I chose.

My office consists of my spare room, where I keep my bookshelves which are crammed with books, a desk with an iMac desktop computer, and a gorgeous antique desk I found in a second-hand furniture store and had restored to its former glory. Then there are my filing cabinets for work stuff.

Drew managed to convince me to fit in a second, smaller desk with a computer and stuff that my assistant will need. It feels a bit awkward trying to find someone who will work out of my house with me, but though my plan for the business eventually includes renting premises to work from, I currently don't quite have the funds. I'm hoping that, with taking on someone to help, I can take on more work. That means more money and hopefully being able to afford the deposit for a small shop in town that used to be a bookstore, but hasn't been open in years.

The boys return from the shop and Drew comes into the office to move some furniture that's in the way of him being able to wallpaper my feature wall. I've gone for a bright, clean look because I don't want the room to feel too cramped.

After finishing the feature wall, Drew makes a start on the other walls while I load the second computer with all the files my new assistant will need. I take him a cup of tea and a bacon sandwich so he can take a break.

"So how do you want to arrange these desks? Neither of you is going to want to be in front of the window," Drew says as he stands and surveys the room.

We come up with a plan and he arranges the desks then calls me back in to double check. It looks perfect so I grab a handful of books to start restacking them on my shelves.

Once the bookshelf is sorted, I turn to look at the filing cabinets that Drew put back in place. Having had to move them out for the decorating, we didn't want to pull out all the files and get them jumbled up, so it had been harder to move them in and out of the room. But Drew has managed to do it and now he's all hot and sweaty. I tell him to take a shower while I arrange some of the smaller items in the room.

"Don't go overdoing it, baby. If you can't lift something, wait for me or get Caleb to help you," he says before leaning down to kiss me.

"Eww, you smell like stale sweat. Go and shower."

I playfully swat him away and he bursts out laughing as he walks out of the room.

The office is finally finished, and I have to admit it looks really good. I still wish I had separate premises for work, but in all honesty, I didn't know if Memories Made would turn out to be a success. Many businesses fail in their first year, so I didn't want to run before I could walk.

Drew, Caleb and I decide to settle down with a film. It's been a long day and we could all use some downtime. The boys debated the film choice and I didn't get a say. I told Caleb to make some microwave popcorn, so we have that in a large bowl and some other snacks. *Storks* is our film of choice, so Caleb puts it in the DVD player and we all sit back and relax, for a while at least.

***

After a long week, I finally found an assistant that I felt would fit well with the business and also with me. Amanda comes across as smart as a whip, has good knowledge of event organisation and she seems to have a sense of humour. Her references checked out and nobody had a bad word to say about her, so we agreed a start date and she didn't seem to mind the idea of working out of the house with me until I could expand to another premises.

It's not long now until Christmas and, as well as the Christmas Ball for the hospital, I also have a few other events to oversee. Thankfully, it's busy this time of year in my line of work and that means I'll be earning more money, but it also means that my shopping for presents has had to be done mostly online. I'm glad my boys are both so easy to buy for.

I have Christmas songs playing on the iPod in my office when the doorbell rings and I step out to answer it. Amanda is dead on time for her first day and I hope her punctuality remains as good in future.

I show her to the office and tell her to get settled in at her desk while I make us both a coffee.

When I return with two steaming mugs, she's singing along quietly to the Lady Antebellum version of *A Holly Jolly Christmas*. She has a good voice but as she turns to see me in the doorway, she goes silent and blushes.

"Don't stop, you have a lovely voice," I say as I hand her a mug of coffee.

"Oh, please, you don't have to be polite. I sound like a strangled cat. I just couldn't help singing along. I love Christmas."

"Please, have you heard yourself? You have a unique quality to your voice. I don't think you should hide your light under a bushel. Don't be modest about it, embrace it. If it makes you feel better, I'll sing along to *I'll Be Home for Christmas*, my favourite track on this album, and you can hear what a strangled cat *really* sounds like."

"Oh, I love that song, too. I love Lady Antebellum actually and can't name a song I don't like."

"Me too!"

She has good taste in music; another thing to add to the list of things I like about her. I do as I said and start to sing along when the song starts to play. I can't help but close my eyes and lose myself to the music. I may not have a good voice, but I love to sing.

We both start to sing along to *This Christmas*. I sing the parts that Charles Kelley sings and Amanda does Hilary's parts.

"We have a few works parties on the books. A few corporate types and one ball for a hospital," I tell Amanda as we get down to work.

"Ooh, a Christmas Ball? Sounds fancy."

"Yeah, the hotel is pretty swanky. I'll actually be attending as well because my fiancé is a paramedic and works at that hospital, as does my best friend Sam, who is a nurse."

"Do you have a ball gown?"

"Not yet. I'm going shopping tomorrow with Sam. She hasn't got her dress yet either. I must admit I don't like clothes shopping, especially for dresses, because I'm more of a tomboy."

"There's this really great little boutique in town; I don't know whether you've heard of it. It's called Bella's. I'm sure you'd be able to find something there."

"I've heard of it, but never had cause to go in there before. I'll check it out, thanks."

"Tell Bella that you know me, she'll give you a discount."

"Oh, I couldn't do that. You hardly know me."

"Sure you could. Just say that Manda sent you. Bella is the only person I let call me that. I prefer my full name, but she's the kind of person to do exactly what she wants, regardless of what I say."

Amanda laughs and I can't help but join in. I don't know what it is, but I feel like we could be friends as well as boss/employee.

***

It doesn't matter how many times I tell Sam that I *hate* shopping, she still drags me round all the shops in search of her perfect dress. I haven't seen anything that I like or think I'll stand half a chance of looking good in. I feel it's imperative to look my very best because I'll be in the company of people that Drew works with.

Coming to a stop in front of Bella's, I gasp aloud as I see a stunning gown in the window. What I would give to have the figure I did back when Drew and I first knew each other. That is exactly the kind of dress I would wear.

"Wow," Sam says softly as I point the gown out to her.

"You'd look great in that, Sam, if only you hadn't bought the one you're holding."

"No, that's so not my style. It's *yours*. You simply must try it on."

She giggles and claps her hands like a gleeful schoolgirl.

"Maybe if I were ten years younger. And slimmer."

"Do I have to slap some sense into you?" she asks as she grabs my arm and pulls me through the door.

A pretty, slightly older lady greets us and introduces herself as Bella, the owner.

"My friend Manda said I should come here to find the perfect evening gown," I say as I take the hand she's holding out.

"Manda? Oh I haven't seen that girl in way too long. Please tell her I said 'hello'."

"She'd like to try on that fantastic dress in the window, please," Sam blurts out before I can stop her.

"Oh yes, I can just picture you in that one. I can always tell when a girl and a gown are perfect for each other and believe you me, once you've tried that one on, you won't be buying anything else."

I don't believe her for a moment, but if it appeases her and Sam, I'll at least try it on.

"Com, dear, let's get you into a changing room. You strip down to your underwear and I'll get the gown for you."

Bella shows me into the back where there is a row of changing rooms. I slip into one and draw the curtain. Stripping down to my underwear as she suggested, I'm glad I wore matching panties and bra.

"I have the dress, sweetie, may I come in?" Bella asks from the other side of the curtain.

"Sure," I say as I try not to look at my body in the full-length mirror.

I might have a little more confidence in myself since getting with Drew, but I still find it hard to look at myself in such a big mirror. I tend to scrutinise every little detail, all the lumps and bumps. The only thing I don't mind is my caesarean scar because that's where my baby boy came into the world. That's one scar I wear with pride.

Bella steps into the changing room with me and holds up the dress. It really is beautiful, but I just don't think I could do it justice. Looking at it, I begin to get anxious. My palms start to sweat and my head starts to buzz. Snapping the band I wear around my wrist helps but Bella notices my panic and calls out to Sam.

"Oh, honey," she says as she steps in beside me.

"I…I just…" I can't get my words out.

"Honey, you need to calm down. Big deep breaths. In through your nose and out through your mouth."

I do as she says and she repeats her instructions as I follow. I feel myself begin to calm and see Sam smile at me.

"You don't have to do anything you don't want to, but, honey, you should at least try the dress on. What's the worst that can happen?"

She's right. It's not like there's anyone but the three of us here. I need a dress and I can't avoid choosing one so I allow Bella to help put the dress on.

Lifting my arms above my head, Bella slips it over my arms and lets the material fall into place. My eyes are tightly closed until she pulls the bottom to flare out slightly.

"Open your eyes, baby girl, you can do it," Sam says, "You look amazing; absolutely breath-taking."

Slowly opening my eyes, I don't focus straight on the mirror. Instead I concentrate on how the material feels on my skin. It's not too tight, but is still form fitting.

Deciding there's nothing else to do, I look at myself in the mirror. The girl in the reflection doesn't look like me. Sure, she moves her arm when I do. She blinks when I do. She even turns when I do. But it's like I'm looking at somebody else.

The dress gives me a flattering silhouette. I can't see the lumps and bumps I saw just a few minutes ago. I turn so I can see the back in the mirror and it falls beautifully. The split up the side of the dress shows my leg, but it's not an open slit; it has a sheer material in the gap.

"Oh, Sam," I say on a sigh.

"I told you."

"And I didn't believe you…until now."

Bella appraises me and smiles the most beautiful smile, and I can see in her eyes that she knows she was right. Now I have this dress on, I won't buy anything else. I don't even want to look. I may not be perfect. I may have my flaws but this dress hides any imperfections and highlights my curves. It shows a generous—but not indecent—amount of cleavage, plus it shows my waist and falls well over my hips. I'm sure Drew will love it as much as I do.

Walking away for a moment, Bella comes back with a pair of nude colour, slip on shoes. I can't wear heels, but these flat pumps are so pretty and they go perfectly with the dress. She also hands me a matching clutch bag so that I can see the whole picture.

Once I'm changed into my normal clothes, Bella rings up the purchases and has everything put into bags for me. The dress is in a black dress bag, so Drew won't see it until the night of the ball. As Amanda predicted, Bella gives me a discount, but she also gives me a rose gold, jewelled headband free of charge. She noticed my engagement ring and said that she had never seen anything quite so exquisite. Then she went to one of her display cabinets and took out the headband, saying it would be the perfect finishing touch.

I thanked her over and over for her generosity and she asked if I would return with a picture of me on the night. I agreed and left the boutique with a huge grin on my face.

It's Caleb's parents evening tonight and I am looking forward to hearing all about his progress. His teacher has mentioned when I've picked him up from school how much of an improvement he's made recently. It seems Drew has had a positive influence on Caleb as well as me. He's done his homework with him, made dioramas with him and generally been a great help. For me, it has been great to see such positive changes, considering the place he was in when Jensen left. I didn't want to be with someone just to give Caleb a father figure, but now he has one in his life and I've noticed the changes in him.

Caleb's teacher, Mrs Munroe, is sitting behind her desk when Drew and I arrive. She smiles and welcomes us before going on to tell us what an improvement these last few months have been. She's noticed a positive change in Caleb's attitude and he's doing better all round. She was great when I told her that what had happened with Jensen had affected him; made him become withdrawn. The school have worked with him to bring him out of himself more and now it's like he's a different person. Not different, he's always been himself; this is just the best version of Caleb.

We leave happy to hear that he's doing so well. He'll be going to high school before we know it and, whereas I was worried about that before, I am not panicking about it now. Instead, I am looking forward to seeing him go on to do just as well there as at his current school. Mrs Munroe seems to think that he'll go on to flourish. Drew and I do, too.

We order takeaway for tea as a treat for such a good parents' evening. Caleb wanted to order Chinese, so that's what we ended up doing. Now the three of us are sitting around, eating and chatting away. Drew asked me earlier if it would be okay to get Caleb something to reward him for all the effort he's been putting in lately, so we decided to go and get him a new phone this weekend. We're going to take him during the day on Saturday before the Christmas Ball.

Drew asked if he could get a sneak peek at my dress before Saturday, but I told him he is in no way to look in the dress bag, on pain of death. I'm kind of joking, but I hope he takes me at my word and doesn't spoil the surprise. I want him to be blown away.

Chapter Twenty-Two
Drew

We took Caleb to get his phone today. He had no idea what we were doing, except going shopping. To say he was pleased when he got himself an iPhone would be an understatement. He was going to need a phone for high school anyway, so I just suggested to Elise that we get it a little earlier than planned.

Tonight is the night I have been looking forward to for weeks. I can't wait to take Elise to the ball. I have no doubt she will look stunning, but she won't let me see her dress until she's got it on. We've got a childminder to look after Caleb. He wished he could come with us, but told us to have a great night and take lots of photos.

I'm sat waiting in the lounge with Caleb and Karl while Sam and Elise get ready upstairs. They've been up there for about two hours, so Karl and I have been chilling out with a beer. I'm really glad that Elise will have the two of them there, because she won't really know anyone else. I don't intend to leave her side, but I want her to feel comfortable. Thankfully, her anxiety hasn't kicked in. Normally she'd feel nervous about going to this kind of thing, but Sam has reassured me that Elise will be fine. After all, she does have us with her and should she begin to panic, she has a paramedic and a nurse on hand as well as a room full of medical staff who won't let anything happen to her. She's my fiancée, therefore they see her as one of their own and would have her back if she needed it.

"Women. Why can't they just shower, shave, put their clothes on and be done? I mean, we manage it, don't we?!" Karl says as he looks at his watch.

"Yeah, but we don't have to straighten our hair, apply makeup; all that shit that women do."

"Sam would look stunning without makeup, I always tell her that."

"Elise would look stunning wearing a bin liner. I keep telling her this but you know what women are like, man."

"And just what are women like?"

Karl and I both jump in our seats as Sam's voice startles us. We look to the doorway and she has her head poked round the door.

"Wonderful, darling. Women are abso-freaking-lutely wonderful," Karl says as he stands.

"You bet your ass we are."

Sam opens the door fully and walks in. Karl's eyes light up as he takes in the elegant crimson dress she's wearing.

"Wow, baby. You look…just…wow."

"You look beautiful, Auntie Sam," Caleb says as he looks up at her and smiles sweetly.

"Thank yo, darling boy," she says as she ruffles his hair.

"And thank you, sweetheart," she says as she walks towards Karl, "but now for the main event, please welcome Miss Elise Swanson."

We look to the doorway and in walks the most incredible, knock-out beauty of a woman I have ever laid eyes on.

"Holy fu…shit!" they are the only words that register in my brain. I recovered from saying 'fuck' when I realised Caleb was still in the room.

"Do I look okay?" she asks meekly.

"Okay? Do you look okay? I have no words for just how amazing you look."

I wrack my brains for something appropriate to say, but come up short. I'm utterly speechless. It takes me back to the first time we went to a Christmas Ball. She bewitched me before that night, but that was the first time I referred to her as my girlfriend and her responding smile as I said that melted my heart.

Feeling tears sting my eyes, I blink slowly and try to stop them from spilling over. If I hadn't already, I would ask her to marry me in this very moment. How the hell did I get so lucky? She has agreed to be my wife and we've talked about the possibility of me adopting Caleb. That's not luck, that's something else entirely.

"Drew," Elise says, catching my attention.

"Sorry sweetie, did you say something? I was thinking about our first Christmas Ball."

"I just said we better get a move on."

"We have to wait for the childminder."

"She's here. Sam just let her in. Wow, you really did zone out. Sam and Karl are already in the taxi."

"Oh, sorry, baby, I guess I was rather lost in thought. You look incredible and it just triggered a memory."

"Thank you," she says as I see a blush tint her skin, "Let's say goodbye and be on our way. We're holding everyone up."

"I didn't even know a taxi had been called."

"We had the childminder's taxi agree to take us, now let's get going."

Caleb comes to hug and kiss us both goodbye and we tell him we love him before venturing into the night.

We climb into the back of the black cab that's waiting at the kerb. The driver sets off and I take Elise's hand in mine, bring it to my lips and place a tender kiss on the back of it.

"I love you," I whisper.

"I love you, too," she replies.

"Aw man, get a room!" Sam says, completely breaking the moment.

"We already have one," Elise responds before sticking her tongue out for good measure.

These two girls will be the death of us tonight. But I'd die a fucking happy man.

***

We've been here for about an hour and barely made it very far into the room. Everyone wants to meet the woman that tamed Andrew Wright, because they all know I've not had many serious relationships. Of course, all the women stop to look at the ring and they look green with envy.

Elise went to the ladies room to get a breather with Sam because some people were a bit full-on. I'd offered to take her outside but Sam had taken her hand and led her away.

She walks back into the room and I take a good, long look at her. The black dress she is wearing is simple, elegant and oh so sexy. It's got a sweetheart neckline that shows a little cleavage but leaves the rest to the imagination It is simple and understated. There are lace flowers going from her cleavage to her waistline, long sleeves that are black at the front and a nude, sheer fabric at the back. The dress falls to the floor and as she walks, the sheer fabric of the split up the side shows one of her sexy legs.

The people behind her can see nude fabric on her back, with a trail of lace flowers down her spine to the waistline where they meet the bottom half of the dress.

Stunning, classy, elegant, sexy…so many words could describe how she looks tonight. I love how she wears her gorgeous red hair loose around her shoulders with only a rose gold and pearl headband adorning her head. Her makeup is minimal, but with smoky looking eyes. This woman screams sophistication but she also screams siren, vixen, goddess and much more. I'm just hoping she's not wearing any underwear because I can't wait to get her naked tonight. If she's wearing underwear, it had better not be expensive because I will tear it from her body.

This woman didn't tame Andrew Wright. She stole his heart over a decade ago and held it hostage until we met again. It wasn't *taming* me, it was giving me my own heart back.

Chapter Twenty-Three
Elise

I'm glad that I was able to secure this venue last minute for the ball. It looks absolutely beautiful and everyone seems to be enjoying themselves.

I'll admit I had a bit of a panic attack at first. I've never been a fan of large social gatherings. I'm not exactly a social butterfly and I don't like to be surrounded by people I don't know. I say never, but that's not quite true. I didn't have a problem until the last few years. Since becoming disabled, I have had issues with things that didn't bother me before. But Sam helped me get through it this evening and now I am trying to remain calm and have a good night. It's important for Drew because he works with these people and I don't want to be an embarrassment to him. He'd be angry at me for even thinking that way; he's done nothing but reassure me that I don't embarrass him. I just don't want his friends and colleagues to look back and remember tonight as the night a woman had a panic attack and fled the room.

Drew has been so great; he hasn't left my side unless I'm with Sam, because he knows I feel tense due to not knowing anyone else here. I've encouraged him to go and mingle, but he'd rather take me along with him. We've had so many people congratulate us on our engagement and it makes me so happy when I see Drew's face light up as he talks about us and Caleb. He's not embarrassed at being seen with the woman with the walking stick, to him it's just an extension of me. I need it, therefore I use it and he doesn't care one bit.

A hand taps me on the shoulder and, as I turn, I come face to face with one of the midwives that helped when I was in hospital having Caleb.

"Elise, I can't believe it's really you. You look so different to when

I last saw you. Someone told me you were here and I had to come and say hi," she says she pulls me in for a hug.

"Zavanna, it's so good to see you."

I wrap my arms around her and feel a big grin tug at my lips.

"How's Caleb? He must be what, ten now?"

"Yeah, he'll be eleven and in high school really soon."

"Wow. How time flies. You're looking well. And your dress, oh my God, it's stunning."

"Thank you, Zavanna, I'd like to introduce you to my fiancé, Drew."

She shakes hands with Drew and I see her appraising him.

"It's a pleasure to meet you, Drew."

"Likewise. How do you two know each other?"

"Zavanna was there when I had Caleb. She was so kind and patient with me. I mean, I know that's part of the job description, but she really was the sweetest person."

"Aw, you'll make me blush. Do you have any photos of Caleb?"

I pull my phone from my clutch and scroll through a bunch of recent photos with her. Drew goes to fetch us another drink as Zavanna and I reminisce.

Her face lights up as she sees photos of my beautiful boy. She asks about school and I'm only too happy to talk about the light of my life. She tells me all about her daughter, Ever, who is four and shows me photos of her. I see a girl who's going to be a heartbreaker when she's older.

"Zavi, honey, there you are."

That voice sends chills down my spine. It can't be him, surely. I have my back to whoever spoke, so I can't be one hundred percent positive, but I don't want to turn round to make sure.

"Oh, baby, sorry. I was talking to Elise."

"I thought you'd got lost or something. I expected you back ages ago."

His voice gives the creeps and the patronising tone he's using makes me shudder.

"Peter, honey, allow me to introduce you to Elise," Zavanna says, completely clueless to the fact that I know the monster to whom she refers.

I turn to look at him and see shock register on his face. Panic spikes throughout my body and spreads like wildfire in my veins. My head feels fuzzy and my palms are getting clammy. I reach for the band on my wrist and snap it hard. I repeat the gesture several times to bring my mind back to reality. He can't hurt me anymore. I'm not his to use and abuse.

"It's a pleasure to meet you, Elise. Now if you'll excuse us, I would like to speak to my wife," his tone drips with venom.

How can someone make something so normal sound so awful? That's Peter all over though. He takes Zavanna by the arm and they walk away. I say 'walk' as though what she's doing isn't being dragged across the room, which is exactly what the prick is doing to her. Controlling as ever. I guess it's true that a leopard doesn't change its spots.

Then it hits me, Ever must be his daughter. That's fantastic; two more women in his life for him to manipulate. He treated his two daughters like shit when we were together and they grew up to hate him and moved out as soon as they could. Now he has another daughter to try and mould in his image.

I want to run to Zavanna and tell her everything that bastard ever did to me. I want to show her my old scars and help her see that she's better off without him. But I can't do that. I know he'd manipulate the situation to his advantage. He could always talk his way out of everything.

Drew comes back to me and the look on his face shows I'm not covering my fright as well as I had hoped. I tell him I'm fine but he doesn't listen. Instead he takes me out into the hallway and sits me in one of the leather chairs. He sits next to me and places our drinks down on the table so he can take my hand in his. I reach out and pick up his Jack and coke. Taking a large swig, I relish the burn as it travels down my throat.

A hand comes up to the side of my face, and though I know it's Drew, I flinch when he makes contact with my skin. The pad of his thumb swipes my cheek and I realise he's trying to dry tears I hadn't even noticed I was shedding. I sigh and sink into his embrace as his arms fold around me.

Pulling myself together, I take a few deep breaths and knock back the rest of Drew's drink. He smiles at me and I lose myself in his gaze. He's my saviour, my anchor, the love of my life.

I take a breath before explaining who it was that upset me. His face turns angry and I put a hand over his, squeezing gently.

"Please don't go after him, Drew. He can't hurt me anymore."

"What's the fucker doing here anyway?"

"He's Zavanna's husband; they have a daughter together. I can't help but fear for them, not myself. He can't hurt me now, but he can hurt them. You should have heard the way he spoke to her. It was exactly the way he used to speak to me, as if she were a child he was chastising."

"Try not to think about it, baby. You can't rush in there and rescue her. She wouldn't thank you for making a scene."

"I know, it's just that…well, nobody deserves to be treated that way and she's such a nice person. Her daughter is only four; so young and innocent. She has the rest of her life ahead of her with a violent bully for a father."

"I know, but it isn't your job to save the day. Didn't you once say to me that no matter what Sam or anyone else said, it had to be *you* that decided to leave him for good?"

"Yeah," I sigh, "In that situation, you're scared to stay because he'll beat you and manipulate you, but you're scared to leave for fear of recrimination. It's not easy and you have to ultimately decide how you want to live your life. I felt like I had to break free of the crap he put me through and thankfully, I did. It took Dave to help me do it in some ways, because he showed me that what Peter gave me wasn't love. Anyway, can we please not talk about him anymore?"

"Sure thing, baby," he says before leaning in to place a chaste kiss on my lips.

We make our way back to the ball and head straight to the bar to replace Drew's JD and coke that I drank to calm my nerves.

Sam and Karl are on the dancefloor and I can't help but smile. They don't care who sees them, they dance like fools anyway.

When *I Won't Give Up* by Jason Mraz begins to play, Drew takes my hand and guides me to the dancefloor. He places an arm around my waist and takes my free hand in his. We begin to move and I lay my head against him as we sway together. Thoughts of anything except us escape my mind and I feel at peace in the arms of the man I trust not to break my heart.

***

This evening has been fun…for the most part anyway. As Sam and Karl dance to *Locked Out of Heaven*, I walk to the ladies room. I know it's a Christmas ball, but I'm glad that the DJ it hasn't played all Christmas songs.

Suddenly I'm being pushed backwards until my back hits the wall. I don't see who is in front of me as it happens so fast. As my mind clears, I see Peter's face contorted in rage. He has me pinned to the wall with an arm across my throat.

"Just who do you think you are?" he demands.

"W-what?"

My panic levels are at a maximum. My palms are sweaty, my head buzzes and I am catapulted back to being the scared little girl he controlled like he was a puppeteer holding onto my strings. I try to reach to snap the band on my wrist, but his body is too close to mine. I can't do anything to help myself and I begin to hyperventilate.

"Let me refresh your memory, it went something like this; I don't know who you think you are or what you want and I don't care. Stay the hell away from me. Forget I exist, the way I have forgotten you."

I search my memory for what he's talking about but come up empty. The panic he's triggered makes it impossible to think clearly.

"I asked you a fucking question, bitch," he spits in rage, "I asked you who the fuck you think you are? Have you forgotten how to talk? You better start talking or you'll regret it."

"W-what?" I repeat my earlier question.

"That message you sent me. I don't know where you get off talking to me like that, but you don't say it to my face. You're not so brave now you're not sitting behind a computer screen are you, little girl?"

Suddenly, I remember what he's talking about. The message I sent him the day he dared contact me. Why the hell it matters, I don't know. I take a deep breath and scream for help as loud as I possibly can.

Peter is ripped away from me and as my body crumples to the floor, I see someone take a swing at him and then everything goes black.

Chapter Twenty-Four
Drew

I hear a scream for help as I'm heading to find Elise. She went to the ladies but hasn't come back. I run to where the scream came from and see that bastard Peter holding Elise up against the wall. He's pinning her with his arm across her throat and I see red. I don't have time to think; I just react on instinct and pull him away from her before hitting him as hard as I possibly can. As I'm about to hit him again, I hear my name called from behind.

Turning to see who called me, I see Sam sat on the floor with Elise's head in her lap. I start walking in their direction but am thrown to the floor. I fall head first to the ground and spin around in time to see him coming for me again. He throws a punch and I hear a high-pitched scream as it connects with my jaw.

Peter is pulled from me by two burly security guards. He struggles against them but it's two of them against only one of him, so his struggle is futile.

Standing up, I look to Sam and Elise, only to find a crowd gathered and Zavanna in tears. I ignore them and rush to Elise's side.

"I'm okay," she says in a whisper.

I kneel next to her and stroke her face gently.

"Were you hurt? What did he do? Did he hit you?"

"No, I fell to the floor when you pulled him off me. I sorted of crumpled in a heap. I'm good though; please help me stand."

Sam and I help her to her feet. Where moments ago all I felt was fury in my veins, now I just feel like I want to hold Elise and never let go.

Everyone starts to disperse and return to the ballroom. The show is over. Peter got his punk ass thrown out and now I'm left with bruised knuckles from hitting him and Elise is left with another emotional scar that she really didn't need or deserve. I can't do anything to take that away, but I can be there for her, no matter what.

"Did he hurt you?" Sam asks Elise.

"Not too badly. I'm just a bit sore from falling where I passed out."

"Do you want to go home?"

"I don't want it to ruin the night, but I don't want to sit around where people pity me."

"Then we're going," I say as I take her arm and begin to walk into the ballroom towards the exit.

"I'm sorry," she says to me or Sam, maybe both.

"You have nothing to be sorry for," we both say, outraged that she would feel that way.

"It's that little prick that should be sorry," Sam says as we approach the table to collect our things and tell Karl what's going on.

"Elise, what happened? Are you okay?" he asks, worry evident in his voice, "I couldn't get through the crowd of people to you."

"It's okay Karl, I'm okay."

"Her ex had her pinned to the wall, his arm across her throat. That was until Drew tore him away from her and punched him in the face," Sam says quietly, filling Karl in without wanting to broadcast it to everyone.

Nobody else matters, as long as Elise is okay.

"Let's not talk about it anymore tonight," I suggest as we all walk towards the exit.

"I would suggest we come back to yours, but I'm guessing you'd rather be alone," Sam says as we walk out of the building.

"I'd rather just take a shower and go to bed. Sorry, is that okay? I promise I'll call you tomorrow," Elise says as we stand outside and I call for a taxi.

"Sure thing, babe."

Elise is quiet during the taxi ride home. She's snuggled into the side of me, her head in the crook of my neck. I'm worried she's internalising it all, but I guess she'd just rather try and forget it happened. When we pull up outside, I pay the driver and we walk up to the house. Angie, the childminder, is sitting in the lounge, but Caleb isn't around so I assume he's gone to bed. That's probably for the best considering how Elise is feeling. She wouldn't want him to see her upset.

I pay Angie and see her to the door before putting the coffee machine on. With two steaming mugs in hand, I walk into the lounge and place them on the coffee table.

"I'm sorry I wasn't there," I whisper as I sit next to Elise on the couch.

"But you were. There's no need to apologise for giving that bastard a taste of his own medicine."

"Oh, trust me, I'm not apologising for that. I'm just sorry I didn't get to you sooner."

"Baby, he cornered me when you and Sam weren't by my side. The one time I leave you both, he decides to get me alone. That's not your fault. Nor is it Sam's or mine. It's Peter, that's just who he is."

"But I…"

Elise cuts me off by leaning over and putting a finger against my lips.

"But nothing. He was angry that I had stood up to him."

"What do you mean?"

"He messaged me via social media a while ago…"

"He did what?" I blurt without letting her finish her sentence.

"He sent me a message saying something about me looking different. I can't remember the exact wording, but I stood up to him. I sent him a message back telling him he had a nerve contacting me. I told him he has no control over me and I didn't hear from him after that. Then tonight he said something like *who do you think you are, bitch,* meaning he didn't like that he couldn't manipulate me anymore. Said I was braver behind a computer screen than in person."

"Wow. I can't believe he even contacted you. Why didn't you tell me?"

"Because I just wanted to forget about it. And I did, until tonight."

I pull her to me and wrap my arms around her. She doesn't deserve to have to explain this shit to me. I can't believe the nerve of that manipulative piece of scum. I'm glad I ran when I heard a scream. I hadn't realised it was her in trouble until I got there and saw it. Now he'll be nursing a bruised face and a dented ego.

"Do you want to go and have a shower or just go straight to bed?"

"I think I'll drink this coffee and then have a shower."

"Need a hand scrubbing your back?" I say in jest, trying to lighten the mood.

"Sure," she replies, surprising me.

Chapter Twenty-Five
Elise

It's been three weeks since the incident with Peter. We had a wonderful Christmas and New Year; just Drew, Caleb and me, celebrating our first Christmas together. I put the incident to the back of my mind because I can't keep going over it. It won't get me anywhere. I told Drew the next day that it would be better if we just forgot all about it. He wasn't happy that I wouldn't report it to the police, but I honestly don't want to have to make a statement and then wait while they decide whether to press charges. Not wanting it to be dragged out longer than necessary, I told Drew that and he agreed with me, but didn't like it much.

His Christmas leave is over tomorrow and Caleb will be back at school too, so we are spending the day curled up watching a movie and eating junk food. Drew chose to watch *Back To The Future*, a film we all enjoy watching.

After Caleb's gone to bed, we pour a glass of wine and watch *The Night Manager* before getting an early night.

I pull my hair from its messy topknot and run my fingers through it. Looking at myself in the bathroom mirror, I make sure the Mrs Claus lingerie I have on looks right with the candy cane striped stockings. I put my Santa hat on and walk into the bedroom.

Drew is sitting up in bed, waiting for me. From the look on his face, he likes what he sees. I try for a sexy pose in the doorway, something I'd been practicing in the mirror so that it looked sexy rather than silly. As he stands and walks towards me, I'm guessing I got it right, judging by the bulge in his boxer shorts.

He pulls me into his arms and kisses my his lips, claiming them in a passionate, bruising kiss. I drag my nails down the length of his spine and a shiver runs through him. Taking my hand in his, Drew leads me to the bed and lays me down. He kneels between my legs and looks up at me with lust, love and admiration in his eyes. Looking from the red and white striped stockings on my legs to the sexy red Mrs Claus outfit that clings to my every curve, he flashes me a salacious grin that does funny things to my insides. He strokes one hand purposefully down my leg and lifts it to place it on his shoulder before repeating the action and lifting the other leg.

With both my legs around his neck, the heat of his breath across my core makes my pulse spike. My nipples strain against the fabric of the red garment covering my body. I reach up and cup my breasts, throwing my head back as Drew grips my ass and manoeuvres me closer to the edge of the bed. He reaches for my panties and peels them off, leaving everything else in place. His first taste of me is slow, languid, a promise of what's to come. It sets the blood in my veins on fire and as he dips to taste me again, it's like he's pouring petrol on the flames. The warmth begins to pool in my abdomen and I relish the tingly feeling. A moan escapes my lips as I arch off the bed with the first touch of his deft fingers. This isn't about raw, unadulterated sex, but it's fiery and passionate all the same. He takes his time as he slowly circles my clit before delving his tongue further down and plunging it deeper into me. The incoherent fragments of words falling from my lips only serve to make him kick it up a notch. He moves faster with his fingers and tongue, working me to the point where my legs begin to tremble at either side of his head. That alone is a sure sign my body relishes his every touch. I begin to unravel further and Drew moans as he tastes me. My hands grip the sheets beneath me as he doesn't relent in his pursuit of my first orgasm. A few moments later, I come undone. I moan long and loud as I spiral. My body feels sated, yet hungry for more. I can never get enough of this man and the way he makes love to me like no other has in my entire life.

He stands and removes the only article of clothing he has on. His erection springs free and I lick my lips at the sight. My body is ready for round two and I can think of no better way than with him sunk deeply inside me.

Standing from the bed, I gesture for him to lie down. As I straddle him, I feel the hard length of him against me. It's begging for my attention and it will get it, when I'm ready. I lean down to claim his lips.

I lick at the seam of his closed mouth and he opens to grant me access. Deepening the kiss brings a groan from him as he firmly grips my hips to hold me in place.

Throwing my head back, I take his hands from my hips and place them over the red material covering my breasts. He pulls down the cups and my nipples are exposed to the cool air. Gently, he squeezes them both, drawing a long moan from my chest. I rock back and forth over him and he responds with an almost feral growl. Moving his hands back to my hips, he guides me down gently onto him, inch by inch. It's almost excruciatingly slow but I relish the feeling as my body stretches to accommodate him. I rock slowly back and forth again, this time with him fully inside me. He bucks underneath me and it takes all my might not to speed things up. I need the friction his thumb is exerting on my clit, I need to climax in sync with him, but I don't want it all to be over too quickly. So I set a pace that gives just enough and holds back at the same time.

Drew drags the lingerie over my head and I ride him wearing just the stockings. The wicked glint in his eye tells me he's about to up the ante whether I like it or not. So I give in and allow him to find a rhythm to suit his needs. I lean down to capture his lips once more as he bucks his hips, pushing himself in and out of me.

He flips us over so that I am lay on my back, plunging deeper inside me. I drag my nails down his back, no doubt leaving deep red scratches. He moans his approval as he appreciates the feel of my nails. I sink my fingers into his hips and bite down on his shoulder gently as he ups the pace and brings me closer to the edge.

Some people think of paradise as I place, but I think of it as a feeling. It's the feeling of being so connected to someone you love, not just on a physical level. It leaves me in no doubt that we were made for each other. He sinks into me once more and that's all it takes for me to explode. I see stars behind my eyelids as they flutter closed. I hear Drew mutter something incoherent and can't help the smile that threatens to split my face in two.

***

I've been so busy with work these last few weeks that Amanda has had a lot on her plate. I thought I'd ease her in gently with just light duties, but we've taken bookings for birthday parties, anniversaries and more wedding receptions, so I've had to throw her in at the deep end. Thankfully, she's swimming instead of sinking. I think I made the right decision choosing her as my assistant. She's been nothing short of brilliant at her job.

Drew asked me if I was going to organise our own wedding or have somebody else do it for us. With my contacts in the business, I decided it was easier to do it myself and, thankfully, Amanda has stepped up to cover some other events while I've been doing things for my own wedding.

Organising an event for someone else is much easier than it turns out to organise your own. Add to that the fact that I got the shop premises in town and have been planning our grand opening, and I'm absolutely shattered all the time. I can't complain, though, because life is on the up. I've well and truly left the past behind me where it belongs.

Before Drew, I think I lived with one foot still planted firmly in the past, but he's been by my side every step of the way as I have cut all ties with the things that held me back. Whatever has gone before, I can truly say that my heart feels lighter these days and my scars are less painful than they were. Some wounds never heal, but you learn to stop nursing them and let them fade into the background. That's what Drew has helped me do.

Chapter Twenty-Six
Drew

Work has been so busy these last few weeks, and when I'm not at work, I've been to cake tastings and traipsed around shops for suits for me and Danny, who I asked to be my best man. He's been totally on the ball in his duties of helping the groom.

I never thought I'd see the day that I stood in front of a full length mirror, wearing a tuxedo that I would be getting married in. But that's exactly what I did yesterday. I found the perfect tux, with a cummerbund in purple, as asked for by my wife-to-be.

Elise has been organising so many events, arranging the grand opening of Memories Made and now planning our wedding. It just goes to show that women can multitask. Amanda has been invaluable to her and they have a budding friendship outside of their work relationship.

Everything has been going so well and the only thing left to do is formally put in the request to adopt Caleb. His biological father isn't on his birth certificate, so if we wanted to, we could proceed without his consent, but Elise contacted him and he responded saying that he was only too willing to allow us to go ahead with our plans. He's not interested in his son since he married a woman with children of her own.

We are planning to get married on Valentine's Day next year and would love the adoption to go through as close to that as possible because we want to start our married life with us all having the same surname. Caleb is so excited that I'll finally legally become his dad and that excitement is contagious. The three of us are feeling it. It's a buzz that I don't think will wear off anytime soon.

I'm sitting here nursing a steaming mug of coffee on my break when Danny comes over to the rig and sits beside me.

"So the stripper for the stag do here is booked, the weekend in Amsterdam is being sorted as we speak and I bought some heavy-duty handcuffs that you have no hope of getting out of."

"Fuck off, Danny. That's not what I want. You know that."

"What man doesn't want strippers, alcohol and a buzzing stag do abroad?" he chides.

"This man," I say, pointing at myself. "I don't want a stripper and I swear, I won't turn up to my own stag if that's how it's going to go."

"Ooh, is the missus putting her foot down?" he says in a sing-song voice.

"No. *I* am. Listen to me, Danny and listen well. I don't want that kind of stag do. I just want to go out with my mates, get pissed and have a laugh. No strippers, no gentlemen's clubs, *definitely* no Amsterdam."

"She has you by the balls. Tell me, what's it like to not be in possession of your own balls, Drew?"

"Fuck off, Danny. Go clean your rig and leave me alone. If you can't organise the stag do, maybe you shouldn't be my best man."

I try to sound stern, but my tone is lighter than I was trying for. I know he's not planning a trip to Amsterdam or any such thing, really, he just likes to get me riled up. But just in case, I'm giving Elise my passport for safe keeping.

Seb and I are on the rig together today and we've had it pretty easy so far. A call comes through on the radio from dispatch and we get our shit together to go.

As Seb drives, I try to forget all the shit Danny was trying to stir up. My mind needs to be clear and focussed on the job.

We arrive on scene and I realise the house is familiar. As we walk up the path, I try to remember why I know this house.

"He's in here, please hurry," a scared female voice says as we reach the open front door.

We walk in and I stop dead in my tracks. It seems one heart attack wasn't enough for this guy. Seb and I get to work quickly and I radio in to control that we have a patient with history of heart trouble who had a heart attack not long ago.

Seb fetches the stretcher and we load the patient into the back of the ambulance. The distressed wife sits in the back with him and I ask

Seb if we can switch so that I can drive. I don't want to do something I shouldn't. If it were up to me, I would let the prick die, so he'll be safer in Seb's hands than mine.

We get to the hospital and the doctors take over. I'm glad he's not in my care because I don't care whether he lives or dies.

I didn't tell Elise last time I saw him because I didn't want to bring up any past hurt. I don't want to tell her now, either, but as I look on through the window and see the doctors failing to save his life, I know she deserves to know that the man who hurt her most in the world is probably not much longer for this life.

Pulling my phone out of my pocket, I send her a text.

Drew: Can you meet me at lunchtime?

The three little black dots show she's typing a reply;

Elise: Why? Something up?

I decide not to tell her anything by text, it's too impersonal. This isn't the kind of shit you want to hear over the phone.

Drew: We need to talk about something, but I don't want to wait until I get off shift.

Elise: You're worrying me now. Is this where you break it off with me? Has it all become too much?

I hate that she's so insecure and that's the first thing she would think it could be.

Drew: No, baby. It's nothing like that, I promise. Just please, drop by at lunch.

Elise: Okay. See you soon. Love you.

Drew: I love you too, baby.

Never have I meant it when I told someone I loved them more than when I tell Elise. She's the best thing that ever happened to me and everything in my life seems to be falling into place. I've never been happier than I am with her.

***

Lunchtime comes all too quickly and I have to take a few deep breaths. Seb kept me informed and let me know when the patient died. I felt at odds with my feelings because, as a paramedic, I do everything I can to save lives, but this guy…I don't feel any empathy. I've never wished anyone dead, but I can't help feeling a little pleased that the source of Elise's pain has been wiped from this earth.

Elise's taxi pulls up and I smile as I see her pay the driver and walk over to me. I take her in my arms and inhale the scent of her. She nestles her head in the crook of my neck and I kiss the top of her hair. She holds me for a few moments before pulling back to look at me. Her baby blues threaten to drown me as I fall deeper into her gaze.

"What is it Drew, why am I here?" she asks softly.

"I need to tell you something."

I pause and take a breath. I don't know how to break it to her. Gently? Quickly like tearing off a Band-Aid?

"Go on," she urges quietly. Her tone sounds like her voice might break.

"We had a patient today, he had a heart attack. Elise, it was Clive."

She gasps and I see fear in her eyes.

"He's dead, Elise. Clive Swanson is gone."

She grabs at my arms as weakness overcomes her. I gently coax her towards the back of my rig and sit her down.

Seb brings out a cup of sweet tea like I asked him to. Handing it to Elise, he nods at me and turns to walk away.

I haven't told him what that asshole did, that's not my story to tell. I just told him that Clive was her stepdad and he didn't pry further.

"He's really dead?" she asks before taking a sip of her tea.

"Yes, baby. Look, I should be honest here. I didn't want to tell you before because I didn't want to bring the subject up and cause you any undue pain. The fact is, Clive had a heart attack before this one. It was a couple of months back, maybe, I'm not too sure. I wasn't aware of who he was until Sam told me. She saw him being brought in and made me aware of just who it was."

"And she didn't tell me she'd seen him?" she asks in a whisper.

"Don't blame Sam. She didn't want to bring the subject of him up for the same reason as I didn't tell you sooner. But I thought you deserved to know this time. You deserve to know that monster is no longer breathing the oxygen he wasn't even worth."

"I'm finally safe."

She looks into my eyes and I see old heartache, but also fresh relief. The monster under the bed can't hurt anyone else. More importantly, she's correct, she's safe. She always has been since we got together but now more so than ever.

I don't know what I expected her reaction to be; whether she'd cry, or if she'd remain stoic. But she sagged against me without shedding a single tear. Clive himself is not—or was not—worthy of her tears, but I thought she might shed a few quiet tears of relief. Instead she takes a few deep, steadying breaths and pulls away from my chest.

"You tried to save him?" she asks softly.

"Not me, Seb. I couldn't. I didn't want his fate in my hands."

"I'm not one to wish anybody dead, Drew, that's not who I am. But I'm glad Seb's efforts were in vain. I'm not sure whether to hope he suffered excruciating pain before he died or to hope it was swift and upon him before he knew it."

"I don't think any of that matters anymore, baby," I whisper as I push a stray lock of hair behind her ear. "All that matters now is he can't hurt anyone else. Most importantly of all, he can't hurt you."

"I thought I'd put what happened behind me and closed the door on that chapter of my life. But it wasn't until now that I actually had that final closure."

***

We're standing at a safe distance so the family don't see us. No doubt they would all rage against Elise and tell her she has no place here. I tried to convince her not to come, but she remained adamant that it was the final piece of the jigsaw. She needed to see his coffin lowered into the ground, to see that he's really gone for good.

As the coffin is lowered, Elise lets out a long breath. I pull her closer to my side and rub small circles on her back.

"We can go now. That's all I needed to see. Thank you for being here with me."

Elise turns on her heels and begins to walk away. She reaches out for my hand and I take it. We walk back to my car. Together we are walking away from the past and towards our future.

Placing her hand on my thigh as I drive, Elise flashes me a small, grateful smile. This was the closure she needed and I'm glad she is dealing with it so well. I expected tears or some form of emotion over the last few days, but I've seen nothing but smiles and relief. She has nothing to be frightened of anymore and she's relishing in that fact.

I sigh contentedly as I take her hand, lift it to my lips and place a chaste kiss on her knuckles. I may not be able to change any of the things that happened to Elise in the past, but I vow with every beat of my heart to keep her safe until the very last breath leaves my body. She and Caleb are my world now and I wouldn't want it any other way.

Epilogue
Elise

Two Years Later

I look at the wedding photos lining the walls of the house and smile. It was one of the happiest days of my life. The only other days that come anywhere close were the day Caleb was born and the day we gave him a little sister, Cassie.

Caleb was overjoyed to find out he was going to be a big brother and Drew was elated that we were going to have another child.

The way Drew looks at our daughter with a love so strong in his gaze makes me happier than I've ever been,

Caleb is such a great big brother. He does all he can to help out and loves to just sit with her and talk or read her a story. He says he can't wait until she's old enough to read the Harry Potter series with him which makes me smile. My two beautiful children and my sexy paramedic husband are my world and I have to pinch myself at times because I wonder how I got to have it all.

Twisting my wedding band around my ring finger, I feel contentment settle around me. The day I vowed to love my husband for the rest of my life—'til death do us part—was the day I found out I was pregnant with Cassie.

"It's just nerves, Sam," I say as she fusses around me.

I asked my best friend to be my matron of honour, but I didn't ask her to cluck around me like a mother hen.

"Elise, that's twice you've been sick. You can't be 'that' nervous, surely?" she asks as she sits by my side.

"Well what else can it be?" I ask as the hairdresser starts to style my hair.

"I have an idea, but it means you peeing on a stick."

"Don't be silly, we haven't been trying that long."

"You know what they taught us in sex education at school, it only takes once."

She leaves my side and comes back brandishing a pregnancy test my way.

"Sam, I'm not pregnant. I'm just a little…" I can't say anymore as I reach for the waste bin just in time.

Sam stands by my side, holds back my hair and rubs small circles on my back. Once she's sure I have nothing left to throw up, she passes me a glass of water to rinse my mouth.

"You're doing this test and you're doing it now," she says as she places the package in my hand.

I do as I'm told and pee on the stick. I'm not convinced for one moment that this sickness is more than nerves, but I'll do it to appease Sam and get her to shut up.

We wait for the result and I'm suddenly afraid to look. I know it says 'not pregnant' on the little screen, I just know it. But that doesn't make it any easier to pick it up and look at it. Drew and I decided to try for another baby and I had my contraceptive coil removed. I'm sure the test will be negative, but that's part of the problem. I'd love to be pregnant so soon. It would make our little family complete.

As Drew and I sit at the top table, people all around us chatting and laughing, I try to summon the courage to show him what I have in my little clutch bag.

I've had to stop myself from blurting it out all day; during the ceremony, during the speeches at the reception. Now drinks are flowing and I'm only drinking orange juice, pretending to Drew that it is bucks fizz.

Deciding it's now or never, I catch Drew's attention as he talks to Danny, his best friend and best man.

I don't say anything, I just hand him the little stick. I'm just grateful it has a cap to cover where I peed on it.

His eyes dart down to what I gave him and I see joy, immense pride and wonderment pass in his gaze. Before I know what's happening, Drew slants his mouth over mine and kisses me like his life depends on it. As he pulls away breathless, he places a hand tenderly over my stomach. The stick said five weeks plus, but I don't know exactly how far along I am. My cycle didn't go back to normal as soon as I had the coil removed, so I didn't even realise I was late.

"Before you, I didn't believe in the whole 'one true love' thing. Then you came along and turned my world upside down, knocked it completely off its axis. I fell hard and I knew that you and Caleb were my world. Now this happens and I couldn't be any happier. You complete me, Elise Wright."

I'm beyond touched by his words and the sincerity in them. After Jensen, I didn't think marriage and another child were what I wanted anymore. He'd left me feeling as though I wasn't worthy and that I shouldn't put my heart on the line. But I couldn't be any happier than I am right now. My whole face beams with pride. Today we are married, in two days' time, the adoption will be finalized and now we are expecting a baby.

When I got with Drew, I knew he was Mr Wright, but I didn't realize how hard I was going to fall or that he'd end up being my Mr Right.

Arms encompass me and I am pulled from my reverie.

"Hey, baby," he whispers close to my ear. The warmth of his breath causes goose-bumps to break out on my skin.

No matter how long we've been together, Drew always makes me feel like a giddy teenager in the first flushes of love.

"Hey," I say as I turn in his arms.

I wrap my arms around him and rest my head on his shoulder. Cassie is asleep and Caleb is at school. We have a little alone time before Drew starts his evening shift. He gently puts his hand on my chin and lifts it so I am looking at him. His hazel eyes with flecks of gold are the kind you get lost in.

"I need a shower before work. Fancy joining me?"

I don't answer; I just take him by the hand and walk to the bathroom. I strip my clothes off slowly as he takes in the sight of me. I have a new tattoo on my right thigh that represents my husband, my son and my daughter but still has a little bit of my own character in it. There's a little watercolour picture of Stitch—from the film *Lilo and Stitch*—with script in the Disney font that reads "OHANA means family. FAMILY means nobody gets left behind." I had it inked on me a couple of months ago and I absolutely love it.

Drew reaches out and brushes his hand over the tattoo and my breathing hitches as his warm skin comes into contact with mine.

He undresses and I see the new tattoo over his heart. It's our children's dates of birth in roman numerals. He doesn't have many tattoos; he always said that to have something permanently etched on him, it had to really mean something. And this does.

His smile warms me from the inside out and I get in the shower, waiting for him to walk in behind me and shut the door. As I turn the water on and the steam cocoons us, I realise that I am the one thing I always desired to be, safe. Nothing can hurt me now. Drew would never let anything happen to me and I am stronger than ever before.

The End

About the author

Keren is a bookworm whose bookshelves groan under the weight of her obsession, but she believes there's always room for "one more book."

She lives in the UK with her son and when she isn't reading or writing, she's nurturing the reader and writer in him as he's currently writing his own book.

Keren loves to connect with her readers. You can reach out to her on social media. She loves to talk anything books, movies and TV.

Her other obsessions include Disney, Marvel, and she's a Potterhead for life.

Coming soon from Keren Hughes

Home

For more of our titles visit

www.blackvelvetseductions.com